D1121297

The Real Town

The Real Town

The Real Town

by

Stephen Doherty

The Real Town

CHAPTER 1

The four young men sat in a new luxurious white 1967 Cadillac convertible, casually discussing sports. Oddly enough, with the temperature well into the eighties, they had the top up.

"I'm telling you," said the red head, who was slouched in the back seat, "this is their year. The Sox are gonna' win the World Series."

Gus, the driver, nodded his head eagerly. "I hear ya', Artie. They're goin' all the way." Then, looking next to him, said, "But Sean don't think so, do ya'?"

The slender baby faced one, sitting in the front passenger seat, just smiled and said, "The Babe's not gonna' let it happen. He's still pissed off. Ya' shouldna' let him go."

The fourth passenger, Tommy, sitting in the back seat, said, "What's he talking about?"

Artie just shook his head, "Ahh, he's nuts. Don't listen to him. He says the Red Sox are never gonna' win a World Series because they traded Babe Ruth to the Yankees. Fuck Babe Ruth, for Christ's sake, that's fifty years ago. Gimme a break, will ya'? Besides, he's a fuckin' Braves fan."

Tommy laughed, looking at Sean, who just smiled back and winked at him. Tommy wasn't much of a baseball fan but he knew Sean. They had been best friends, and partners, since they were kids.

Artie was going on about the Red Sox when Sean suddenly said, "Here we go."

The Real Town

Instantly, the car went quiet, all of them looking to the left. They were parked in a shopping mall, filled with hundreds of cars. As they watched intently, an armored car pulled into the lot and parked in front of a large bank. Two guards got out of the side door, in the back of the truck. The first one, with his pistol drawn, scrutinized the parking lot. The second one had two good sized money bags, one in each hand. From the deft manner in which the guard carried the bags, it was obvious that they contained paper, not change.

They walked around the truck and into the bank. A few minutes later they came out and got back into the truck - no bags, no gun.

As they were coming out of the bank, Sean was looking around, carefully scanning the lot. He said, "We're on."

Gus, who'd been waiting to hear this, immediately put the top down and pulled out of their parking space. As the armored car pulled away from in front of the bank and turned back out onto the highway, the large white convertible smoothly pulled into the same spot.

Sean, Artie and Tommy casually got out of the car and strolled over to the bank. As Sean pulled the door open and stepped inside, he suddenly slid the large dark sunglasses down from his head which was already covered with a thin, black ski cap down to his eyebrows and simultaneously pulled up the neck of the black turtleneck jersey that he was wearing. The jersey covered his face, tightly, right up to the bottom of the sunglasses. Tommy and Artie were each wearing wigs, dark glasses and fake moustaches.

Exploding into action, Sean sprinted towards the counter, and, without breaking stride, grasped the counter with one hand and easily leaped over it.

The Real Town

It was a long counter with many tellers. There were lines at all of them -- except for the first teller's station, which was empty. That was where Sean went.

As Sean was going over the counter, Artie and Tommy had split up, each pulling two guns. Artie yelled loudly, "Don't anyone move. Just stay where you are and nobody gets hurt."

There were close to a hundred customers who, for the most part, looked stunned and frightened. One elderly woman, who was standing just in front of Tommy with a frantic look on her face, was tightly clutching her large old pocketbook. In a low voice, Tommy said to her, "Don't worry, Ma'am. We don't want your money."

Then, with a smile, and a slight wave of his pistol, he said, "Just theirs."

Then he heard, "Let's go, Charlie."

Glancing towards the first teller's station, they saw Sean coming back over the counter. Artie and Tommy each started walking backwards, towards the door, guns still pointed at the crowd.

As soon as Sean had gone behind the counter, he'd pulled a large folded shopping bag from underneath his jacket. Snapping it open, he knelt down and swung open the door of the safe that was below the counter. There, stacked neatly on three shelves, was the money that had just been delivered. Standing the shopping bag up against the front of the safe, he smoothly swept the money into the bag. Even though it was a reinforced, oversized bag, the money packets filled it nearly to the top. Packing them down firmly, he stood up, and pushed himself back over the counter.

As he did, he yelled, "Let's go, Charlie."

The Real Town

The three of them dashed from the bank. Without opening the convertible's doors, they simply went over the side and into the car.

Pulling out of the parking lot onto the highway, they turned right and, in less than a hundred yards, the road curved to the right and they were out of sight of the shopping mall.

The mall was in a rural section of western Massachusetts. A couple of hundred yards down the road, they suddenly took a sharp turn into an almost invisible dirt path, and disappeared into the woods. They drove along the path for a few miles and then swung off of the road into an ancient, long abandoned, barn. There were two cars parked there, waiting for them, totally blocked from the sight of anyone who might happen to come down the dirt road. They had placed them there at four o'clock that morning.

Quickly changing cars, Tommy and Artie got into the black four door hardtop, nodded to Sean and took off.

Gus started the other four-door sedan. This one was dark blue. Sean took one last look into the white convertible to make sure that they weren't accidentally leaving something behind. Nodding his head, he picked up the bag containing the money, got into the car with Gus, and said, "Let's go."

As soon as Sean got into the car, he removed the ski cap and the black jersey and put them into the shopping bag, on top of the money. He meticulously tucked the jersey down along the sides of the bag, completely obscuring the packets of money. He was now dressed appropriately for the summer weather, wearing a bright orange sleeveless tank top.

The Real Town

The dirt road continued on for about another five or six miles before they came to a highway, a different highway, two towns removed from the town where the bank was that they had just left.

They were a good couple of hours away from Boston, even more so, because they had decided to take the 'back roads' home. Tommy and Artie were heading for the Mass Pike and would probably beat them back by an hour or so.

The route that they were taking would bring them through a series of small towns. As they were entering one town, Sean saw a petite, young girl up ahead, maybe eighteen years old, standing by the side of the road, with a knapsack on the ground next to her. She had her thumb out, trying to hitchhike a ride.

Turning to Gus, he said, "Pick her up."

Gus, looking incredulously at him, said, "Are you nuts?"

Sean murmured, "Uh huh. Just pick her up."

Muttering to himself, Gus pulled over a few feet past the girl.

Sean, smiling at her, said, "Hi, how far you goin'?"

The young girl, smiling brightly back, said, "Cambridge. But I'll take a lift as far as you're going in that direction."

Grinning, Sean said, "This is your lucky day. We're going to Cambridge, too. Hop in."

"Oh wow," she said, "That's so cool. Kismet." Opening the back door, the girl placed her backpack in, and then slid in herself. It was summertime, in 1967, and she was aptly dressed for the time -- sandals, cut-off jeans, and a skimpy halter top that barely reached her midriff -- and no bra. With a face that matched. She was beautiful.

Her backpack was rather large and, as she was getting situated, they pulled into the center of town. As they approached the town's one large intersection, they pulled up beside a middle-aged, rather rotund police officer, who was closely watching the traffic with a gleaming eye as he spoke into a hand held radio. As they stopped for the red light, the cop was actually standing no more than three feet from Sean. Fortunately, there was a good deal of traffic for him to focus on and his one quick glance into the car was at the girl who was sitting behind Sean with the rear window open.

Turning his back to the door, and the cop, ostensibly to speak to the girl in the back seat, Sean said, "So, what's your name and what are you going to Cambridge for?"

Scooting over to the middle of the seat, she said to Sean, "My name's Jenny. What's yours?"

Sean smiled and said, "Steven, and this is my friend, Bill."

Jenny said, "Hi, Bill."

Tersely, Gus said, "Hi."

As the red light changed and they moved on, Gus, repeatedly glancing into the rear view mirror, was visibly relieved. The cop never looked at them, as they drove off.

Sean repeated his earlier question, "So what are you going to Cambridge for, do you live there?"

Jenny smiled happily and said, "No. Well, yeah, I am staying there for now. I spent the weekend with some friends, in Sturbridge, but I'm in a play in Cambridge - in Harvard Square. It's a great part. I get to play the part of the innocent girl who goes bad. But she's not really bad, you know?"

Then, cocking her head, and smiling brightly, she went on to describe the part. For the next hour or so, Sean and the girl went back and forth. There was an obvious connection.

At one point, Jenny asked him, "Do you smoke grass?"

Sean said, "Sometimes."

Jenny nodded, as if confirming her thoughts. Then, "Would you like to buy some?"

Outwardly smiling, Sean said, "If it was any good, I might. But I couldn't do it right now. We don't have any cash on us."

Jenny nodded, understandingly.

After a minute she said to Sean, shyly, "Would you like to go to my play tonight?"

Sean said, "I'd love to."

Jenny beamed and said, "Great. I'll leave you a ticket at the booth."

A while later, they pulled into Harvard Square and dropped her off, as she was getting out, she said, "The play starts at seven-thirty. So try to get there around seven."

Sean said, "I will. I'll see you then. Take care,"

As they drove off, Gus said, "I can't fuckin' believe you. Every place we go, you meet broads. If you went to a fag bar, you'd find a broad."

Then, "And, man, she is sweet."

Sean, staring up at the sky, said, "I can't believe it. I pick up a goddamn cover and she turns out to be a fuckin' dealer."

Gus said, "Huh?"

Sean just shook his head.

The Real Town

A few minutes later, they were going over the Prison Point Bridge into Charlestown. Parking across the street from the Bunker Hill Monument, Sean looked up to the third floor of the old fashioned brownstone building and saw Tommy looking down at him. Smiling, Tommy gave him a thumbs up.

The buildings on one side of the monument were, for the most part, rooming houses. Sean had rented two of the rooms on the top floor of the corner building, mostly for business purposes, although, as one of the rooms did have an oversized bed, he had been known to end up there occasionally, after the clubs closed, at night.

The other room had a large table in the center and that was where they dumped the money. After carefully counting it out, Sean looked up smiling and with a shrug said, "O.K., so I was wrong. There's no two hundred grand."

The other three looked disappointed. Artie said. "Shit. How much is there?"

Sean said, "There's only a hundred and ninety-six thousand."

After a second of confusion, they all burst into grins. Gus said, "You fuckin' asshole."

Tommy laughed, saying, "You are a ball buster."

Then, he said, "Forty-nine grand each instead of fifty. I guess we can live with that."

"You're fucking right we can", said Gus.

Then, looking at Sean, he said to the others, "And on top of that, we pick up this beautiful young broad, hitchhikin', and he's got a fuckin' date with her tonight."

Tommy looked at Sean, "You picked up a hitchhiker on the way back from the score? With the money in the car?"

The Real Town

Sean nodded, "Yeah. I figured they're looking for four guys. They see two guys and this cute little girl, they're not gonna' give us a second look."

Tommy nodded his head, smiling. Then, raising one eyebrow, "And you got a date with her tonight?"

Sean glanced up from the money that he was separating into four piles and gave him a half a grin. "Yeah," he said. "Right."

Gus, looking slightly confused, said, "You ain't gonna' go?"

Sean just continued dividing the money.

Tommy said, "She was just a cover, Gus. If he sees her again, she could be a witness."

Then, looking at Sean, he said, "Nice?"

Making a face and shaking his head, Sean said, "You wouldn't believe it."

Tommy just laughed. Then, looking at Gus, he said "And don't you even think about going over to take his place."

Gus, trying to look innocent, said, "Well, I was just thinkin', the poor kid's feelin's are prob'ly gonna' be hurt."

They all just laughed.

Sean, leaning back from the four completed piles of equally divided money said, "Trust me, Gus. I'd like nothin' better than goin' over there tonight. But don't worry about her feelings. I doubt that anyone's ever stood her up before. I'm sure she'll get over it real quick."

Then, after a moment's reflection, "Probably quicker than I will, she really was delicious."

Shaking his head again, Sean said, "To make matters worse, she tried to sell me some grass."

He then went on to describe the incident.

When he finished, Tommy and Artie were both laughing. Tommy said, "So lemme get this straight. You pick up this cute kid for cover an' she turns out to be a fuckin' dealer an' she got her shit on her an' you gotta' ride all the way back with the shit in the car?"

Sean gave him a rather sheepish look as he nodded his head.

As Tommy picked up his money he said, "Anybody mind if I go first? I gotta' get in town to see a guy."

Gus and Artie both nodded and Sean said, "Okay with me. I'm in no hurry."

They had a routine. Whenever they met at the apartment, especially after a score, they would leave at ten to fifteen minute intervals.

CHAPTER 2

Sean and his partners were all in their mid-twenties. Sean and Artie were twenty-six and Tommy and Gus were twenty-five. Tommy and Artie were both around six feet tall. Tommy had blonde hair and was well-built, while Artie was a redhead and would best be described as long-limbed and lanky. Sean and Gus were both around five feet ten inches tall. Gus was slightly stocky with black hair, while Sean was slim with light brown hair. They had all grown up together in Charlestown. When they were teenagers, they were part of a street crew known as 'The Jokers'. They had stuck together ever since.

Charlestown was a neighborhood in Boston -- about as insular as you could get. You literally had to cross a bridge to get into the town -- and the insularity didn't stop there. The town was all white, and mostly Irish.

Initially, Charlestown had been a city by itself. Charlestown was first settled in 1628, before Boston, and was the Massachusetts Bay Colony's initial seat of government. It became a part of Boston in 1874.

If you're a historian, and you hear Charlestown, you think of things like the Battle of Bunker Hill, Paul Revere's Ride, which started there, and the Boston Navy Yard, where the U.S.S. Constitution, the oldest commissioned warship afloat, was - and still is - berthed.

But, if you're a cop, you think bank robbers, armored truck robbers, Irish gang wars, and the revered /reviled code of silence - the town where no one talks.

The Real Town

Legend has it that the town was once listed somewhere as having more barrooms per square mile than anywhere else in the country. Which, by the way, is how big Charlestown is, one square mile.

Even in the sixties, there were about forty of them left. From the 'ALIBI' to the 'BLUE MIRROR' to the 'SHAMROCK VILLAGE', to 'KELLY'S', 'SULLIVAN'S', 'J.J. McCARTHY'S', 'JACK'S LIGHTHOUSE', and the best of all of the after-hours clubs in Boston, the 'STORK CLUB' -- which didn't open up till all the other bars closed.

Actually, the Alibi closed at the start of the sixties, after the McLean/McLaughlin war started, in 1961. Buddy McLean killed Bernie McLaughlin - at high noon, on Chelsea Street in City Square - with at least a hundred people standing around.

No witnesses.

Sean and Tommy had just walked over the bridge that day, from the North End, into City Square. They had just crossed over to the other side of Chelsea Street when they heard the shots.

It was October and Tommy's immediate reaction was, "Who's got firecrackers this time of year?"

The Real Town

Then they looked up and saw someone running down the other side of Chelsea Street, in the opposite direction. As they didn't know just what had happened, they kept on going in the direction that they had been heading. But they kept glancing across the street. About halfway down the block they saw someone on the sidewalk, on the other side of the street, lying in a pool of blood. As this was none of their business, they just took off; taking the first left, past Joe Monroe's joint, The Eight Bells, onto Joiner Street. One block down Joiner Street, on the far corner, there was a gas station. As they were going past it, a friend of theirs, who was working there at the time, came out the door and yelled, "Hey. Didja hear? Buddy McLean just killed Bernie McLaughlin."

This was no more than two minutes after it happened. Word does travel fast.

They kept going until they were about in the middle of the town, in Thompson Square. They stopped at Brassil's Flower Shop -- which happened to be right across the street from the Alibi.

At that point, the Alibi was temporarily closed. Tommy Ballou had had an altercation with another patron and had stuck a broken beer bottle through his cheek -- in the process, chopping off a piece of the guy's tongue -- and the place had been temporarily shut down. But, about a minute or so after they got to Brassil's, the door to the Alibi flew open and a half a dozen guys came running out. Shortly after that the Alibi closed.

Small wonder, the main players on both sides of the war that had just begun had all hung out there. Over the next four or five years, depending on who you listened to, maybe a hundred guys were killed. The body count, (the ones that were found), was someplace in the seventies by the time that it ended.

The Real Town

Originally, the ALIBI's name had been the THOMPSON SQUARE SPA. Which made sense seeing as it was in Thompson Square and connected to the Thompson Square Theater, (a.k.a. The Hippie).

It was just a regular neighborhood bar/restaurant, and you could run into anyone in there -- from legitimate citizens to rogues to cops.

One thing did stand out, though. It seems that a large percentage of suspects who were picked up for questioning by the police in Charlestown back in the early 1950's, happened to have been at the Thompson Square Spa at the time that the events, which they were being questioned about, had occurred. Inevitably, the patrons of the bar would verify the suspect's presence.

As the story goes, one day the police had a 'Townie' down at the local police station, Station 15, and were questioning him about an incident that had occurred the night before. The gentleman told them that he knew nothing about the occurrence in question, that he had spent the entire evening at the Thompson Square Spa.

At which point, one of the cops said, "Yeah, right. They oughtta call that fuckin' place the 'Alibi'." And, from then on, they did.

So, when the time came that the theater wanted to expand, (they owned the block), the proprietors of the Thompson Square Spa moved across the street and built a new building. They named it the Alibi.

The Alibi was the only building in a large empty lot on Main Street, except for an old wooden three-decker apartment building that stood in the middle of the lot, a couple of hundred feet behind the Alibi.

The Real Town

One night, when they were about fifteen or sixteen, Sean, Tommy and Artie were sitting in the doorway, on the steps of the old building, drinking beer, when a car pulled up to the back door of the Alibi. Not unusual. That was where some people went to pick up pizzas to go, except this night. As soon as the car pulled up, the back door of the Alibi opened and a man stepped out. He looked around and then opened the trunk of the car. As soon as he did, two others came walking out carrying someone, and stuffed him in the trunk.

As the car pulled away, the one who had opened the trunk was just standing there looking around, when he spotted Sean, Tommy and Artie on the steps. It was dark and he hadn't seen them at first. He turned back to the other two, and said something. They all looked over at the three-decker.

At this point, with the three of them staring over, Sean, Tommy and Artie were ready to make a break for it. But, after a moment, one of the three guys at the back door said something to the others and then, looking like they were laughing, they waved and walked back inside.

In point of fact, all three of the kids had recognized one of the guys who'd been carrying the body -- and, obviously, the recognition was mutual.

It was Tommy Ballou.

Tommy was a known rogue. The Jokers hung in the court, behind the building where he lived, in the projects, on Bunker Hill Street. They used to see him all the time, coming and going, and, of course, they all knew who he was.

Tommy was a large, burly, quiet guy. Whenever he'd walk by the corner, they would all say 'Hi.'

He'd just nod. He'd never respond verbally.

Yet, one Seventeenth of June, (more commonly known, outside of Charlestown, as Bunker Hill Day, complete with parades, carnivals, and all of the trimmings), he saved some of them from spending the day in jail. They were just a bunch of kids, without a lick of sense between them - and the cops did not like the Jokers.

The Bunker Hill Day Parade, appropriately enough, would start off by coming up Bunker Hill Street, past the housing project and right by the corner of Monument Street, where they hung out. On this particular Seventeenth, shortly before the parade was due to come by, a half a dozen cop cars came swooping in to the project courtyard behind the building on the corner. They were going to lock up all the Jokers for the day.

Everybody scrambled, but the cops had the place surrounded. Still, most of them got away. But a few of them ran through the middle hallway of the project building, only to find that the cops were waiting outside the door on the other side of the building. With nowhere else to go, they ran upstairs for the roof. But they knew that they were going to be caught. There were three different stairways down from the roof, and they just knew that cops would be waiting at each of them.

But, as they were going past a door on the top floor, it opened up. It was Tommy Ballou. Obviously, he'd been watching what was going on, out the window.

He just said, "Get in here."

Which, of course, they did.

After closing and locking the door, Tommy walked over and looked out the window for a minute. Looking back at them, standing in the middle of his parlor not quite knowing what to do, he laughed.

The Real Town

He went into the other room for a minute. When he came out, he was buttoning his shirt. He said, "I'm goin' out, now. Sit down an' make yourselves comfortable. There's beer in the refrigerator. Don't make any noise, don't answer the door and make sure the cops are gone before you leave. Then get the fuck outta here."

He stood by the door for a minute, listening. Then he opened the door and looked out into the hall. Looking back at them, he said, "And don't fuck anything up.", and walked out the door.

You can bet that nobody fucked anything up.

The next time that he walked by the corner, everyone said, "Hi, Tommy."

As usual, he simply nodded.

There were at least a dozen bars in City Square alone -- which was only a block away from the Navy Yard and a couple of thousand thirsty sailors. City Square was where you came into the town from over the bridge that ran to the North End -- which was the main Italian section of Boston -- and the Boston Garden. You came off of the bridge into the Square, took a right onto Chelsea Street and there were bars as far as you could see, on both sides of the street.

One of them was the Stork Club, which was on the second block coming down Chelsea Street, on the left hand side. Unlike most normal sidewalk bars, the Stork Club was on the second floor -- and it took up the whole block. It was also open all night.

The Real Town

Downstairs, were your regular neighborhood stores; grocery store, TV repair shop, Army-Navy store, a movie theater, etc., that all fronted out onto Chelsea Street. The rest of the block was surrounded by an empty lot, with one short side street that led into the heart of Charlestown. There was one plain door on the side of the building that was barely noticeable. It only opened from the inside, where two 'doormen' decided whether you could get in, or not. Inside was a flight of stairs, about fifteen or twenty steps up, then a U-turn to the right for another five or six steps, then, into the club itself.

The U-turn in the stairway could be helpful during the occasional disagreements that are bound to occur when you've got a couple of hundred 'night people' indulging, at four o'clock in the morning. If you should find yourself going ass over teakettle down the stairs, the bend in the road could slow your journey.

Like the night the Yankee's were in town and Mickey Mantle and Billy Martin were having a few cocktails at the bar -- a large oval bar, maybe thirty or forty feet long -- and Billy Martin started a fight with Stevie Hughes.

Not a good move. In a bar filled with legitimate tough guys, Billy Martin picked a fight with the one guy that the tough guys wanted no part of -- and poor Mickey Mantle had to jump in to help.

Unfortunate for Mickey; not that he didn't do the right thing, Martin was his pal and he was getting his ass kicked.

So, as Stevie escorted Martin down the stairs, a friend of his, 'Silky' Sullivan, encouraged Mickey to join him. I'm sure that they both appreciated the bend in the road as it slowed their trip to the bottom of the steps.

The Real Town

A few years later, Stevie was killed in the Irish gang war. Actually, the war ended when he did. He was riding shotgun with a guy, in the wee hours of the morning, when a car pulled up beside them and blew them away with rifles.

Later on, one of the shooters from the hit car said, "You know, I really didn't like Stevie. He was a dangerous bastard. He was scary. But I'll give him this: He had balls. When the car pulled up beside them and he turned around and saw them? He knew it was over. Son of a bitch didn't flinch or try to duck or anything. Shit, he didn't even blink. He just stared. It was like he was saying 'Fuck you'."

It's doubtful that Billy Martin ever had a clue as to just how lucky he was to walk away from the Stork Club that night with just a couple of bruises.

The war - known as the McLean/McLaughlin war - ended with not one person ever being convicted for any of the murders. After one such incident, a television reporter was interviewing a detective at the scene of the murder. The interviewer, who happened to be a woman, asked the detective, 'Officer, this is the thirty-seventh gangland slaying in the Charlestown Irish gang war. Can you explain why none of these crimes have been solved? Why nobody has been caught?'

The plain-clothes detective, with a rather cynical look, just shrugged his shoulders and said, "Lady, who cares? . . . . There ain't no innocent people dead here. They're just killing each other. So who cares?"

A rarity, an honest cop.

That was the Charlestown in which Sean, Tommy, Artie and Gus grew up.

CHAPTER 3

The day after they robbed the bank, Sean walked into Kelly's Bar. It was a Saturday afternoon. Kelly's was a men's tavern on the corner of Concord and Bunker Hill Streets. Bunker Hill Street was the main street in town. It was a regular neighborhood bar across the street from the project. During the week, it did a pretty good business. But, on Saturdays, it was packed. Everyone was there to bet on the horse races. They had the best bookie in town. As usual, it was mobbed.

Sean spotted Tommy at the far end of the bar, and walked down.

Tommy motioned him close and, in a hushed voice, said, "Did you read today's paper?"

Sean shook his head. "Not yet."

Tommy said, "You gotta' see this."

There was a copy of that day's newspaper on the bar. Tommy picked it up and opened it to a particular page.

"Here", he said. "Check this out."

Sean had moved around the end of the bar, by the back door, so he was standing slightly behind the bar, with his back to the wall. He quickly scanned the article on the previous day's score, until he came to the part where they were describing the bandits' escape.

The eyewitnesses, at the bank, had described the car that they had gotten into as they ran out of the bank as 'either a black or dark blue four door sedan'.

The Real Town

He glanced up at Tommy who was trying not to grin. He quickly finished the piece, and found no more surprises. He glanced back at the description of the getaway car, then closed the paper and looked at Tommy.

"Can you believe that?"

Grinning, Tommy said, "Eye witness testimony, ain't it swell? I read that this morning, I got a fuckin' chill up my back. Here we are ridin' all the way back here, thinkin' they're lookin' for a white convertible an' we're drivin' what they're lookin' for!"

The bartender, a friend of theirs named Becky, brought them a round of beers. "Here", he said. "Sammy sent these down."

They looked down the bar and saw Sammy and a couple of other guys standing about halfway down the bar. Just then an older guy, around forty, joined them.

Sean recognized him immediately. His name was Joe O'Rourke. He was better known as 'Rockball'.

Sean had recently heard that Rockball was getting out of Walpole State Prison, but had yet to see him. They had only met once before. Rockball had just done about fifteen years, with about a six month break in between, about half-way through, when he was out on parole. Sean had met him one night during that break, back around 1960.

Sammy and Rockball came walking down.

Sammy said, "Hey Sean, you remember Rockball?"

Sean nodded his head. "Oh yeah".

Turning to Rockball, he stuck out his hand, "Good to see you, Joe. I heard you were gettin' out."

O'Rourke nodded back, smiling. "Yesterday," he said.

Turning to Tommy, Sean introduced them.

The Real Town

Shaking hands, Tommy said, "It's good to meet you. I've heard a lot about ya', all good things."

Even though he'd been gone all of those years, Rockball was still well known throughout the town. He had been part of the crowd that had hung down the Alibi. If he hadn't been away all during the Irish war he would have been right in the thick of it. Stevie Hughes had been his best friend.

Turning to Sean, Tommy said, "I didn't know you knew Rockball. Where'd you two meet?"

Sean, Sammy and Rockball each looked at each other, and smiled. Sean said, "A few years back, when he was out on parole."

Sammy said, "Lemme tell it. You remember, years ago, maybe six or seven years ago, some skinner was ridin' around town late at night, tryna' pull girls in his car?"

Tommy nodded his head, "Yeah, I remember it. I think he had a green car."

It was the sort of thing Tommy would remember. He had four sisters.

Sammy continued, "Yeah, that's right. A Buick, if I remember right."

Rockball and Sean both nodded their heads.

"Anyways", Sammy went on, "this night, it's about one or two in the morning, I'm out takin' a walk, just lookin' around. You know, see if I can maybe run into a green Buick. I'm comin' down Bunker an' I meet Sean comin' up the other way. Just a couple a' blocks up the street, on the corner of Green Street.

"So we're standin' there shootin' the shit, an' I ask him, "Hey, you ain't seen a Green Buick around, have ya'?

The Real Town

"Sean starts to laugh and reaches in his back pocket and pulls out a pistol. He says, 'I was just gonna' ask you the same thing'.

"Now we're standin' there talkin' about it, an' I see Sean look up the street. He says, 'Who's that?'

"I look, but I can't tell who it is. It's some guy walkin' down Bunker on the other side of the street, over by the graveyard. But it's so dark, I can't tell who it is.

"Then Sean says, 'Is that that fuckin' Ellsworth? He better not try to shake me down or we're gonna' have a problem.'

"He thought it was Ellsworth. Remember Ellsworth, the cop?"

Tommy nodded his head, "Of course, I do."

Sammy continues, "So now I'm lookin' and the guy starts to cross the street towards us, an' I realize it ain't him. It's Rockball.

"When he comes up to us, I says, 'Hey, Joe. How ya' doin'? Sean, this is Joe O'Rourke, 'Rockball'. Joe, this is Sean Brady'.

"Then, I tell Joe, 'Sean thought you were Ellsworth -- the dick.'

"Joe says, 'Son of a bitch. That's the third time someone's said that to me. I gotta' see what this guy looks like.'

"So, we're standing there talking, and, after a few minutes, Rockball says -- like he's just looking for some friend a' his -- 'Hey, you guys ain't seen a green car around, have ya'? A Buick?'

"Me an' Sean bust out laughin'. Then we tell Rockball why we're laughin' and he reaches into his belt and pulls out a pistol."

Rockball nodded his head, grinning. "Yeah, I remember. Hey, did anybody ever get him? I got busted right after that and I never heard nothin' more about it."

Sean and Sammy glanced at each other. Then Sean said, "He just sorta' went away. We kinda thought you mighta' got him."

Rockball just smiled. "I wish. But, ya' know, when I was back inside I was tellin' a guy about it an' he said, 'Well, at least ya' know the town ain't changed',"

The fact was, regardless of everything else that was going on, when it came to women, Charlestown was the safest neighborhood in Boston. A girl could walk home at four o'clock in the morning and feel perfectly safe. If you bothered a woman, or a child, in Charlestown you did not have to concern yourself with being arrested. That was the best that you could hope for.

They had another couple of drinks, and then Artie and Gus came in the front door and started walking towards them. Half-way down the bar, Artie half-nodded his head to Sean. Sean excused himself and went to meet him.

Artie said, "I was just talkin' to Barney outside. He wants to talk to you. I think he wants ya' to go for a ride with 'em."

Sean glanced reluctantly back at the guys with whom he'd been drinking. He was in a good mood and felt like partying. But, business was business.

He said to Artie. "Do me a favor. Go tell him I'll be out in a minute, okay?"

Artie nodded and left.

Turning back to the others, he said, "Listen, I gotta' take off. I gotta' go someplace."

Nodding to his partner, Tommy, he said, "I'll see ya' when I get back."

Tommy said, "Everything okay?"

Sean nodded and, as he turned away, turned back saying, "Hey Joe, it's good to see you out. Welcome home."

As he said it, he held out his hand. Rockball had had to turn around to respond, thereby placing his back to the others. So, nobody saw the money that Sean discreetly placed in his hand when he shook it.

Rockball just winked, and smiled, as he palmed the money, saying, "Thanks a lot, Lad. It's good to see you too."

It was a common practice, an acknowledged facet of the code of behavior, if you will, in Charlestown, to give money to someone who had just gotten out of prison. It didn't have to be someone that you were close with -- those people automatically got something. But, even if it was someone that you didn't know well, as long as he'd been a stand-up guy, and had done his time right, it was a way of showing respect. Everyone needs a little help when they first get out.

CHAPTER 4

Sean Brady was almost twenty-seven years old. He'd been robbing banks since he was nineteen. When he was twenty-four, he robbed his first armored car.

One day, about a year after that, he was approached by an old time rogue, named Barney Johnson. Sean had known Barney since he was a kid.

Barney told him that they had a score coming up and that they needed someone who was quick and who made the first move. That was Sean.

It was a three man score. Barney told him that the third guy was from out of town, a guy that Sean had never met.

At first, Sean declined. He had his own crew. Guys that he had grown up with, Tommy, Artie and Gus -- and a couple of others, if need be. Why would he want to work with some stranger?

Barney said, "Look Sean, I know you usually only work with 'Townies', me too. But I've known this guy for years. He's not from around here. But I knew him in Walpole, and I've worked with him before. And besides, it's his score. One thing I give ya' my word on, he's a stand-up guy."

Sean thought about it for a moment. Then he asked him, "Does this guy know me? Does he know you're askin' me?"

The Real Town

Barney shook his head. "Uh uh, like I said, he ain't from around here. I just told him I was gonna' talk to someone about comin' in. Look Sean, he don't even have to know your name. All he has to know is that I say you're a stand-up guy. And I'm tellin' you, it's a nice lookin' score."

Sean thought about it and decided to meet the guy. Even though he'd never worked with Barney, he respected him.

The guy's name was Jack Laby. Sean met him a few days later and they took a ride down to Connecticut.

Jack was older, somewhere in his fifties. But Sean took to him right away. By the time that they reached their destination, they were both comfortable with each other. Sometimes your gut knows, right from the start.

Their target was a bank which sat by itself in the middle of a good-sized lot with plenty of parking room. Jack and Sean parked on the other side of the street, about a half of a block away, facing the bank.

As they sat there, waiting for the armored car to deliver the money, Jack laid it out for him. "The truck comes down this way." He said, as he pointed his thumb over his shoulder. "It'll go right by us and pull into the lot and park right in front of the bank. The guard gets out and brings the bag inside. The thing is, when the truck guard leaves, they don't lock the bag up right away."

Glancing in his rear view mirror, Jack said, "And here they come, right on time."

As the armored truck went by them, Sean noted, from the name on the side, that it was a different armored car company from the ones with which he was familiar.

The Real Town

The truck pulled into the bank parking lot and came to a stop right in front of the bank door. A minute later, the side door in the back of the truck opened. A guard hopped down to the ground. He had a large money bag in his left hand. He had nothing in his right hand.

That caught Sean's attention. Usually, the guard who got out first was the one who had his pistol drawn. As Sean sat staring intensely, waiting for the second guard to get out of the truck, the guard with the bag of money casually strolled around the back of the truck and walked into the bank. He had left the side door open. From the angle that they were watching, Sean could see into the truck. He was literally staring at the back of the driver. There was no barrier between the driver and the money.

Eyes darting around, from other parked cars to rooftops, Sean said, "Get the fuck outta here. It's a set-up."

When the car didn't move, Sean's head snapped around. He was glaring at Jack. "What the fuck's goin' on here?"

With half a smile, Jack said, "Take it easy, Sean, ain't nothin' wrong . . ."

Sean interrupted him, curtly. "Nothin' wrong? One guard, no gun, no screen between the driver and the money . . . and he left the fuckin' door open? *Get me the fuck outta here.*"

Staring at Sean, with a slight grimace on his face, Jack said, "You never took a truck outside a' Boston, did you?"

Without waiting for an answer, he went on. "Probably all Brinks, right?"

Slowly, eyes still flickering around, Sean nodded his head in response.

The Real Town

Jack nodded back. "Figures. Lemme tell you something, Sean. They don't do trucks anywhere else like they do in Boston - especially Brinks. They're the worst. Outside of Boston, most of the trucks only use one guard with the driver. And most of them don't have that screen between the driver and the money."

While listening to Jack, Sean was staring at the truck. He could not believe that he was sitting there looking *into* an armored car, at the back of the driver. Then the other guard came walking out of the bank, walked around the rear of the truck, jumped back in and closed the steel door.

As the truck pulled away, Sean said to Jack. "What the fuck is that all about?"

Jack said, "Like I told you, this ain't Boston. They don't do it like that anywhere else. Just up there."

Sean's mind was racing. "Listen", he said, "Why bother just taking the bank? Why not do the truck?"

Jack shook his head. "By the time the truck gets here, it's almost empty. It's only got one more stop and it's a small drop. Most of the money's goin' in here. It's a lot easier. This place ain't even got a guard."

"Besides", he went on, "I am looking at a truck, a different truck. It'll be a while. But, if this score works out okay, we'll talk about it."

The Real Town

They watched the truck drop off the money again the following week, this time from a different angle. Sean was out of the car, walking in the direction of the bank as the truck pulled up. He timed it so that he was walking by the front door just a few seconds after the guard had brought the money inside. A quick glance allowed him to see the guard standing at the counter. He was talking to a young female teller behind the counter. A heavy set man in a suit was standing next to her, leaning over the counter apparently signing a piece of paper.

After the truck was gone, Jack said, "We're on for next week, okay?"

Barney was with them this time. He and Sean both agreed.

Barney said, "Hell, we could've done it this week."

Jack said, "Yeah, we could've. But next week we'll get twice as much money. There's a big housing project right behind the next block. Most of 'em are on welfare. They get their checks on the first and the fifteenth of the month. So every other week they drop off twice as much money. Next week's a check week."

During the week, Sean drove down twice by himself to check out the routes getting out of the area. He would have preferred to cross the state line into either Rhode Island or New York, and then swing around. But, Massachusetts was closer than both of them and his priority was getting out of the state as quickly as possible.

On the day of the score, Sean met Barney and Jack in a shopping mall a few miles from the bank. As he got into Jack's car, Barney said, "The swap cars are in place. We took care of them this morning."

It was essential to have extra cars in place, in case something went wrong. Jack drove them around to each of the cars so that they would know where they were.

The Real Town

They were in place, up the street from the bank; about a half an hour before the truck was scheduled to be there.

The plan was for Sean to enter first, with Barney behind him. Sean would get the money. Barney would cover his back. Jack was the driver.

The armored car pulled up in front of the bank about fifteen minutes later than usual. The guard got out, just like before, and trotted around into the bank with the money bag in his hand. This time, however, he was back out almost immediately.

They were ready. As the truck pulled away, Jack was on his way down the street. As the truck was pulling out of the exit from the far end of the lot into the street, Jack was pulling up in front of the bank.

Sean stepped out of the car and walked the few steps to the door. Just before he pushed the door open, he reached up to his neck and pulled a dark blue head-band up over his face. It covered his face from his chin to just underneath his eyes and the dark sunglasses that he was wearing, the dark ski cap on his head came down to the top of the glasses.

As he stepped through the door, he turned slightly to his right and walked quickly to that end of the counter. The counter was about ten feet from the door. It was open on both ends with three or four desks in a roomy area behind it. There were three female tellers, one on each end of the counter and one in the middle.

The bank manager was standing next to the end teller on Sean's right, chatting, with his hand casually resting on the bag of money which was just sitting on the counter.

Without pulling a pistol, Sean marched to the counter in three or four quick steps, snatched the bag, and spun back around towards the door.

The bank manager, obviously shocked, yelled, "Hey!"

At that point, Barney was just coming through the door. As Sean strode by him, Barney pointed a pistol past him and said, "Hold it right there."

A few seconds later they were back in the car and heading down the street. Barney and Sean were both on the floor in the back.

Moments later they were on a small side street, changing cars. After they got into the second car, Barney said, "Jesus Christ, Sean, I knew you were fast, but you were almost back out the door with the money, before I even got in there!"

When they got back to their own legitimate cars, Barney took the money and they split up, all three of them heading for Boston in separate cars.

They stopped at a motel, just outside of Boston, where Barney had rented a room, earlier. They went inside and counted the money. They had a total, of one hundred and twenty-one thousand, three hundred dollars.

They were standing by the bed, as Barney divided the money into three piles. As the piles reached forty thousand each, Sean glanced over at Barney with a mischievous grin on his face.

Barney grinned back. "Whatta you wanna' do, play a hand?"

Still grinning, Sean said, "Sounds good to me."

Jack was glancing back and forth between the two of them. "Whatta yez' talking about?"

Barney said, "His crew, when they're cuttin' up a score, an' get down to change, they round it off and play a hand of cards for the rest."

Jack said, "What kinda cards?"

Sean shrugged, "Don't matter to me. Five card showdown's good. That way everyone can see what's happenin'."

Reaching into his shirt pocket, Sean pulled out a new, unopened deck of cards. "Here", he said, tossing the deck to Jack. "You deal."

Looking at Sean rather skeptically, Jack said, "You took a deck of cards on a score with ya'?"

Sean laughed. "No. They were in my car. I buy a deck before every score."

Shaking his head as he finished shuffling the cards, Jack asked, "Anyone wanna' cut?"

Sean reached across and cut the deck saying, "Positively. As Grampa Bill always told me, 'Have faith in your fellow man. But always cut the cards'."

Jack dealt the cards slowly and, on the last card, Jack won, ironically, with a pair of Jacks. He beat Barney, who was winning with a pair of nines.

When the final Jack turned up, Barney said, "Oh, you sonofabitch!"

But all three of them were laughing.

Turning to Barney, Sean said, "Now tell the truth. With forty grand in your pocket, ain't that the best hand of cards you ever lost?"

They all laughed again.

The Real Town

After that, Sean started looking at scores out of state. He found out that Jack was right. Armored cars were far less security conscious outside of Boston. They were almost lackadaisical compared to the trucks in Boston. Even their reaction was different. When you got the drop on a Brinks guard, in Boston, it wasn't as if he wasn't expecting it, because he was. But, if you did it right, there just wasn't anything that he could do about it. When you got the drop on an out of town armored car guard, he was, invariably, shocked and surprised. It was as if he had never expected it to happen.

CHAPTER 5

When Sean came out of Kelly's he saw Barney parked across the street. Barney waved at him.

He walked over and got into the car. "What's up?"

Barney said, "I want you to take a look at somethin', a Brinks truck over in Chelsea."

Sean said, "On a Saturday?"

Barney shook his head. "No. The truck won't be there. I want you to take a look at a place where it makes a pick-up, when the place is closed."

They drove over the Mystic River Bridge, into Chelsea. A few minutes later, they pulled into the parking lot of what appeared to be a warehouse. It had a long loading dock where about fifteen to twenty trailer truck vans were parked.

As you entered the lot, the loading dock was on your right. Cruising slowly by the trucks, they came to the end of the loading dock. At the end of the dock, blocked from sight by the parked vans, was a small flight of stairs up to the dock, which led to a doorway, going into the building.

Pointing at the doorway, Barney said, "There's the stairs up to the office. That's where they pick up the money."

Pointing to the secluded area between the first parked trailer truck and the stairs, he continued, "That's where the Brinks truck parks when they go up to get the money"

Looking around, Sean immediately realized what Barney was showing him. The Brinks truck, being much smaller than the trailers, would be totally obscured from sight. He said, "I like it."

Barney went on. "It gets better. It's the truck's last pick-up of the day. It gets here about five o'clock on Mondays. I figure we take a couple of months to get ready. We hit it after Daylight Saving Time ends, when they turn the clocks back. By that time, it'll be dark, an' they'll never see us comin'."

Sean said, "You know how much, yet?"

Barney shook his head, "Not really. I don't know the whole route yet. But we got a couple a' months to find out. I do know this: I know two banks, a supermarket, and a department store that it picks up from. The last bank, the one it gets just before it comes here, the smallest amount that ever come outta there on a Monday, is three hundred and seventy-five grand, at least in the last three years. An' that's the *smallest* amount."

Sean raised an eyebrow, inquisitively. He was curious. But it wasn't a question one asked.

Barney shrugged his shoulders, "I know a woman who works there. Good broad. I take her out sometimes."

Barney had turned the car around. They were facing back towards the street.

Sean asked, "How many of these trucks are here when it comes in?"

Barney said, "Usually all of them are back by that time. An' if any of the slots are empty it'll be the one's down by the gate. They start parking at this end."

Sean said "Perfect. It'll be dark, so we can come in on foot and wait underneath the trailers right next to the Brinks. We'll be right next to them and they'll never see us."

The Real Town

Sean said, "How many guys ya' figure?"

"I don't know", he replied. "at least four, countin' the driver, maybe five. Figure one guy for the guards and we might need two for the money. We don't know how many bags there's gonna' be. An' I was thinkin' maybe one for the driver. I know we can't get to him, but maybe we can scare 'em into not hittin' the alarm."

Something that most people never realized about robbing an armored car was that the main problem was not the guards, it was the driver. In a Brinks truck, the driver would be partitioned from the two guards and the money. He also had access to a deadbolt that would lock the back section and make it impossible to open the rear door with a key. So, even if you got the drop on the guards when they were out of the truck, it was meaningless. The driver would just throw the deadbolt and the game would be over. The trick was to get the drop on the guards while the door was open. It's all in the timing.

Sean asked, "Does he park facing in or facing out?"

"In." Barney replied."

Sean nodded his head. "Sounds good, why don't we take a ride over here on Monday? I'll meet you down Kelly's about two."

CHAPTER 6

When they got back to Charlestown, Sean had Barney drop him off up at his mother's house. She lived at the top of Bunker Hill Street.

When Sean was twenty-two he had bought the house. At the time, he lived there with his sister, Anne, and their mother, Grace. Anne was two years older than Sean.

Then Anne got married. For a time Grace lived on the first floor, Anne and her husband, Pat, lived on the second floor, and Sean lived on the third floor.

Then Anne had her first baby. A little girl named Bridget. When Anne got pregnant the second time, Sean decided to let them have the two top floors.

When Anne had her son, Patrick, Sean bought another three family house, about a block from the Bunker Hill Monument.

On paper, his mother, and his sister and her husband, were all paying Sean rent. As were the tenants in the first two floors of the new house, who actually were paying rent. Sean lived on the third floor. On paper, Sean had the rent from five apartments as a legitimate income.

*

Sean spent the rest of the afternoon at his mother's house doing chores and chit-chatting. Anne, Pat and the kids came down. As it was Saturday, they were all having supper at Grace's. Every Saturday, Grace baked her own beans and bread. You could have your choice between steak and hot dogs. The kids usually took the hot dogs and the grown-ups took the steak. Sean took both.

The Real Town

After supper, Sean said that he was going to walk down to Kelly's to pick up his car.

Anne said, "I'll drop you off. I've got to take a run down to the store."

As they pulled up in front of Kelly's, Anne said, "Look Sean, I wanted to talk to you about something, but I didn't want to say anything in front of Ma . . . or Pat."

Sean immediately perked up. Anne might keep things from Ma - everybody kept some things from their mother - but not from Pat.

He said, "What's up? You got a problem?"

She shook her head. "No, not me, Meg."

Meg Doyle was Anne's best friend. They had grown up next door to each other. Sean had known her all of his life. She was a little bit of a thing, barely five feet tall, with shoulder length reddish-blonde hair and a face that would stop a clock -- and a body to match. She was also the sweetest person he knew, filled with energy, always smiling and sharp as a whip.

Sean asked, "What's the problem?"

Anne said, "There's a guy that's bothering her . . ."

Sean interrupted, "In Charlestown? Who?"

Anne shook her head. "Not in Charlestown. Meg's living over in the Back Bay, now. You know she got a promotion. So she got a place near the hospital."

Meg was a nurse. Even though she was still in her twenties, she was already in a supervisory position.

Anne went on. "There's a guy that lives upstairs in her building that's been bothering her. The problem is, he's a foreigner, from somewhere in the Middle East, and he's a big shot. He's got diplomatic immunity. Meg talked to the police about it but they said that there's nothing that they can do. See, he hasn't really done anything physical. But he keeps making remarks to her. She was on the elevator with him the other day -- just the two of them -- and he kept moving close to her and saying things. Things that he wanted to do to her. No, not what he *wants* to do to her, *what he's going to do to her*. But he never does it when there are people around. It's so weird. He's got a wife and kids. Meg ran into his wife and tried to talk to her about it but the woman just put her head down and kept on walking, muttering something in a foreign language."

Sean was openly angry. "That son of a bitch."

Taking a deep breath, Anne said, "Sean, you know Meg doesn't scare easily. But she's scared. She says that it's just a question of time. She's afraid that he's going to rape her."

Sean said, "Do you have her address?"

Anne nodded, taking a pen and a piece of paper out of her pocketbook.

"Here", she said, as she wrote it down on the paper. "Do you want her phone number?"

Sean shook his head. "No. Do you know his name?"

Nodding again, she said, "Uh huh."

She quickly wrote it down and handed it to him.

As Sean took the paper, he said, "Don't tell her that you told me."

Looking slightly baffled, she said, "Why not? It would make her feel a little safer and you know you can trust Meg."

"I know that," He replied. "But it's for her own good. The less she knows the better."

Nodding her head, slowly, she put her hand on his forearm and said, "Sean, I don't want you to get in any trouble. Jesus, Ma would kill me. But I'm so afraid for Meg. I've never seen her afraid of a guy like this."

With a bitter twist of her mouth, she said, "I wish the Hell she'd move back to the town. This would never happen here."

Then, eyes opening wide, clearly showing that something had just occurred to her, she said, "Sean, you're not going to kill him, are you? Jesus, now I wish I hadn't told you."

Fear and panic were obvious in her voice.

Sean took her hand in his and said, "First off, if you hadn't told me, I'd be mad at you. Second, I'm not going to kill him. Don't worry about it. There'll be no problems. Just don't tell anybody anything, okay?"

Anne smiled as she nodded her head. But her eyes were filled with tears.

"I couldn't even if I wanted to," she said. "Meg's gonna' be out of town until Friday. She's at a nurse's convention down in New York."

Sean thought for a moment, then smiled. "Really," he said.

Giving her a kiss on the cheek, he said, "Go on home, now, and take care of the kids. Everything's gonna' be okay."

CHAPTER 7

Sean walked back into Kelly's. The crowd had thinned out some, but his crew was still there. Rockball and Sammy were still with them.

Joining them, he bought a round of drinks.

Gus asked him, "Where's Barney?"

Sean just shrugged. "He dropped me off at my mother's a couple of hours ago. We just went for a ride to talk about a couple of things."

Sammy said. "You shoulda' stayed. Flaza and Butch Harkins had a fight."

Sean said, "What! Flaza had a fight with Butch? How the fuck could he do that?"

They all started laughing.

It wasn't that fights were uncommon in Kelly's but Butch Harkins was in a wheelchair. He had been wounded, and crippled, in the Korean War. Butch was a good-sized guy, at least from the waist up. He had big muscular arms and huge hands. He was also a miserable son of a bitch, which, in reality, was understandable. Being in a wheelchair, could certainly make you as cranky as he was. He was a pain in the ass. He'd bang into guys with his wheelchair, or run over your foot and then tell you to 'get the fuck out of the way'.

Occasionally, someone would get pissed off enough to say something to him. He'd immediately call them out and challenge them to a fight. But, of course, you couldn't. How can you hit a guy in a wheelchair?

The Real Town

Flaza Flynn, on the other hand, was a pretty easy going guy, but he could also fight a little bit -- and he liked to fight.

Sean said, "Okay, what happened?"

Sammy said, "Well, Butch was being his usual nasty self, and he runs his wheelchair into Flaza. He knows Butch so he tells 'em to knock it off, to stop being an asshole and to look where he's going. And Butch tells him, if he don't like it to do something about it.

"Now Flaza's getting more and more pissed off, and the madder he gets, the more Butch is bustin' his balls. He's telling Flaza that if he could get up and get his hands on him he'd kick his ass.

"Finally, Flaza loses it. He grabs Butch's chair and wheels him over to the wall, a coupla' feet out from the corner, then turns the chair around so Butch is facing out. Then he goes and gets himself a chair, brings it over to the corner, and puts it right next to Butch, facing the other way, so they're sitting side by side, but they're facing each other.

"Flaza says, 'You wanna' fight? O.K., let's fight. I won't get up outta this fuckin' chair. So, it's a fair fight.'

"And punches Butch in the face.

"They must've sat there punching each other for ten minutes, maybe fifteen. And Flaza never moved out of the chair. It was a fair fight, and in the end, Flaza won.

"But I gotta' give Butch this, he didn't quit. He reached the point where he had nothin' left. Like I said, they punched the shit out of each other for about fifteen minutes. They were both covered with blood. Finally, Butch was done. He couldn't even throw any more punches. So, Flaza stops hittin' 'em.

"He says, 'Ya' had enough?'

"Butch says 'Fuck you!' an' tries to hit 'em again.

"Flaza just blocked it. He knew he was all done. He said, "Aw, fuck it, I don't want any more, we'll call it a draw."

They were all grinning. Artie said to Sammy, "Didja see the look on Sean's face when ya' first told him who had a fight? He looked just like Pebbles did when Flaza told him."

They all started laughing again.

Tommy said to Sean, "When Flaza went to get the chair, he went over to the card table. Pebbles was sittin' in the chair at the end a' the table, an' Flaza asks him if he can use the chair for a coupla' minutes.

"Pebs says, 'Hey Flaz, I'm playin' cards.'

"Flaza leans over an' says something to him, we can't hear. All we hear is Pebs say, 'Ya' gonna' fight with Butch Harkins?' And he looked just like you did when he said it.

"Then Flaza says somethin' else we couldn't hear, an' Pebs turns around an' looks at Butch, then he looks back at Flaz an' says 'That's a good idea. I wish the fuck I thought a' that.' And he gets up and gives Flaza the chair."

Sammy said, "Yeah, Butch ran inta' Pebbles a coupla' times, too.

Sean asked, "What happened after? Were guys bustin' his balls?"

The Real Town

Tommy said "No, not really. Flaza went in the bathroom to clean up. Like Sammy said, they were both covered with blood. A couple a guys got wet rags from behind the bar an' Butch cleaned himself up. Then, when Flaza came outta the shithouse, he bought them both a drink an' they started shootin' the shit. Guys kept sendin' them drinks. We sent 'em a couple. And guys kept telling' him what a good fight it was. I don't think I ever saw Butch talk as much, or to as many guys, as he did today, even after Flaza took off, guys kept doin' it.

"Ya' know, I think afterwards Butch was glad it happened. For most of the fight he gave as good as he got and, even though in the end he did get his ass kicked, for a while, he got to be a guy again."

As they were standing there shooting the breeze, a piece came on the television, up over the bar, about Sacco and Vanzetti. It was about the anniversary of their execution. They had been executed forty years ago that month, right there in Charlestown. They all went quiet, watching it.

As the narrator of the show described the world-wide demonstrations that had protested their executions, the television screen was filled with an overview of Charlestown State Prison, where they had been executed in the electric chair.

The prison had been torn down about ten years earlier, after a series of riots, but, on screen, it was just as ugly as they all remembered it. Time Magazine had once described it as "a cramped compound of blackened granite and dilapidated brick buildings in the Charlestown section of Boston, [it] is the oldest, most disreputable prison in the U.S. It was built in 1805, has been damned for 80 years as a verminous pesthole, unfit for human habitation."

The show was a recap of the controversy that had been argued since before their execution: Were they framed and falsely executed, or was it a legitimate conviction?

After it was over, Rockball said, "They were bum-beefed."

Sean said, "Yeah, I always thought so, too."

Rockball said, "I don't think so. I know so."

"Yeah?"

"Yeah. I was with an old timer when I was in Charlestown. He told me about it."

Rockball had begun serving his lengthy sentence in the old Charlestown State Prison, where Sacco and Vanzetti had been executed, but had finished it at Walpole, which was built and opened, during his stay. Charlestown State Prison had been torn down as a result of the notorious "Cherry Hill Riots". Another result of those riots was that Rockball had wound up in the 'hole' for a couple of years. The allegation being that he was one of the leaders of the riot.

He went on. "He was an old school guinea from Rhode Island, a good guy. He's gone now. He musta' been in his seventies by then. He said they took the score an' then made it right back to Rhode Island. He said nobody knew Sacco or Vanzetti. No one had ever even heard of them till they got busted."

Sean said, "Yeah, and I heard that they both went out like guys. They didn't snivel."

Sammy said, "Yeah, like 'Trigger' Burke. I love the way he went out."

Gus said, "Who was he?"

Sammy said, "He was a guy from New York. I heard he use to come up here sometimes."

Turning to Rockball, he asked, "Did you know him, Joe?"

Nodding his head, Rockball responded, "Yeah, but not well. I met him one night down the Alibi. He was in town seein' some friends. Good guy."

Gus said to Sammy, "Whadda ya mean, ya loved the way he went out? Did he get fried, too?"

Sammy said, "Yeah, in New York. He got busted up here for machine gunning 'Specs' O'Keefe, over in Dorchester - you know, the rat in the Brinks score over the North End. After he got busted they had him over the Charles Street Jail and he escaped. Later on, they caught him down in South Carolina and brought him back to New York and tried him for a murder. No big deal, just a barroom beef. Some guy got dead, but they gave him the death sentence. They were tryna' get him to talk. They told him if he'd give up everyone in Boston and New York, they'd let him off. Of course, he said 'No'.

"It went right up to the night they were gonna fry him. They had him strapped in the chair and, from where he was sittin', he could see the phone. The Warden told him if he'd talk, he'd call the Governor right from there and get him off the hook. Just before they fried him, the Warden came over and tried one last time. He said, "This is it, Mr. Burke. Do you have a last request?"

"Trigger said, 'Yeah. Sit in my lap.'"

They were all laughing and grinning.

Rockball said, "Ya know how ya said he escaped from Charles Street. Didja know it was a guy from the Alibi that broke him out?"

Sammy said, "No. I never heard that."

They were all smiling.

Rockball said, "Yeah, ballsy move. There was a little back door on the back street between Charles Street and the Mass. General Hospital. The guy broke into it. It went into a hallway that came to a door that opened up into the back of the jail. It was a door that they never used. He broke in, in the middle of the night, and undid the inside door. I think he mighta' took the hinges off it. He'd already gotten word into Trigger and Trigger knew he was coming. When Trigger came through the door, the guy was waitin' for him, and they were gone."

Sean said, "Nice move."

Then, finishing his drink, he said, "Okay, it's Saturday night. I know we ain't gonna' spend it in Kelly's. Anybody hungry? I feel like pizza."

Everybody immediately agreed.

Tommy said, "Let's go over the Regina."

Turning to Rockball, he asked, "You been over the Regina since you come home, Joe?"

Smiling, Joe said, "No. But, it's about time. Let's go."

The Regina was over the bridge, in the North End. They had all grown up eating pizza at the Regina. It was the best pizza in Boston.

*

After stuffing themselves with pizza, they walked down the street a couple of blocks to a local nightclub up the street from the Boston Garden that Rockball wanted to see, The Batcave.

The Batcave was a good-sized saloon with a round bar in the middle of the room, just a few feet from the door

The place was crowded and, as they walked in, a majority of the people at the bar turned around to stare at them.

The North End was as Italian as Charlestown was Irish, and just as insular.

As they approached the bar a short, stocky, Italian man stepped into view on the left-hand side of the circular bar.

"Joe?" He said, as he walked towards Rockball. "I'll be a son of a bitch. I don't believe this. I just heard you got out, a couple of hours ago."

Joe reached out to shake hands. The man, with a large grin on his face walked past his hand and hugged him.

Still grinning, he stepped back and said, "I just called a guy I know over in Charlestown and told him I hadda talk to you. You didn't get my message this quick, did ya'?"

Joe shook his head. "No. We just come over the Regina for Pizza an' I figured I'd take a walk down an' see if you were around."

Turning around to the others, he said, "Guys, this is a friend of mine, Larry B."

After he completed the introductions, Larry led them all to a large round booth. As they were sitting down, he nodded his head to Rockball, saying, "I gotta' talk t' ya' for a minute."

Waiving a waitress over to the table, he said, "Give these guys anything they want."

Then, glancing at Sean, he said, "We'll be back in a minute."

Larry and Rockball went into a back room. Larry said, "I wasn't shittin' ya' when I said I sent you a message. A couple a' guys from Winter Hill came over the office a little while ago. They wanted t' let us know that you were out an' that there might be a problem. I think they're afraid you're gonna' pick up the beef again, because a' Stevie Hughes gettin' whacked."

Joe shook his head. "It's not a problem, as long as they don't make it one. As far as I'm concerned the beef's over. If I was out when it went down? Yeah, I woulda' been with Stevie. But I wasn't. So why start somethin' up again that wasn't my beef in the first place? Like I said, as far as I'm concerned, it's history."

Just then a waitress brought them over a round of drinks. She placed Larry's on the table in front of him and said to Rockball, "Your friends say this is what you're drinking."

He tasted the drink and said, "That's it. Thanks."

After she walked away, he looked back at Larry and said, "On the other hand, if they want a problem, they can have one."

Larry shook his head, "Nah, they don't want no more trouble. Everyone's happy that shit's over.'

Raising his drink, he grinned at Rockball, "Salud, Joe. Welcome home."

Tipping their glasses towards each other, they each took a drink, then got up and went back out to the bar to join the others.

They sat around for another hour or so, swapping stories and having a good time.

At one point, Larry said, "Hey, did you guys see that thing on Sacco and Vanzetti on the TV tonight?"

The Real Town

When they acknowledged that they had, he turned to Rockball and said, "I was thinkin' a' you when they mentioned how the joint finally got torn down after the Cherry Hill Riot. Tell them about the medical records yez' found."

Rockball grinned, "When we had the joint, we were goin' through everything and we found these old medical records. You know the joint was built way back in 1805, and according to the medical records, every guy that died in there up to 1912, or maybe 1920, I forget which, anyway, they all died from the same thing, every one of them.

"What'd they die from?"

He replied, "Masturbation."

They all started laughing.

"No shit."

"Get outta here."

He was still grinning. "On every medical record for the guys that got dead, under "Cause of Death", it said "Masturbation"."

Larry said, "Ya know, when I was watchin' the Sacco/Vanzetti thing I was thinkin' about Georgie Mac. I always heard he got bum-beefed too."

Rockball said, "Yeah, he did. Everyone knew it. But with all the heat he had from the beef with the Hill, he never had a shot. Ya' know the feds hated him and his brothers."

Larry nodded, "Yeah, they wanted him off the street. Now they're gonna fry his ass, too."

George McLaughlin had been convicted of a murder that had nothing to do with the Charlestown/Winter Hill Irish war. He was now sitting on death row, waiting to be executed.

CHAPTER 8

As they were walking back to their cars, Rockball told them what Larry had said about Winter Hill.

Artie asked him, "You think ya' got a problem?"

Rockball shrugged his shoulders. "We'll see. If I do, the problem'll be theirs."

They headed back over the bridge into Charlestown. They had agreed to meet at the Blue Mirror

The 'Mirror' was a nightclub located down by the water, beside the Navy Yard. According to the fire laws, it could legitimately hold three hundred and seventy-five customers. That was okay during the week. But, on the weekends, by closing time there would inevitably be at least five hundred people jammed in there.

They parked their cars out in back and walked around to the front door. Halfway around, they came to the end of a line of people waiting to get in, that stretched down around the corner to the door. As they approached the door Rockball said, "Fuck, we gotta' wait in line to get in here?"

The 'Mirror' had not been opened when he had gone back to Walpole so he only knew of it by word of mouth.

Sean said, "No. Just keep goin', follow Tommy."

They walked on by the front door and Tommy turned into the door of the adjoining diner, the Blue Bonnet. There were a number of people sitting at tables, and at the counter, eating. It was obvious from their body language that this was simply a quick snack stop, a 'chew and screw' joint.

The Real Town

As Tommy made his way past the counter he waved to a young lady, behind the counter, who was setting a sandwich down in front of a customer. "Hey Sally, how ya' doin'."

Smiling, she winked at him and turned back to her customer.

They walked through a back door into an office, then through the office, out another door and into the middle of the Blue Mirror. The place was packed and the band was blaring.

As they made their way to the bar Rockball said, "Jesus, ya' think it's a little crowded?"

Sean said, "Yeah, it's like this every weekend. But it ain't really the kinda' crowd ya' mind is it?"

Looking around, Rockball shook his head and said, "Uh uh, there really are lot a' good lookin' broads in here."

As they reached the bar, Tommy passed them both a drink. For the next couple of hours they drank and partied. The majority of the guys in the bar were from Charlestown. There were a couple of different crowds from out of town. For the most part, out of town guys came from Somerville, Cambridge, or South Boston, and they usually had friends from Charlestown.

It was different with the girls, though. A far greater number of them came from out of town.

As Rockball had spent the last seven years locked up and this was his first time in the 'Mirror', Tommy was telling him about the place As Sean returned from the dance floor, Tommy said, "Hey Sean, tell Joe what that girl told you about the 'Mirror' that night over the Sonesta."

Sean was smiling at the girl that he'd been dancing with as she returned to her table, smiling back. He said, "Aw, she was this cute kid from West Roxbury. At least that's where she said she was from.

"Anyways, we wound up over the Sonesta one night after closin' time, down here."

Joe said, "Where's the Sonesta?"

Sean said, "Right over at the end of the Prison Point Bridge, in Cambridge."

With a half smile, he said, "I'm sure you remember where that is."

Grimacing slightly, Rockball said, "Yeah, I think I remember."

The Prison Point Bridge was called that because it began in Charlestown, right where the old Charlestown State Prison had been located, and ran over the railroad tracks, into Cambridge.

Sean went on. "So we're in bed and, at one point, we're sorta' catchin' our breath an' havin' a cigarette an' just talkin' an' I ask her how she wound up down the 'Mirror'.

"She gives me this big smile an' says, 'You kiddin'? Everybody knows about the 'Mirror'. If you want to go out an' fool around, it's not like downtown where you can get into trouble or run into someone you know. I mean, for all the fighting and stuff that goes on down the Mirror, guys only hit guys. And you know you're not gonna' run into your boy friend, or your husband.'

"I said, 'Why not?'

"She started giggling. She said, 'Come on, guys from outside of Charlestown don't go down there.' Then she rolled her eyes and said, 'I know guys from West Roxbury don't'.

"By that time, we were done with our smoke and we started foolin' around again. But I always remembered what she said. I'd never really thought about it like that before, but she was right."

Rockball looked around the club and said, half jokingly, "She ain't here tonight, is she?"

When Sean just smiled, Tommy grinned at Rockball and said, "He wouldn't tell you if she was. He thinks that guys that tell ya' who they fuck, are stool pigeons."

Rockball looked at Sean with a raised eyebrow. "That's kinda hard, ain't it?"

In Charlestown, being a 'stool pigeon' was the equivalent of being a 'diddler' or a 'skinner' i.e. a child molester or a rapist.

Sean looked back at Rockball and shrugged, saying, "What's the difference between rattin' on a girl, or rattin' on a guy? A rat's a rat."

Just then, a tall, slender, very good-looking girl, with long straight blonde hair, poked Sean's shoulder with her finger.

"Hey you," she said, "how come you're not dancing?"

Looking over his shoulder, he said, "Hey Lee, long time no see."

Kissing him on the cheek she said, "I've been out in California for the past couple of months and I'm leaving town again in a few days. C'mon, let's dance."

"Sure", he said, as he turned towards Rockball. "Joe, this is a friend of mine, Lee. Lee, this is Joe. He's been out of town, too."

The Real Town

They both said 'Hi'. Then Sean and Lee went to the dance floor. It was a slow song and as soon as they started dancing Lee snuggled up against him. She was almost as tall as Sean and could easily nuzzle his neck, which she did.

After a minute, she leaned her head back and, with a curious look, said, "Whereabouts out of town has he been?"

Sean said, "Walpole."

Her eyes brightened up. With a catch in her throat, she softly asked, "For how long?"

"Oh, I don't know exactly", he said. "About seven years or so, he just got out yesterday."

She caught her breath and actually shivered.

Lee was a rather unique young lady. She lived on Beacon Hill and came from old Yankee money. Well educated, highly intelligent and one of the most fiercely independent girls that Sean knew - and very curious. She led various lives which she kept separate from each other.

Sean had first met her at The Sevens, a bar on Charles Street, at the bottom of Beacon Hill. Charles Street was Boston's version of Greenwich Village and The Sevens was a bar that was populated mostly by 'beatniks', back before they became 'hippies'. Lee had been going through her beatnik/hippie phase.

The Real Town

They had had a short torrid fling that ended quite amicably, two people, from two different worlds, who were looking for nothing more than sex. Afterwards, they remained friends who ran into each other occasionally. At one point, long after their affair had ended, they ran into each other in town and, after a few drinks, Sean brought her down to the 'Mirror'. She loved it. It was entirely different from anything that she had ever known. She began dropping in on her own. Not often, but occasionally. Sean came in one night and saw her sitting at the bar. He went over and joined her.

In the course of the evening, she told him that she had been there a number of times, by herself, since the night he had first brought her there. With a coy smile, she said, "I always sit at the bar and as soon as I sit down I ask whoever I'm sitting next to, if they've seen you. That always breaks the ice. You wouldn't believe some of the things that people have said in front of me."

Then, in a low whisper, filled with wonder, "I can't believe how many of them have been in prison. I was in the ladies room one night and a girl asked me if I knew that the fellow that was sitting next to me -- *the guy I was talking to* -- was a bank robber. I was so excited. But when I went back out, his girl friend was there. That sort of ended the conversation. But he seemed like such a nice guy. I never would have guessed. It got me thinking."

As if to compose her thoughts, she stopped talking and took a sip of her drink. After a long moment of silence, with cheeks faintly blushing, she said, "I kept wondering what it would be like to be with a guy who just got out of prison - to be the first one."

Then, looking up at him, freely blushing and giggling, she said, "You haven't been in prison, have you?"

"No", he'd replied, as he knocked three times on the wooden bar.

Now, as they finished dancing, that conversation was in the forefront of both of their minds.

She said, "Why did you tell me that he'd been in prison?"

With a half smile, he said, "I thought you might want to know."

She thought for a moment and then, smiling back, said, "Why don't you buy me a drink?"

They went back to the bar, got another round and began to chat with the others. Within a little while, Lee and Joe were talking quite amiably. After a few dances and a few more drinks, Lee went to the ladies room. Rockball leaned over and asked Sean, "Listen, Sean, is Lee, uh . . ."

Sean interrupted softly. "Lee's a good kid an' she's a friend of mine. That's it, just friends. Go for it."

A few minutes after Lee came out Rockball took her to the dance floor again. They never returned.

CHAPTER 9

The following Thursday, Sean called Tommy and arranged to pick him up at his house.

When Tommy got in the car, he said, "Where ya' been? I ain't seen you since ya' left the 'Mirror' Saturday night..

Sean said, "I been keepin' the peek on a guy that's been botherin' a friend of ours."

"Who?" Tommy asked.

"Meg Doyle," he replied.

"Meg? Who the fuck's botherin' Meg?"

"Some guy in the Back Bay, some kind of Arab who's got immunity. I been sittin' on him all week."

"Whaddaya mean he's got immunity?"

"He's got some kind of diplomatic immunity. I didn't bother getting into it too much. It's not like I'm gonna' call the cops. I just wanted to clock him. I pretty much know where he'll park when he gets home tonight."

Tommy asked, "Ya' gonna' whack him?"

Sean said, "No, not unless I have to."

"Shit", Tommy responded. "It'll be a lot quicker."

"Yeah, I know. But it probably won't be necessary. We'll see"

Smiling, Tommy leaned back in his seat, "Okay then, you wanna' do the good guy or the bad guy?"

Glancing sideways at him, Sean said, "I'll do the bad guy."

Now grinning, Tommy said, "I figured that. You had the hots for Meg since we was kids."

Half smiling, Sean said, "Fuck you."

In fact, he *had* had a crush on Meg Doyle when they were kids. Unrequited, of course, in Meg's eyes, Sean was simply her best friend's little brother.

They were cruising down Beacon Street, in the Back Bay. Sean pointed to a rather tall building, on the right hand side of the street. "That's where he lives."

Tommy asked, "Where does he park?"

Sean said, "The closest spot that's open. Handicapped, fire hydrant, crosswalk, it don't matter. He parks wherever he wants. Like I said, he's got immunity."

Smirking, Tommy said, "Not from everything."

Then, in a more serious tone, "Okay, how ya' wanna' play it?"

Sean outlined the impending scenario. When he was through, Tommy said, "Sounds good. You got the van ready?"

Sean said, "Uh huh, right over the bridge."

Tommy looked up and realized that they were pulling into South Boston. "We gonna' leave the car in Southie? Good. We can stop off an' have a drink with 'Neezo' afterwards."

'Neezo' was a friend of theirs, named Tommy Nee, whom they had not seen in a while.

They parked on a side street and walked about two blocks and got into a black van. Before getting in, they each put on a pair of transparent surgical gloves, just one of the many ways that they had of avoiding leaving fingerprints.

As they drove back into the downtown area, Tommy asked, "So, you wanna' take him at his work or at his house?"

The Real Town

"It all depends on what time he leaves work. If he leaves before it gets dark, we'll wait till he gets home. But if he stays till it's dark, the parkin' lot's perfect. The building where he works is in the financial district an' it's got one of those small parkin' lots that's blocked in by buildings on three sides. We're comin' up to it now."

Slowing down to a crawl, Sean pointed over to a small parking lot in the middle of the block on his left. "Right there, that's his car in the back, the Caddy."

There were only three cars left in the lot, the Cadillac, a small sports car and a van. They were all parked at the back.

They parked the van across the street from the lot. Sean said, "He comes out the door on the far end of the building, on the corner. So I'll get there just before 'em. Let's swap seats so he don't see me gettin' out."

After they changed seats, Sean reached into the glove compartment and took out a small pink and white flowery looking cloth bag, about a foot or so long. He then took out a long flat, leather covered, lead blackjack with a leather strap on its end. Sliding it into the flowery bag, he tightened the drawstring at the top of the bag, leaving the leather strap hanging out.

They patiently waited for over an hour. During which time it got progressively dark. At one point, Sean smiled and said, "Perfect. We're on for here."

Finally, the corner door at the far end of the building opened and a rather tall man came out. He turned right, and started walking in the direction of the parking lot.

Sean said, "Here we go."

Quietly sliding out of the van, he walked around the back and ambled across the street. He reached the lot a half a dozen steps before the oncoming target. Stopping on the sidewalk for a moment, just outside of the lot, he pulled a set of keys out of his pocket with his left hand and held them up to glance at them and then put them back into his pocket as he continued into the lot. It was obvious to anyone who might be watching that Sean was totally unaware of the man who entered the lot only a few steps behind him, slightly to his right. In the moment that Sean had ostensibly stopped to check his keys, he had peripherally glanced to his right. A move his target completely missed as he was contemptuously staring down at the bright pink and white flowery bag that was dangling from Sean's right wrist.

About half-way to the back of the lot, Sean started patting his pockets with his left hand. He was obviously having difficulty finding something. Looking down towards his pockets, he stopped for a second. In that second, as Meg's stalker drew up next to him, Sean's right hand snapped up and backwards.

The pretty flowery bag caught the target flush across the point of his jaw. He dropped like a sack of potatoes.

Immediately, the black van backed into the lot. Sean opened the rear door. He easily lifted his prey and threw him into the van. Jumping in behind him and closing the door, he said, "Go."

As Tommy pulled back out onto the street, he and Sean both vigilantly scanned the area. There was no one in sight. Moreover, all of the windows in the building across the street were dark.

Sean quickly stripped the Arab of all of his clothes. Rolling him over, he taped his wrists behind his back. Finally, he taped his eyes shut. Then he got back into the front seat.

After a while, they heard their passenger moaning, then muttering.

They began their conversation.

Tommy said, "So, whatta we gonna' do with him?"

Sean replied, "Just take 'em down the docks. We'll kill him down there, then just dump him inna water."

At this point, their passenger, who was lying on his back, with his feet down towards the front seats, cried, "My God, what is happening?"

Sean said, "Shut the fuck up", and smashed him across the front of his exposed shin bone with a craggy iron bar.

The unexpectedness of the assault brought on a loud scream of pain.

The intensity and sharpness of the pain caused the screaming to continue, Sean struck him again, this time across the front of the other shin. "I said shut the fuck up. You scream again, I'll rip ya' fuckin' nuts off."

That reduced the screaming to whimpering.

Sean and Tommy continued their routine.

Tommy said, "You sure ya' wanna' whack 'em? I thought the boss said to just give him a message?"

Sean said, "Yeah, yeah, I know. But it's our call. He said if we don't think he got the message, we just whack 'em. I don't think he got the message."

Tommy said, "C'mon Mike, ya' didn't even give him the message."

Sean said, "Look Lou, ya' know he's gonna' say he won't bother the broad no more. Then when he does, we just gotta' come back an' whack him anyways. So why don't we just do it now an' save the time?"

At this point, the Arab, interjected, "What are you talking about? Oh my God, please tell me. Please!"

Sean said, "You been botherin' some broad that lives downstairs from ya'. Some broad ya' keep tellin' yer gonna' fuck 'er? Well, you ain't, pal. She got friends."

The Arab immediately denied it. "It is not me. I did not do it. I swear. It is not me. You have the wrong person."

Sean said, "Ah, shut the fuck up. See what I mean. Mike? ya' think he got the message?"

The Arab yelled, "I tell you. It is not . . . *arrrrrrgghh!*"

Sean cut him short with a blow from the craggy iron bar across the pelvic region. That definitely stopped him.

As he lay there, curled into the fetal position, sniveling, gasping and gagging. Tommy said, "Yeah, I guess yer right. If he's tryin' t' bullshit us that it wasn't him, I guess we gotta' dump him."

Sean climbed into the back and rolled him over, sitting him up against the side of the van. Taking out an automatic pistol, he held it close to the Arab's face and, loudly pulling back the slide, cocked the gun. "I'll finish him here. Just pull down the end of the dock an' we'll dump him in the water."

The reaction was instantaneous. As his entire body stiffened with obvious panic, the Arab opened his mouth to speak. "*Wait . . . I . . . mmmhh*"

Whatever he had to say was cut off as Sean jammed the barrel of the pistol into his mouth, breaking his two front teeth in half.

At that point, Tommy interjected. "Hey, wait a minute, Mike. You ain't gonna' waste the gun on him, are ya'? I like that gun, Just strangle 'em, or cut his throat."

Keeping the gun in his mouth for another long moment, Sean finally removed it, slowly, saying, "Yeah, awright, gimme a cord, or a knife."

As the gun came out, the Arab, blood splattering from his mouth, sputtered, "Oh . . . oh . . . please, please, do not . . . do not kill me. I swear I will not do it again. I will never see her again. I will never talk to her again. Please. Oh my God. I swear it."

Sean said, "Yeah, right. I thought ya' didn't do it?"

Sobbing, he said, "I am so sorry. I was wrong. I swear on God's name I will not do it again."

After three or four long seconds of silence, Sean said, "You believe him?"

Tommy replied, "I don't know. The boss did say that if he'd move out of the building and never see her again, to give him a chance."

Another long silence, then Sean said, "Aw fuck. I'd just as soon dump 'em now. Lemme tell ya' somethin', '*Akbar*'. If I have to come back for you, you ain't gonna' like the way I kill ya'. You'll think today was a *good* day. I'll fuckin' chew you t' death. Here's the deal. You go home tonight an' pack yer shit and be outta there by tomorrow. I don't give a fuck where ya' go. But ya' better be gone. You ever even go near that place again, you're history. Ya' hear me?"

"Oh yes, yes", he replied, relief flooding his voice. "I will be gone. I swear."

Tommy said, "Don't forget the other thing the boss said."

Sean said, "Oh, yeah. We don't want the broad to know anything about this. If she hears about it, you're gone. If you ever run into her anyplace, you just get the fuck outta there. You got that?"

"Oh yes, yes", he said.

Pulling up to the sidewalk on a deserted street in Roxbury, Sean opened the rear door and, in one fluid move, slit the tape that bound the wrists and brusquely shoved him out door, still naked and unseeing, throwing his clothes out onto the street behind him.

They pulled around the corner and were out of sight before he even had the tape removed from his eyes.

CHAPTER 10

That Saturday, when Sean went to his mother's house, his sister was waiting for him. After being greeted by his mother, Anne said to him, "Listen Sean, Pat's down the park with the kids. You wanna' come upstairs and give me a hand moving something?"

"Sure", he answered.

As soon as they got upstairs, she said to him, "The Arab moved out. When Meg got home last night he was gone. The landlord told her that he didn't even know that the guy was moving. He said that he happened to look out the window and saw this big moving truck out there, with the guy's wife talking to the movers as they loaded their furniture and stuff. When he went out to ask them what was going on no one would talk to him. She just told him they were moving. When he asked her where her husband was, she got all 'plexed up. He said she started waving her arms an' talking in some foreign language."

Sean said, "Well, that's good. It'll save me the trouble of having to talk to him. Unless she still thinks he's a problem?"

Raising her eyebrow, she looked at him skeptically and asked, "You haven't talked to him, yet?"

Sean shook his head, "No. I've been busy all week an' I figured where Meg was out of town it wasn't a pressing matter. I was gonna' grab him this weekend. Guess I won't have to, now."

Looking skeptical, Anne said, "Well, that's good. By the way, seeing as you're not going to have to do anything, I can tell Meg that you know, right?"

Sean said, "I don't know. Maybe you better not. Just in case this guy keeps on bothering her, ya' know? I still might have to speak to him."

Anne nodded her head, as if confirming her thoughts and, with a slight knowing smile, said, "Uh huh, sure. I won't mention it. C'mon, let's go downstairs. I can hear Pat and the kids. And Ma must have supper ready by now."

CHAPTER 11

On Monday, Sean and Tommy met Barney at Billy Driscoll's, the bar where Barney hung out, down on Medford Street. They got into Barney's car and drove over the bridge into Chelsea, then continued on into Revere.

After parking on a side street, off of Broadway, Barney said, "I'll show you the stops I know so far. The truck'll be by in a couple a' minutes."

About ten minutes later, a large gray Brinks truck came down Broadway and went by the street where they were parked. Barney let three other cars go by before he pulled out to follow the truck.

The next stop was at a shopping mall where they made three stops, picking up bags of money at a supermarket, a bank and then a department store.

After leaving the mall, they proceeded back down Broadway, stopping at another bank, a small bank. After about ten minutes inside they came out carrying six money bags.

Glancing over at Sean, Barney said, "This is the bank I told you about."

Then, looking into the back seat at Tommy, he continued, "The smallest amount that's come outta here in the last three years is three hundred and seventy five grand."

Tommy nodded. "Sean told me."

The Real Town

They followed the truck down Broadway, into Chelsea, with six cars in between them. As they approached the intersection a few hundred yards before their destination, the light turned red after the truck went through, but before they could make it. After the light changed they drove up to the warehouse, slowly going past the gate. The loading dock was already filled with parked trailers. The armored truck was nowhere in sight.

Tommy asked, "Is it in there? I can't see anything."

Barney said, "It's in there. The trucks are blockin' it."

They continued on for about a quarter of a mile then did a U-turn and pulled over and parked, facing in the direction of the truck. A few minutes later, the truck appeared, coming towards them. Suddenly, about a quarter of a mile away, it took a left turn.

Tommy said, "Where's it goin'?"

Barney said, "It's headin' for Logan Airport. That's where they drop the money off at night."

Turning around to look at Tommy, he said, "Whaddaya think?"

Tommy smiled. "I love it. I wanna' take a look in the warehouse yard, behind the trucks."

Sean said, "We will. Not yet though, there's still people workin' in there, upstairs. We'll come back later tonight and check it out. Feel like gettin' somethin' to eat?"

Barney said, "Yeah. There's a place up on Orient Heights that's got great lasagna. Wanna' try it?"

"Sure. We love lasagna. Who don't?"

The Real Town

CHAPTER 12

After the waitress took their orders and brought them their drinks, Sean was looking around the restaurant. It was a typical old school Italian place, dark, yet clean, with bustling waitresses and a wonderful aroma. As his gaze drifted over the scene, he became aware of two women, in a booth on the other side of the room, who were staring in their direction. They looked to be in their late twenties, and were both quite pretty. He looked back.

They both smiled at him and one of them playfully pointed her finger at him. Not quite getting it, Sean raised his eyebrow. Smiling even wider, she turned her hand and made little side-ways pointing gestures. Sean thought for a moment and then, still staring at her, he raised his eyebrow inquisitively again and pointed across the table at Barney.

She started laughing and nodded her head.

Barney and Tommy were sitting on the other side of the booth talking and had been unaware of Sean's byplay until he pointed at Barney.

Before Sean could say anything, Barney turned and looked across the room. His face broke into a large smile. "I'll be a son of a bitch."

Sliding out of the booth, he ambled across the room. As he approached their table, the one who had been pointing, stood up and greeted him with a warm embrace.

He came back about ten minutes later, as the waitress was delivering their food. When she was done laying out their dishes, Barney said to her, "Send those two girls over there a round and just add their check to our bill. I've got it. Give 'em anything they want."

The waitress smiled at him. "You know Laura and Gina?"

Barney, seeming slightly distracted, nodded. "Yeah, we're old friends."

After she left they began eating. They all agreed that the food - they'd all gotten the lasagna - was delicious, as they finished eating, Laura and Gina appeared at the table.

Laura said, "We're on our way out of here. We just wanted to thank you for supper."

Smiling back, Barney introduced them to Sean and Tommy, and said, "You wanna' stick around and have a couple a drinks?"

With a meaningful look, shaded by a slight grimace, she said, "I'd love to, but I have to pack. I really do."

Nodding, Barney said, "I know. I understand."

Then, glancing at Sean and Tommy, he said, "But you know you'd be safe here."

Smoothly sparing Laura from having to answer, Gina intervened. With a coy smile she said, "We know. Did you tell your friends I know them?"

Barney grinned, "Not yet. We've been eating."

Looking at Sean and Tommy he said, "A friend of Gina's was goin' out with a guy from the North End that got whacked. When the cops took her in town to question her, Gina went with her. They made Gina wait in another room."

Still grinning, he turned to Gina. "You tell 'em."

She said, "It wasn't a real big room, but all four walls were covered with pictures. One wall was all guys from the North End and another one was all guys from Charlestown."

Then, with an impish little grin, she looked at Sean and said, "You were there."

Shifting her glance over to Tommy, she said, "And so were you."

Then, glancing at Barney, she said, "You all were."

Looking innocently back at her, Sean said, "Musta been school pictures."

She giggled and said, "I'm sure they were."

After they left, Sean asked Barney, "What's up with Laura? She got a problem?"

Barney frowned. "Yeah . . . maybe . . . I don't know. Harry Gannon's gettin' out this week. She's scared of him."

Looking rather doubtful, Sean said, "Why's she scared a' Harry. I know Harry. I never heard of him botherin' any girls."

Barney looked off for a moment. Then, "Look Sean, I know you and Harry are friends an' I don't wanna' start anything or get in the middle of anything . . ."

Sean interrupted him. "Look, Barn, first off, Harry an' I ain't what I call friends - not like you an' me, okay? We get along. I got no problems with him. An', yeah, years ago, when I was a kid, I did a coupla' scores with him - high-jacked a coupla' trucks. I was eighteen an' he was one of the older guys an' he came to us with a couple of easy scores that he set up with the drivers. But when I started doin' banks, we went our different ways."

Barney seemed to ponder for a moment, and then said, "Do you remember Chuckie Flynn?"

Sean said, "Yeah. I didn't really know him. He was older than me. I heard he was a rat."

Frowning, Barney asked, "Did you ever hear that before he got whacked?"

Sean thought for a moment, and then said, "Yeah, I think I did."

Nodding his head, Barney said, "Do you remember who told you it?

Sean said, "Yeah, Harry Gannon."

Barney said, "Yeah. You sure it was *before* he got clipped? I can't see him sayin' it while Chuckie was alive."

Tommy cut in, "Where ya' goin' with this, Barney? Whatta ya saying? You sayin' he wasn't a rat?"

Barney said, "I knew Chuckie all my life. He never ratted on no one. Harry Gannon spread that story after Chuckie got dead. Laura was Chuckie's girlfriend. Harry had a thing for Laura but she was goin' with Chuckie and Harry wouldn't fuck with Chuckie. But as soon as Chuckie was gone, he started hittin' on her."

"So, whaddaya' sayin', Harry whacked Chuckie to get . . .?"

Shaking his head, Barney "Uh uh, that's one thing I ain't sayin'. I know he's whacked a half-dozen guys, but they were all in the back. Maybe if Chuckie was shot in the back . . . maybe. But whoever did it, did it face to face. Chuckie was shot in the front and he had his gun in his hand. Ain't no way Harry Gannon would ever go face to face with Chuckie.

The Real Town

"But the thing is, he's gettin' out this week, so Laura's movin'. She's scared of him. She said that before he got busted he wouldn't leave her alone. She said that one night she was out with a bunch of girls and they ran into him and a bunch of other guys over in Southie, at Blinstrub's, and they all wound up sittin' together. Afterwards, they all went to the Stork Club. He wanted to take her home, but she didn't want to go with him. He wouldn't leave her alone and they wound up having an argument outside. She said that, while he never actually said that he killed Chuckie, by the time they were done fightin', she knew it was him. She moved up to New Hampshire and didn't come back for a coupla' years - till after he got busted. But now he's gettin' out an' she's scared to stay around here."

The three of them sat in silence. Finally, Sean said, "Why don't we take off? I gotta' do a coupla' things back in town."

Shortly after that, Barney dropped them off in front of Kelly's. They stood there staring at each other. Then, without saying a word, they got into Sean's car and drove off.

After a while, Sean said, "You didn't know, man. Ya' thought he was a rat. We both did."

Tommy said, "He played us. I let him use me."

"C'mon, man, you were eighteen years old. What the fuck did we know?"

Nodding his head, and glancing over at Sean, Tommy said, "Yeah, but we know now."

CHAPTER 13

On Friday, Harry Gannon got out and, like so many others, even guys from other neighborhoods, he came straight to Kelly's. He got the usual treatment, guys welcoming him home, calling him off to the side and slipping him money. Sean and Artie each gave him a thousand dollars. Tommy wasn't there. When Harry asked for him, Sean told him that Tommy was out putting something together, that they might have something going that night.

As the night progressed, they wound up down the Blue Mirror. Around midnight, Tommy came in the back door. As he approached the bar, Harry stepped out and said, "Hey Tom, how ya' doin'?"

With a look of surprise on his face Tommy said, "Hey Harry, when the hell did you get out?"

Grinning, he answered, "This morning."

Tommy said, "Well, Hell, let's have a drink."

After ordering a round, he nodded his head to Sean and they stepped off to the side. After talking for a minute they came back to the bar. Sean said to Artie "It's on."

Then, turning to Harry, he said, in a hushed voice, "We got a truckload of cigarettes waitin' for us. You want in? You can just ride in the follow-up car with Tommy."

"Sure", he replied. "I can use the bread."

Tommy said, "The truck's gonna' be there at one o'clock, so we got a little time. Let's all leave separate."

Sean said, "Okay, where'd ya' park?"

"Out back, it's a brown Buick."

Sean nodded and said, "See yez' in fifteen or twenty minutes. The truck's only over in Somerville."

Artie casually walked away from them and went to the telephone which was right next to the front door. Sean strolled over to a table filled with girls and asked one of them to dance.

Tommy said softly to Harry, "I'm gonna' head out the back now. Go out the front door in about ten minutes or so and walk around the back. I'm parked in the lot across the street."

*

As Sean and Artie pulled into the dark empty lot between two large warehouses in Somerville, they saw Tommy and Harry sitting in the brown car at the far end of the lot. He drove down and pulled up behind them. The four of them got out.

Sean said, "You ready?"

Tommy nodded. Turning to Gannon, who was about five feet away from him, he said, "Why'd ya' tell me Chuckie Flynn was a rat?"

Gannon was caught totally off guard. He stammered, "I . . . He was . . . I . . . Honest t' God, he was a fuckin' rat."

Tommy said, "For a fuckin' broad. I whacked a good guy 'cause you wanted his girl friend."

Looking quickly to Sean, Gannon said, "Sean, it ain't true. He was a rat. Lemme tell ya' what happened. He . . ."

Whatever else Harry Gannon was, he wasn't stupid. He knew what time it was. In the middle of the sentence, he suddenly threw himself back and to the side, drawing a pistol from his belt as he did.

Tommy shot him twice in the chest, then walked over and emptied his gun into Gannon's head.

Opening the trunk of the brown Buick, they gingerly lifted the body and stuffed it inside, careful not to get blood on their clothes.

As Tommy started to close the trunk, Artie stepped in and said, "Hey, hey, hey, you forgettin' something'?"

Giving Tommy a slight hip check to move him out of the way, Artie reached into the dark trunk for a moment. He came out with a wad of hundred dollar bills in his hand. He quickly counted out ten for himself and ten for Sean.

Glancing up at Tommy he said, "What'd you give him?

Tommy said, "A grand."

Counting out ten more, Artie handed them to him, then said, "Whadda ya' wanna' do with the rest of it?"

Sean smiled and said, "He can buy the house a couple 'a rounds down the Mirror."

Then, turning to Tommy, he said, "You wanna' dump him any place special?"

Tommy shook his head, "Nah, I don't give a fuck where he goes."

Sean said, "Let's take him up that project between Mystic Ave. and Winter Hill."

Artie said, "You wanna' leave him in Somerville?"

Grinning, Sean said, "Why not? Whenever they whack anyone out here, they dump 'em in Charlestown."

Laughing, they got into the cars and drove nice and slowly out onto the street, looking in all directions before entering the empty highway. Rules of the road, always drive carefully when you've got a body in the trunk.

CHAPTER 14

The following Monday was labor Day, so they didn't go over to Chelsea to watch the truck. They told Barney that they had something to do on Tuesday so they'd meet him the following Monday and start their surveillance.

In fact, Sean had another score set up and ready to go. Sammy had come to Sean a few months earlier with a friend of theirs, a guy that they worked with occasionally, Teddy Hurley. Teddy had gone up to New Hampshire, to vacation for the summer, and had gone into a shopping center in Manchester to pick up some groceries. As he came out of the supermarket, and was getting into his car, an armored car pulled up in front of the store, right outside of the front door. It was a different armored car than he was used to seeing, a small green truck. As a matter of habit, Teddy sat and watched.

Two guards got out of the truck and went into the Supermarket. There was nothing unusual about that. However, one of them was the driver - at least, he appeared to have gotten out of the driver's door - that was very unusual.

So unusual, that Teddy had to know. Although he thought that the guard had gotten out of the driver's door, the angle from where his car was parked prevented him from actually seeing the door open.

He got out of his car and, with the daily newspaper in hand, walked back towards the store. As he walked by the door, he casually glanced into the driver's window of the truck. Both seats were empty, and there was no partition between the driver's seat and the rear of the truck. As he reached the next store, he stopped in front of the door and, as he nonchalantly lit a cigarette, glanced back. Leaning against the wall, he opened the newspaper to the Sports section and appeared to be reading the horse racing page.

A moment later, the two guards emerged. They were each carrying two bags, and neither one of them had his pistol out of the holster.

Ostensibly unaware of the truck even being there, Teddy was vividly staring at them peripherally, out of the corner of his eye, from behind his dark sun glasses. He could not believe what he was seeing. Two armored car guards casually flipping four money bags - two of which were obviously paper money, not change - into the side door on the back of the truck, and neither of them had their pistol in hand.

After locking the door, they both got back into the front of the armored car and drove away.

Needless to say, Teddy followed them.

For the rest of the summer, Teddy simply vacationed, except for Monday afternoons. The armored car picked up money at four more stops after they picked up the money at the supermarket; a bank, a department store, and another supermarket, all on the main street. At each of these stops, the driver stayed in the truck. His associate would usually bring one bag out of the bank and two out of the other two stops.

The Real Town

Then the truck would leave the main drag, take a right turn, and go three blocks down a side street, turning into a parking lot at the rear of a large brick building. The lot was surrounded by a high brick wall. The truck parked in front of the only door, a small regular-looking back door. At this stop, they both got out and went into the building.

Teddy hadn't discovered this stop until the fourth week, as he only followed the truck one stop per week. As the stops were moving into the late afternoon, he had almost decided to just take the two bags of money at the supermarket where they both got out of the truck. For the most part, Teddy stuck with banks. He had only tried to rob an armored car once and that had turned into a horror show. Now, where both guards were getting out of the truck, in an obscured location, he revised his thinking. That was when he went to Sammy. Sammy went up with him and checked it out. Then he came to Sean.

Sean and Teddy had known each other since they were kids and had always gotten along. Teddy had worked with all of them, Tommy, Gus, Artie, Sammy, all of their old crowd. Earlier that year Teddy had done a score with Tommy and Gus. It was a spur of the moment thing, that almost went bad, and they had had to ditch their car in South Boston and duck into Teddy's girl friend's apartment for a few hours, where they cut up the money.

After Sammy described the score, Sean took a ride up to Manchester with them and watched the armored car pull into the lot. About a week and a half later, they went up again, on a day that the truck wasn't coming. Sean got out of the car and walked into the lot, and tried the door. It was unlocked and opened easily. He had waited for a rainy day, a heavily rainy day, so he would be less apt to be noticed.

He opened the door and walked in. A hallway ran straight for about twenty feet and then stopped at a blank wall. About ten feet down the hall was a set of stairs, going up, on the left. On the right side of the hall, directly across from the staircase, was a door. Sean opened it. It was a large closet, maybe eight feet by ten feet, containing tools and cleaning materials. There was one light bulb in the hall, hanging from the ceiling, between the steps and the closet door.

When Sean got back out to Teddy's car he said, "I like it. But I wanna do it different."

When Teddy had described the score to Sean he had said that, when Sean and Sammy got the drop on the guards inside the hall, one of them could hold the guards inside while the other one took the keys and went out and cleaned the money out of the truck. Teddy would be the getaway driver. He would pull into the lot as soon as the guards went into the building.

Sean said, "Did you look inta' that room across from the steps?"

"No. I didn't even see it. I didn't really go into the hall. I just peeked in and saw it was an empty hall with a flight of steps up. I figured yez'd just wait inside an' grab 'em when they come through the door."

The Real Town

Sean shook his head. "There's a good-sized room across from the steps. We can tie 'em up or cuff 'em to the pipes in there. It'll give us more of a head start."

They had decided to wait until the day after Labor Day weekend. That would give them more time to watch, and prepare, and there would probably be more money after a long weekend.

On the day after Labor Day, Sean, Sammy and Teddy drove up early and went to the cottage that Teddy had rented for the summer, to pick up their equipment. The cottage was on Beaver Lake, in Derry, a little town about halfway between Manchester and the Massachusetts state line. They each drove a hot car, with clean plates. Sean and Sammy had gone up there the day before, getting things in order and reconnoitering their escape route. Teddy had spent a good deal of the summer cruising back and forth between Derry and Manchester exploring the back roads. He had it down pat. He could now go from Manchester to Derry without ever coming out from underneath the trees.

By noontime, they had the cars in place, in Manchester. The armored car's schedule would bring it to the designated parking lot between three-thirty and a quarter to four. At twenty minutes past three, Sean and Sammy got out of the car, about a block down the street from the entrance to the parking lot. Casually strolling up the street, they turned into the lot and walked to the door, quietly opening it, and entered the building.

They stood silently for a long minute, waiting to see if anyone had noticed them entering the building, and showed an interest in their presence. They then went into the maintenance closet and turned on the light. Sean took out a small hand drill and bored a tiny hole in the door, right next to a slight ridge which would prevent the guards from noticing it, but would allow him to watch them as they reached the stairs. Then, placing himself in position where he could peer through the hole, with his hand on the door knob, he turned the light out.

After a long few minutes, Sean's walkie-talkie softly beeped. He pressed the respond button and then placed it in his pocket. A minute later, they heard the back door open. They listened, as a half-dozen footsteps approached them. Then the first guard appeared in front of the door, turned to his left and started up the stairs. As he reached the second step, his partner came into view through the little hole in the door. Sean silently turned the knob and stepped out, placing his pistol against the second guard's right temple.

"Don't move, either of you."

The first guard whirled around on the step, reaching for his holster. Then he froze. Sammy was standing to the left of Sean and the other guard, pointing his pistol directly at the guard on the steps.

Cocking his revolver, he said, "Don't touch that gun."

The guard slowly raised his hands over his head.

They had considered not taking them until they were leaving, after they had picked up the money upstairs. But they decided that they were better off trading the extra money for the advantage of getting the drop on them from behind, while they were both in sight.

They quickly hustled them into the closet, removed their uniform shirts and hats, and handcuffed them to the pipes over their heads.

Taking the guards' guns and keys, Sean said succinctly to the driver, "You're going to tell me which key is which. If you lie I will be back in to hurt you badly."

Holding up one key, close to the driver's face, he said, "Which?"

The driver gulped, as if he were having trouble responding, then said, "That starts the truck."

He quickly identified the other keys.

They had placed the guards back to back when they cuffed their wrists to the pipes over their heads. Now they quickly wrapped duct tape around their legs, taping them together. The last thing that they did was to place a piece of tape over each of their mouths.

A moment later, wearing guard's shirts and hats, Sean and Sammy stepped into the hall. Walking swiftly, yet quietly, to the outside door, Sean peeked out. The truck was parked right outside, with the driver's door just two steps away.

As Sean walked around to the passenger side, Sammy took two steps, smoothly inserted the key into the door lock and unlocked the door. Sliding into the driver's seat, he reached across and opened the passenger door. Sean slid in and immediately crawled into the back of the truck, scanning the money bags lying on the floor. They were neatly lined up against the wall, four on one side and seven on the other side. A quick hefting of the bags showed that the four bags were paper and the seven were change. As Sammy pulled the truck out of the lot, Sean packed the four bags of paper money into a plastic garbage bag. Teddy followed them.

Three blocks away, they turned the truck into an empty lot between two dilapidated deserted buildings. Leaving it at the back of the lot, they walked back to the street and hopped into the back seat of the getaway car and slid down to the floor. About a half-mile away, they swapped cars again. Shortly after that, they pulled into Teddy's place in Derry.

Sean took the wheel of the hot car while Sammy and Teddy got out and got into their own cars, which they had left there the day before. Sean had driven the three of them back to Boston in his car.

Driving south, they were across the state line into Massachusetts in a matter of minutes. Shortly after that, they pulled into the City of Haverhill, where they had gotten one of the cars that they used in their getaway - one of the other cars, not the one that Sean was now driving. Parking the car on a main street, Sean walked up the street about a block, before Teddy pulled up beside him. Sean got in and they took off.

The Real Town

Less than an hour later, they were approaching Charlestown from the direction of Everett, a city slightly to the northeast of Charlestown. As they were entering the rotary at Sullivan Square, another car was coming around the rotary from the Charlestown side, rather quickly. Although the car did have the right of way, it had been coming so fast, it had come out of nowhere and Teddy didn't see it until it was too late. Both cars slammed on their brakes and tried to swerve away from each other. They almost made it, but the car's right fender did hit Teddy's left fender. In truth, they barely touched. That was the good news. The bad news was that it was a Charlestown detective's plain cop car. Charlestown Detective Jimmy Reed was driving and Detective Tony Anthony was in the passenger seat. They all exchanged glances for a fleeting second, then grinning, Sean said to Tony, "It coulda' been worse. It coulda' been you drivin'. At least Jimmy only speeds, he don't fly."

Tony laughed and shook his head. "You guys alright?"

Sean said, "Yeah, it ain't nothin'. You wanna just let it go?"

Nodding his head imperceptibly, and glancing past Sean, Tony said, "I would, but I think we better swap papers."

Glancing over his shoulder Sean became aware of the crowd of people standing outside of the Sullivan Square Train and Bus Station, staring at them. They had seen the accident. Witnesses.

Sean said, "I hear ya'. Where ya wanna do it? This is a bad spot. We're in the middle of the rotary."

Tony responded, "Just follow us. We'll head down the Station and do it there."

The Real Town

The Charlestown Police Station, Station 15, was at the other end of the town, in City Square.

Sean said, "That's cool. See ya' there."

As the cop car pulled away into the rotary, and they followed them, Teddy said, with an anxious glance at Sean, "Whatta we gonna do? We got the money in the back seat."

"Just follow 'em around the rotary. See if they're goin' down Rutherford Ave. or Main Street."

A few seconds later, as they followed the detectives around the rotary, Sean said, "Alright, they're goin' down Rutherford, just stay with 'em. But don't get too close. Let 'em get a little distance between us. Take the turnaround by Cappy's and head for the project."

About a quarter of a mile down Rutherford Avenue there was a one way turnaround, just past Cappy's Diner, an all night restaurant. After that there was no way to turn around for another quarter of a mile. By the time that Sean and Teddy reached it, the cops would have gone by it.

The worry was obvious on Teddy's face. "Fuck. I'm gonna get busted for leavin' the scene."

Sean said, "No you're not. Just drop me off and head right down to 15. Tell 'em I had you drop me off. Tell 'em I said I had a date".

As they approached the turnaround, the cop car was well past it. Sean said, "Go."

Teddy hit the gas and breezed into the turnaround. As soon as they came out of it, going in the other direction, there was a right turn which led to Main Street, one block away. Teddy took it and the cops were out of sight.

As they had gone into the turn, Sean had clicked on his walkie-talkie and called Sammy.

Sammy answered, "Yeah?"

Sean said, "Where are you?"

The Real Town

"I just dropped the guns off."

That meant he was in Charlestown.

Sean said, "Pick me up down the project on O'Reilly Way between Monument and Polk Streets. *Right now!*"

Sammy asked no questions. "I'll be there in two minutes."

As they were coming up Polk Street, Sean said, "Just drop me off on the corner of O'Reilly Way and head right down to '15'. If they ask, tell 'em you dropped me off at my car on Bunker Hill Street, up by my sister's house. Tell 'em I said I had a date, an' I couldn't wait."

As Sean was getting out of the car, he saw Sammy coming up Polk Street behind them. As Sammy pulled up beside them, Sean opened the back door of both cars, reached in and lifted the black plastic bag up off of the floor of Teddy's car and climbed into the back of Sammy's car with it.

Both cars took off in different directions. Teddy turned left on Bunker Hill Street, heading for City Square. Sammy turned right and headed up the hill towards Sullivan Square. As they were going by Anne's house, Sean said, "Let me out. I gotta get my car outta here."

That night, the three of them met at the Top of the Hub, a restaurant on the 52nd floor, the top floor, of the Prudential Building in the Back Bay. Sean and Sammy were already there when Teddy arrived. They had a table by the window.

As he reached the table, Sean made eye contact, then glanced under the table at a large soft-leather brief case that was on the floor by the empty chair.

Sean said, "We got fifty-one grand and change . . . each."

For one second, a look of part disappointment, part incredulity, crossed Teddy's face. Until Sean said "each". That made him smile.

As Teddy sat down he was staring out the window at all of downtown Boston. "Jesus Christ", he said, "I never been up here. What a fuckin' view. I can even see Charlestown."

Then, turning to Sean, he said, "They wanted to know where you went. I told 'em I hadda' drop you off, you had a date. They just laughed. Tony said, 'That cute prick.' The other guy, Jimmy, said, 'What? Was he the one with the guns this time?' But he was laughin'. Ya' know what else they did? They squared the accident. Ya' know they had the right of way, even though they was speedin'. But they fixed it so that neither one of us was at fault."

Although Tony and Jimmy were detectives, Sean got along with them. More importantly, they had done business together on more than one occasion. Once, it had even included Teddy, ironically enough, on Rutherford Avenue. That was what spurred Jimmy Reed's crack about guns.

One night, after the bars closed, Sean was driving down Rutherford, heading for the Prison Point Bridge, with a very cute girl that he'd just picked up at the Blue Mirror, when he saw Teddy standing by his car, with Detectives Reed and Anthony. He went by them and pulled in about fifty feet past them. He told the girl that he'd be right back and got out of the car and walked back to Teddy's car.

Teddy had been pulled over for speeding and it turned out that he'd had a little too much to drink. Worse, the cops had seen a pistol on the floor of the back seat, and when they looked in the car, they found another one under the front seat.

The Real Town

When Sean got to the car, he saw that Teddy was already cuffed. Detective Reed was placing him in the cop car.

He said, "What's up?"

Tony said, "Drunk driving, and we found a coupla' pistols."

Sean glanced over at Teddy, then back at Tony. "How much?"

Tony stared at him for a moment, then said, "Can he keep his mouth shut?"

Sean nodded, "That won't be a problem. He pretty much keeps to himself, anyways. But he won't say nothin'."

Tony said, "Alright, give us a grand. Another five hundred each, if he wants to keep the pistols."

Sean nodded his head, as he reached into his pocket and pulled out a roll of bills.

After shuffling through them, he said, "Shit, I only got about fourteen hundred on me. Lemme talk to Teddy."

Tony called Jimmy off to the side as Sean went over to the cop car. Opening the door, he leaned in and said, "How much money ya' got on ya'.

Teddy's eyes widened. "About eight hundred. Is that enough?"

Sean said, "Yeah, but ya' gonna' owe me somethin'. It's a grand to get outta here. Ya' wanna keep the pistols, it's another five hundred each."

"I wanna keep the pistols. You got enough on ya' to cover it?"

Sean nodded his head. "If you got eight hundred, I do. Where's your money?"

Turning away from Sean and stretching out his left leg until he was almost lying on the seat, he said, "In my wallet, in my back pocket."

Sean dug into the back pocket and removed the wallet. There was eight hundred and sixty-two dollars. He removed eight hundred and replaced the sixty-two, putting the wallet into Teddy's jacket pocket.

Getting out of the car, he took out twelve hundred of his own money and added it to Teddy's eight hundred as he walked over and handed it to the detectives, "We're on. We got enough between us. He's gonna keep the pistols."

Within two minutes, Teddy and Sean were standing at Teddy's car. The cops were gone. Teddy started to say, "Man, thanks. I'm gonna . . ."

Sean interrupted him, "I'll see ya' tomorrow down Kelly's. I've got someone waiting in the car - and keep this to yourself."

Then, glancing at the car, he said, "Probably not in the morning."

Now, as they sat at the Top of the Hub, Teddy said, "Ya know, they was laughin' but I don't think they went for the 'date' story. I think they really did think you had guns, or somethin', on ya'."

Sean said, "I'm sure they did. They're not stupid."

"Hey", Teddy said, "the dick Jimmy said to tell you he's ready for a rematch with Pebbles. What's that all about?"

Sean grinned. "They had a fight one night outside the Stork Club. I'll tell ya', that Jimmy can fight. "

Teddy interrupted, "He had a fight with Pebbles an' he done good? Did he beat him?"

Sean shook his head. "No, but he gave him a hell of a fight. It musta' lasted a half hour. Pebs finally wore him down."

Teddy asked, "Did he pinch him?"

The Real Town

"No. It wasn't like that. We were all up the Stork Club drinkin', an' Jimmy comes in with the other dick, Ellsworth. Jimmy was new at the time. He'd only been stationed in the town about a month or so. So we're all standin' at the bar shootin' the shit an' somehow him and Pebs get off inta' who can fight the best. Now, we all know Pebs can fight his ass off, an' Jimmy tells him he heard he could fight, but that he could kick his ass. Now they're goin' back and forth and Jimmy tells him, he ain't sayin' Pebs can't fight but he ain't never met anyone smaller than him who could stay with him, and he's about an inch or two taller than Pebs. I mean, neither of 'em's that big. Pebs is maybe five-six and Jimmy's what, five-seven or eight?

"Anyways, we all go downstairs, out the back in the lot, an' they square off. Maybe the best fight I ever saw. It musta' lasted a half hour. When it was over, Jimmy got up an' they shook hands. That was that."

Teddy said, "Shit, I wish I seen it. Hey, I met Tommy and Artie up Kelly's after I swapped papers with the cops."

Then, looking at Sean, he said, "We're all goin' out to dinner tonight at that steak place you like in-town, the Beef & Ale. You guys wanna come with us? We're bringin' our girls."

They both declined as they each had something else to do.

CHAPTER 15

The next afternoon Sean walked into Billy Driscoll's looking to catch up with Barney. He wanted to know if Barney had checked the truck in Chelsea the day before. But, before he could ask him, Barney said, "Have you seen Tommy? He was down here looking for you this morning. Rita was with him. They were drinking over at the Coliseum last night and then they went for breakfast."

The Coliseum was an after-hours club in-town, between Haymarket Square and Faneuil Hall - the North End's version of the Stork Club.

"They said if I saw ya' to tell you to give them a call."

Sean called them from the pay phone at Driscoll's. Tommy said that he didn't really want to talk on the phone, so Sean told him that he'd drop over as they had just woken up.

Tommy and Rita were living out of town, in Everett. When Sean got there, he brought them each two large Dunkin' Donuts coffees. They were both slightly hung over.

As they were sipping their coffee Sean said, "We had a good night, did we?"

Tommy said, "Yeah, we went in town to eat at the Beef & Ale. We had a coupla' drinks there, then we went down the Mirror an' after closin' time we went over to the Coliseum. Rita wanted to go there."

Smiling sleepily, Rita said, "I'd never been there before. I was curious. I liked it."

Tommy said, "Yeah, but tell him what happened."

The Real Town

Rita sort of perked up a little, sitting up on the couch where she had been lying down. "This is kinda' weird, and I'm really not all that comfortable talking about it, but I guess I gotta.

"Teddy's girlfriend, Bernie, made a remark earlier, when we were down the Mirror. We were in the Ladies Room and she said something about Teddy robbing a bank that day. There was nobody there when she said it. But, right when she was saying it, two other girls came in. I hushed her up and we walked out.

"Later on, when we were over the Coliseum, and we went to the Ladies Room, she said it again. I didn't really catch what she had said the first time, back at the Mirror. The toilet was flushing when she said it. I got it this time, though. She said that she had told him before that she didn't want him to be robbing banks. She said that she told him that, the day that him and Tommy and Gus split up the money over at her house. She said that he didn't tell her that he robbed a bank yesterday but she knows that he did because of all the money he's got all of a sudden. She said that if he does it again she's going to call the cops."

That got Sean's attention. "She's gonna call the cops?"

Rita nodded her head. "Uh huh, that's what she said. I tried to talk to her about it but she got indignant. Like, it's her house and if he's gonna be coming to her house then he's going to have to do what she says. Like I said, it was really weird."

"Did she say anything to Teddy? Did he hear her say anything like that?"

Rita shook her head. "No. As far as I know, I'm the only one that she said it to. But Artie's girl, Jeannie, heard her say it, at the Coliseum. I didn't really know her before last night and she tried to make it look like she didn't hear anything. But we swapped looks, and she rolled her eyes.

"Later on, when Tommy and Artie were up at the bar for a few minutes, talking to a couple of the wise guys from the North End and Teddy and Bernie got up to dance, Jeannie and I had a chance to talk. I said to her, 'Can you believe what she said she was gonna do?'

"She kinda looked away for a minute, then she looked at me and said, 'I like Artie. He's a lotta fun. But I really don't know him well enough to have any idea what he does for a living. Now I've got this crazy girl - and she is a crazy girl even if what she's saying is true - talking about them robbing banks. I don't want to hear it. I don't want to know anything about them.'

"Then she looked me in the eye and said, 'So I didn't hear anything, okay?'

"When I nodded, and said, 'I understand', she said, 'Unless you need me to back you up. But if you do, we'll keep it between you, me, Artie and Tommy, okay?'

"I said, 'Sure, thanks', even though I knew I wouldn't need her to back me up. But I like her for letting me know that she would, even though she doesn't want to get involved."

Sean asked, "Has anyone talked to Teddy about it"

Tommy shook his head, "Nah, we talked about it but we figured you could do it better than us. We don't know what to say to him. He really likes this broad. I mean, she might be nuts, but she is drop-dead good-looking."

Rita, in an obviously squeamish mode, cut in, "I gotta ask you somethin', and don't lie to me. Ya' gotta tell me the truth."

The Real Town

Sean nodded his head, "Alright."

"Am I a rat 'cause I told on her?"

Sean stared at her for a moment. Her wide open eyes were glistening with hesitance. Rita was a great girl and she was one of their own. But she was also a citizen. She was uncertain of the rules.

Sean reached over and took her hand. "No, you're not, she is. Or, at least she wants to be one. You did the right thing. If you didn't, we could have gotten in trouble."

Tommy said, "That's what she was talking about when she said she was uncomfortable talking about it. I told her she did the right thing, but she wanted to hear it from you, too.

Looking over at Tommy, Sean said, "Let's go for a ride."

As Tommy was putting his shoes on, Sean sat down next to Rita. "You know I trust you?"

She nodded her head.

He continued, "There are some things that you do not want to hear. That way, if they should ever question you, you can honestly tell them that you know nothing, without getting in trouble."

Nodding her head, she started to smile. "I get it."

CHAPTER 16

When they got out into Sean's car, he said, "Let's take a ride over to Southie. I wanna' talk to Neezo."

"Ya think he knows her?"

"I hope so."

They found a parking spot on Broadway, the main street in South Boston, which didn't happen that often, and walked into the Penn, a saloon where Neezo tended to hang out. He was standing at the bar with his friend, Matt.

After ordering a round, Sean asked them, "Do you know a broad named Bernie - I think it's Bernice - Dalton?"

Neezo and Matt exchanged glances.

Neezo said, "Yeah, 'Mouthy from Southie'. Where d' you know her from?"

This time, Sean and Tommy exchanged glances.

Sean said, "I don't. I've never met her. But Tommy has. They were all out drinkin' together last night. She goes with a guy from Charlestown."

Matt said, "Yeah, I know, a bank robber."

Sean said, "You know him?"

"Nah, but my brother met him the other day. Is this guy a friend of yours?"

"Yeah, we've known him since we were kids. How the Hell did you know he robs banks?"

The Real Town

"Like I said, my brother met him the other day. My brother, and two of his friends, just came back from a tour in 'Nam. The three of them spent the night with her. They got back into town on Sunday and they were drinkin' down the street at The Tunnel, when they ran into her. When the bars closed she took them back to her place. She told them the guy she was goin' out with was outta town for the weekend. She didn't think he was comin' back till Tuesday, but he showed up on Labor Day. She just told him that my brother was an old friend that she grew up with who just came back from 'Nam with his friends, and had just dropped by to say 'Hi'. My brother introduced the other two guys - they're from outta state. He said he figured the reason the guy went for the 'old friend' story, was because there was three of 'em there. He said it was a good thing he showed up late in the day. By that time, they were all dressed. But sometime the night before, when she was talkin' about him, she told them that he robs banks. Like Neezo said, 'Mouthy from Southie'. She can't keep her mouth shut."

Frowning, Sean said, "Swell."

Matt said, "I hope you guys ain't got a problem with my brother. He's just a kid that wanted to get laid and she brought them back to the house."

"We ain't got no problem with your brother. Good luck to him. I'm glad he made it back. We just had to know about her."

Neezo said, "Just don't let her know any of your business."

The Real Town

By the time that Sean and Tommy got back to Charlestown, they had talked it over and decided that it would be best if Sean and Teddy sat down alone. Still, Rita would have to be nearby, in case they had to verify what Bernie had said. They drove over to Everett to pick up Rita and explain what had to be done.

Sean called Teddy on the telephone and arranged to meet him down the Mirror. Where it was a Wednesday night the Mirror wouldn't be that crowded and there would be plenty of room to get off alone, yet have Rita within striking distance.

When Teddy showed up, he and Sean got a drink and went into the back section, which was almost empty. As soon as they sat down, Teddy said, "What's up?"

Sean went straight to the point. "Last night, when you guys were all out drinking, your girl friend, Bernie, made a statement that she doesn't want you robbing banks. How much have you told her?"

Teddy was stunned. "I ain't told her nothin'. The only reason she even knows anything is because me and Tommy and Gus had to duck in there after our car got fucked up in that score we pulled before. You know about it. She heard us talkin'."

Sean responded, "Last night she said that she told you back then that she didn't want you robbing banks and that she knew that you just took another one because of all the money you showed up with."

Defensively, Teddy said, "She can think anything she wants, she don't *know* nothin'."

"She knows that you and Tommy and Gus grabbed a bag. They ain't too happy with what she said last night. She said that if you take another bank she's gonna call the cops."

"No fucking way! She'd never call the cops on me."

Then why would she say it."

"Who did she say it to?"

"Rita."

"I don't believe it."

Sean lifted his drink and took a sip, then a second sip. "She said it, Teddy. You know Rita wouldn't lie about something like that. She's coming over now. She'll tell you."

Rita and Tommy had come into the Blue Mirror after Teddy and sat at a table out in the front section, from where they could see Sean and Teddy. When Sean raised his drink to his lips for the second sip, Rita and Tommy had gotten up and headed for the table. By the time that they got to the table, Teddy was staring at Rita.

She said, "I'm sorry, Teddy, I hate to do this, but when she said it, I couldn't let it go."

"What did she say?"

"She said that if you rob another bank, she's going to call the cops."

Shaking his head, looking totally befuddled, Teddy said, "Look, even if she did say something like that, she'd never do it. She was just drunk and talking stupid."

Sean intervened, "Do you believe Rita - that Bernie said it?"

Without saying a word, Teddy half shrugged and half nodded.

Looking up at Rita, Sean said, "Thanks, I'll talk to you guys tomorrow."

After they left, Sean and Teddy sat quietly, for a long moment. Then Sean said, "Teddy, you know you're my friend and you know that I trust you."

At which point, Teddy looked up and their eyes met.

Sean went on, "But, if you're going to stay with her, I can't work with you. I'll have to stay away from you. And the other guys feel the same way. It's your choice."

Beseechingly, Teddy said, "Sean, she won't rat on us. I know she won't. Lemme talk to her."

Sean held up his hand. "That's the one thing I don't want you to do, Teddy. I don't want you to tell her about this. If you're gonna break up with her, you can do it in a way that she won't connect it with us. If you want to stay with her, that's your choice. But, either way, ya' gotta keep us out of it. The last thing you want is for guys to think that she's going to rat on them."

Staring into Sean's eyes, Teddy suddenly found himself in 'no man's land'. He knew no one who treated girls more respectfully than Sean. He had always been that way. At the same time, he knew no one that he would consider more life threatening, when it came to dealing with a stool pigeon, than Sean.

Taking a deep breath, Teddy said, "I can't break up with her, Sean. I'm sorry, I just can't. But I promise you, she won't know anything about anything that you and I ever did. I give you my word."

After a long moment of silence as they stared into each other's eyes, Sean slowly nodded his head. "Alright, I'll take your word. I'm sorry it's gotta be like this Teddy. But it's the only way I can handle it."

When Sean saw Tommy and Rita the next day, he described how it had gone. When he was finished, they sat there in silence for a minute, trying to absorb what had gone down.

Finally, Rita said, "You didn't tell him about Bernie and the other guys?"

The Real Town

He shook his head. "Uh uh, that ain't got nothin' to do with us. That's between them. That's their business."

CHAPTER 17

A couple of weeks later, on a Monday, Sean and Tommy met with Barney and headed back over to Chelsea. They were sitting in the shopping mall, waiting for the truck.

Barney said, "I backtracked the truck another stop last week. It picks up at a church, too."

Tommy said, "You shittin' me? We're robbin' a church? Is it a Catholic Church?"

Barney shrugged, "I don't know. I wasn't really payin' that much attention. I was watching the truck - an' we ain't robbin' a church, we're robbin' a truck."

Looking cynically into the back seat at Sean, Tommy said, "You fuckin' with me?"

Sean grinned.

Barney said, "Whadda ya' talkin' about?"

Tommy nodded his head in Sean's direction, saying, "He's been watchin' the Arch Street Church - says it's a great score. And when I said I wasn't gonna' rob no church, he said what you just said, 'We ain't robbin' a church, we're robbin' a truck'."

Barney turned around, staring disbelievingly at Sean. "The Arch Street Church?"

The Arch Street Church was a twenty-four hour a day Catholic Church set squarely in the middle of downtown Boston. Actually, it was three chapels, all in the same building, with masses going on at all hours.

Sean answered, "No, not the Church, the truck that picks the money up after the masses - in this case, the Christmas masses."

The Real Town

From the look on Barney's face it was obvious that he got it. The Arch Street Church, which was actually Saint Anthony's Shrine, had become, to all intents and purposes, *The* Catholic Church of downtown Boston. In a city filled with ancient, magnificent cathedrals, the Arch Street Church was a large, impressive looking modern building set in the heart of downtown. In essence, Arch Street's parish was all of Boston. Everyone came there for the holiday masses - especially 'midnight masses' on Christmas Eve, which went on all night long. People always gave more money at Christmas, especially at the midnight mass.

Sean went on, "The truck usually picks up the money on Wednesdays an' where Christmas falls on a Monday this year, it'll probably be a regular pick-up. Ya' know that little alley that runs down beside the church? It parks in there an' they come out the side door, into the alley, with the money."

Barney said, "Sounds good. I gotta' take a look at it. But I'll tell ya', that's a tough area to get out of - traffic really sucks there."

Sean agreed, "You're right. It does. But, if you go through the alley ya' can take a right an' come out onto Summer Street. Then you're only a coupla' blocks from South Station an' you're right inta Southie. There's a dozen places to swap cars as soon as ya' get into Southie."

Just then, Barney said, "Here comes the truck."

CHAPTER 18

Each Monday they met, carefully reconnoitering and backtracking the truck's route. When they met on the Monday that Columbus Day was being observed, they didn't bother going to Chelsea. They decided to pass that week.

Barney said, "Hey, are you guys interested in goin' to a Red Sox game if they come back to Boston?"

Sean said, "I guess. I know Artie and Gus would love to go, But ain't they down three games to one?"

The Red Sox had won the American League and were playing the St. Louis Cardinals in the World Series. Artie and Gus were ecstatic. That was the good news. The bad news was that, after the first four games, the Sox were down three games to one. They were playing the fifth game, today, in St. Louis. If they lost, the Series was over. If they won, they would come back to Boston for the last two games.

"Yeah, they gotta win today's game or they're out. A guy owes me some money and he ain't got it, so he asked me if I'd take four tickets to game seven. He ain't a bad guy so I figured I'd give him a break. 'Course, it don't count if they don't make game seven. They gotta win today and then come back an' win on Wednesday. Anyway, I ain't goin', so if ya' want 'em, I got the tickets."

"Sure, lemme have 'em."

The Real Town

Sure enough, the Red Sox won Monday and then they came back and won on Wednesday. Gus and Artie were blown away. On Thursday, they headed for Fenway Park. They got there early, so they stopped for a drink at The Rathskellar, which was a rocking club, just down the street, in Kenmore Square. The place was mobbed. Shortly after they got there, they worked their way into a table and, of course, they wound up sitting with some college girls, Ginger and Rachael. As things progressed, Sean and Ginger hit it off and were brazenly flirting with each other. When it came time to leave for the game, they were off in their own world, giggling and smooching.

Artie could not believe it when Sean said that he'd just as soon stay.

"You gotta be kiddin' me? We got tickets to the seventh game of the World Series an' you ain't gonna *go?"*

Sean said, "I'll tell ya' what, why don't you guys take Rachel. She's like you, Artie, she's a Soxaholic. Me and Ginger are Braves fans."

Which was partially true. Rachel really was a Red Sox fan. Ginger, on the other hand, wouldn't know the difference between the Braves and the Red Sox if she met them.

Rachel popped up, "Oh, I'd love to go. Can I? Can I come? Please."

Sean said, "Of course you can. I'm sure they'd rather have *you* with them than me. Besides, it's my ticket. Here."

Handing Rachel his ticket, he waved them on their merry way - which also freed up Ginger for the evening.

The Red Sox got killed. St Louis beat them seven to two. Even worse, Bob Gibson only allowed the Sox to get three hits.

The Real Town

A few days later, Sean and Tommy happened to be driving by the area and went up Brookline Avenue, past Fenway Park.

Tommy said, "Man, were they bummed out after the game the other night, especially Artie and Rachel. We walked her back to her dorm after the game - it's right up the street here."

"Yeah, I know. I walked Ginger back after the bars closed."

Traffic was especially heavy, so they were just barely crawling along. They were stopped next to the vast Sears and Roebuck parking lot at the huge intersection, where Brookline Avenue crosses Park Drive, when Tommy pointed across the intersection and said, "That's their dormitory right there. That's where we left Rachel. Is that where you took Ginger?"

Sean said, "Yeah, prob'ly."

But he wasn't really paying attention to Tommy. He was focused on two large hedges, which flanked an open walkway from the sidewalk, on the corner of the intersection, into the open parking lot. Each was maybe seven or eight feet high, three or four feet thick and about ten or twelve feet long. They were the only foliage anywhere near the parking lot. The walkway was about six feet wide and led to three steps down into the lot.

Then he said, "Oh my God,"

"What?"

"That's gotta be where we were makin' out."

"Who, you and Ginger?"

"Yeah, I was so drunk, I barely remembered it. I remembered we wound up makin' out between two big bushes that were across the street from her dorm. I just figured we were in some kind of a yard or a garden or something. But those are the only bushes around here."

The Real Town

The light turned green and they moved right up to the corner before it turned red again. They were parked just past the hedges. Looking over his shoulder, Tommy could see clearly through the hedges, Tommy said, "You tellin' me you were fuckin' right there? You coulda' got busted for flashin'."

"I didn't say I fucked her anywhere, I said we were makin' out."

Tommy was laughing, "Yeah, right, as drunk as you two were? Gimme a break. You gonna call her?"

"No. She told me she's got a boyfriend and she usually don't fool around on him, but they had a fight that day."

Looking over at the wide open entry between the two hedges, Sean shook his head. "I cannot believe it."

CHAPTER 19

On the Monday after Daylight Saving Time ended, they were ready. They were more than ready to go as they were sure that the truck was carrying over a million dollars. This was going to be the largest score that any of them had ever made.

They spent the day getting cars and putting them in place. Because of the timing of this particular score, they decided to alter their usual technique. They had different ways of getting their cars. Sean's preferred method was to take them from the Metropolitan Transit Authority (MTA) subway parking lots. They had a set of master keys which could start any car. There were a number of MTA parking lots around the city. Almost invariably, a number of the lots would be full by nine o'clock in the morning. At which point, the lot attendant would leave. Many days were spent keying up cars. That way, they always had at least a half-dozen cars in each lot that they could take on a moment's notice. They simply kept track of which commuters left their cars in the same lot every day and then kept track of which keys started the cars. There had actually been days when they took cars for a score which, for various reasons, did not take place. As soon as it became obvious that the score was not going to go down, they returned the cars to their original parking spots. Why waste them?

The Real Town

Ordinarily, the score would be long over before the cars were even missed. This time, however, because the score wasn't going to go off until around five o'clock at night, Sean decided to slightly alter their routine. One of their other practices was to collect license plates. It wasn't too difficult to obtain them, in the middle of the night - only one, mind you, the front one. That way it could simply be chalked up to having fallen off of the car. After a plate was collected, it would be put away for months. While the police officers did keep a list of stolen cars, and plates, in their vehicles, the lists were kept in a chronological order. By the time that a collected plate was used, it was many pages down the list - if it was even on the list at all.

So, on the day after daylight saving time ended, the cars that they needed had been appropriated, their plates removed and the back plate was replaced. They were good to go.

There were about fifteen long trailer trucks parked at the loading dock. Between the time that it got dark and the time that the armored car pulled into the lot, Sean, Tommy, Gus and Artie had each slunk into the lot, discreetly sliding between, and then under, the trailer trucks.

Shortly after, when the armored truck pulled into the lot, it cruised down past all of the trailers, turning right after passing the last one, and winding up between the long truck and the short stairway leading up to the door and into the building. It was totally out of view of anyone on the street.

Lying flat on the ground under the last trailer, Sean stared under the armored truck and watched the footsteps of the two guards as they got out on the other side of the truck and strolled over to the steps. Although it was already dark, the other side of the truck was quite observable, from a light that was on, over the door. The wait was on.

The main difference between robbing a bank and robbing an armored truck was the level of timing involved. Of course, both required timing. But, with a truck, one had to be much more meticulous. The window of opportunity was quite narrow. If you wanted the contents of the truck you had to catch them when the side door was open. Otherwise, the most that you were going to get was whatever the guards were bringing either to, or from, the truck. If you did not catch the door while it was open, and keep it open, the driver would trigger the deadbolt. End of story.

After what seemed to be an eternity of waiting, Sean faintly heard the door opening. Without taking his eyes off of the bottom of the steps, he slightly raised his hand, making a fist and slowly rocking his thumb back and forth. The other three placed themselves in position to make their move - none of them taking their eyes off of Sean.

A moment after the guards footsteps reached the truck, the slight click of the side door lock unlatching brought them to their feet at the back of the trailer. Gliding swiftly, yet silently, past the rear of the armored truck, they stepped around to the side and caught the guards with the door wide opened. The guard with the money bag in his hand was in the process of raising his leg, to climb back into the truck, when Tommy said, "Don't move."

The Real Town

The other guard, with a pistol in his hand, instinctively started to raise his gun and spin towards them. He half-turned and found himself looking directly into the barrel of Artie's pistol, no more than two inches from his face. Very carefully, the guard lowered his pistol. Sliding around, so he was behind him, Artie took the gun from his hand.

Tommy had the guards lie down, between the front and rear wheels, half-way under the truck. Gus had immediately gone to the front of the truck, pointing a large-barreled intimidating assault rifle at the driver. The tip of the barrel was actually touching the window.

Gus said, "Do not move your hands."

The driver froze. Even though he was safely locked inside the truck, behind bullet-proof windows, the shock of the moment froze him

Sean had flown by all of them, into the truck, with a couple of large black plastic garbage bags in his hand. For the next few seconds, as he jammed gray cloth money bags into the plastic garbage bags, the scene seemed frozen into silence, with Gus standing pointing his rifle at the driver, Tommy covering the incapacitated guards, as he confiscated their weapons, and Artie standing by the truck door watching everything else.

Passing the first bag down to Artie, Sean quickly repeated the process with the second bag. Then he was out of the truck, moving swiftly towards the car that had pulled up behind them, and turned around, with Barney at the wheel.

Throwing the bags into the car, Sean and Artie piled in behind them, with Tommy and Gus close on their heels. The chase was on.

Coming out onto the main road, they turned right and, within a few blocks, veered to the right onto a neighborhood street that ran parallel, but on an angle, with the boulevard that they had just left.

As they approached the first intersection, Barney said, "Shit!"

Cars that were coming along the crossroad, which was heading towards the parallel road that they had just left, were backed up. The last car was dead in the middle of the intersection. It was a new black Cadillac. As they pulled up to the intersection, Tommy, who was in the front passenger seat, leaned out the window and called over to the driver, "Excuse me, Sir, could you back up a little so we can get by?"

The driver, a swarthy, rather corpulent looking man, with a large oversized cigar in his hand, stared arrogantly at Tommy and, with a scornful sneer, took a long slow drag of the cigar, then flicked the ashes out the window, in their direction.

Then, they all heard the ominous sound of a police car's siren, coming from the distance.

Sean said, "They're playing our song."

Tommy stuck his hand out the window and fired three shots. Each of them bounced off of the hood of the Cadillac, leaving it vibrating.

The Cadillac immediately flew backwards.

As they flew by the Cadillac, the driver was sitting there, eyes bulging with disbelief, the cigar stuck in his mouth.

Artie said, "Wow, that was quick. I don't think he even put it in reverse. I think he stuck his feet through the floor and picked it up an' ran backwards."

The Real Town

Less than a minute after that, they were swapping cars. On a small side street, with only one street light - which they had broken the night before - they left the first car and hopped into three others. Barney went by himself, taking one bag. Sean and Tommy took the other bag and Gus and Artie followed them in the third car.

About a half-hour later, after having swapped cars again, they met two towns away, in Winthrop, where Barney had a summer cottage on the beach. By this time, they were driving their own cars.

Barney had a pool table on the rear porch which faced out onto the beach. The porch was screened in well enough so that, while they could see out, people outside really couldn't see in. That was where they counted the money.

Placing both plastic bags beside the table, Sean, who was standing with his back to the beach, began removing the cloth money bags, one at a time. He would remove a bag, dump the contents on the table, hand Tommy the empty bag, and begin counting, out loud, all the while stacking the money neatly along the far side of the table.

As he finished the first bag and started on number two, he glanced up at his compatriots. They were all standing silently, staring back at him. They were already well over a half million dollars.

A while later, counting out loud, as he placed the last stack of bills along the side of the table, he said, "One million, six hundred thousand, that 's three hundred an' twenty grand each."

Then, almost as an afterthought, he waved his hand at the last of the uncounted bills in the middle of the table, "And change."

None of them said anything. Mostly, they just exchanged glances and grins. Then Tommy said, "You got the cards?"

Sean smiled and reached into his pocket, removing a new deck and tossing it on the table. "How much you figure is left?"

They all stared at the last of the money.

"I don't know."

"I'll bet there's ten grand there."

"I ain't got a clue."

Barney looked at Sean. "You wanna' count it?"

Sean shook his head, smiling, "Nah, let whoever wins it count it."

Tommy opened up the deck of cards and, as he began shuffling, said, "Anybody wanna' deal?"

They all just stared at him, grinning.

Barney said, "Wait a minute."

He walked over to the refrigerator and took out five bottles of beer.

"Anyone want a glass?"

They all just shook their heads.

As they all sipped from their bottles, Tommy leisurely turned the cards over. Artie won with three fours. As happened so often, the game was won on the last round of cards. His last card was a four, beating Barney who had been winning with two pairs, Aces and tens.

Barney said, "Oh you sonofabitch! Whenever I play this fuckin' thing I lose - an' it's always on the last fuckin' card."

But, like all of them, he was laughing.

CHAPTER 20

Meg and Anne were having a late lunch at Jack & Marion's, a Jewish Deli, out in Brookline. It was a little out of the way but the food was excellent and they loved the atmosphere.

After they'd finished eating, Meg asked, "How did you find this place? I love it."

Anne said, "Sean took us here, last week. You know how he is about restaurants."

Just then, Meg glanced over Anne's shoulder and her demeanor abruptly changed. One minute she was sitting back, relaxed and smiling, suddenly she was sitting up rigidly, with an alarmed look on her face, as she stared intently past Anne.

Anne was instantly aware of the difference, and turned around to see what Meg was gawking at.

Three men were standing just inside the door. As one of them spoke to the hostess, one of the others, a tall, swarthy man, was looking around the room with an outwardly arrogant attitude. As his eyes passed their table, they suddenly darted back. The rigidity that had come over Meg, as alarming as it had been, was nothing compared to his instantaneous reaction. With his wide eyes filled with fear and panic, his mouth open with no sound coming out, he unconsciously stepped back, stumbling.

The misstep caused him to break eye contact with Meg. Without ever looking back in her direction, he turned coweringly towards the door. The third man, who had been standing behind him, held his arm out and appeared to say something but was brusquely shoved out of the way as the tall one broke through the door. Then they were gone.

Anne and Meg both stared at the door for the next few moments, then, turning back to Meg, Anne said, "That was him, wasn't it? Akbar."

Still staring at the door, Meg nodded her head. "That's the first time I've seen him since he moved. I thought that he'd gone back to his home country or moved to Washington or somewhere else."

Meg's face was like an open book, as it radiated relief, curiosity and confusion. Staring at Anne with a baffled look, she said, "What happened? He ran out. He was more scared than I was. What happened?"

Then, eyes flickering towards the door, something else occurred to her, changing her attitude back. "Could he be outside waiting?"

Anne reached across the table, taking her hand. "I don't think so. I think someone 'spoke' to him.

After a moment of silent rumination, with Meg staring at her with wide, questioning eyes, Anne said, "I'm not supposed to tell you this, but I think I have to now. Wait a minute, though, I have to make a phone call."

When she returned from the phone booth, she had the waitress with her, with a bottle of wine on a tray. Smiling, she said, "This is that wine you like isn't it?"

Meg nodded, half smiling, still glancing at the door.

As she sat back down, the waitress filled their glasses, and left. Picking up her glass, she held it out for a toast. As they clicked glasses, she said, "Here's to the end of your problem with Akbar."

The Real Town

After they put their glasses back down, Anne said, "Remember when you came back from New York and you told me that Akbar was gone? Well, what I never told you was that, while you were gone, I had spoken to Sean about it. He told me not to say anything to you about it."

Eyes widening, her voice barely above a whisper, Meg said, "And Sean . . . 'spoke' . . . to Akbar?"

Tilting her head to the side, eyebrows raised and half-smiling, Anne said, "Who knows? He said that he was going to, then, when you came back and said that Akbar was gone, and I told Sean, he said that that was good, 'cause then he wouldn't have to speak to him. But I know him. I didn't buy it for a second that he hadn't already taken care of it. So I told him that, seeing as Akbar was gone, I could tell you that he knew."

Meg said, "Then, why didn't you? It's been a couple of months."

Anne just sat there with a slight smirk on her face.

After a long moment, recognition appeared in Meg's widening eyes. Nodding her head, smiling, she said, "What did Sean say when you told him that you were going to tell me?"

Wrinkling her forehead, with a thoughtful, yet exaggeratingly ingenuous look, obviously mimicking Sean, she said, "He goes, 'I don't know. Maybe you better not, just in case this guy keeps on bothering her, ya' know? I still might have to speak to him'.

They just sat there, exchanging knowing looks and then they both began to grin, widely.

Leaning forward, Meg asked softly, "What do you think   he   said   to   him?"

Leaning forward, in the same undertone, Anne said, "I don't think we'd really want to know."

They were sitting there, sipping their wine, giggling and speculating, when a voice intruded into their conversation. "You rang?"

They both looked up, caught slightly off-guard, at Sean, who was standing there grinning at them.

Meg's eyes sprang wide open in obviously delighted surprise, "Oh, how did you . . ."

Looking sharply at Anne, she said, accusingly, "You called him! Why didn't you tell me?"

Anne said, "Well, I didn't want you to get upset, but, when you said that Akbar might be outside waiting, I really didn't think he would be. But, just in case, I figured I'd call Sean."

Looking down at Anne, with a raised eyebrow, Sean said, "Akbar?"

With a slight shrug of her shoulders, she said, "I had to tell her."

Sean's face took on a look of innocence. "Tell her what?"

The look was so close to the look that Anne had had on her face, when she had been mimicking Sean earlier, that Meg burst out laughing. That set Anne off.

As the two of them sat there, giggling back and forth, Sean said, "I gather we've had a little wine?"

Still giggling, Anne said, "You want a glass?"

Glancing at the bottle, he said, "Do they have S.S. Pierce Asti Spumante?"

Rolling her eyes, Anne said, "We can ask."

When they asked the waitress, she told them that they didn't but that they had other kinds of Asti Spumante.

He politely declined. "I find the others all too sweet. S.S. Pierce is just right. It's the only one I really like."

Then, turning to Meg, he said, "You're a wine drinker. You really ought to try it. It's delicious. It tastes like apple juice with bubbles."

Smiling, Meg said, "I'd love to try it. Where do they have it?"

Anne interrupted, "At the S.S. Pierce store in town, across from the Common, on Tremont Street."

Meg said, "I meant what restaurant, or bar, would carry it. Somewhere we could go now for a drink?"

Then, with a sly smile, she said, "While Sean tells us what he said to Akbar."

The bland unknowing look that instinctively appeared on Sean's face caused eye contact between the two girls, making them both break out into laughter, which gradually turned into suppressed giggling.

Anne happened to glance up at the clock. "Oh my God, look at the time. It's almost suppertime. Ma's gonna' kill me. She's minding the kids. I told her we were just going for lunch."

Turning around, she waved to the waitress, "Could we get the check, please. Thanks."

As the waitress brought the check over, Sean took it out of her hand. "I've got it. Are you both driving?"

Meg said, "No. Anne picked me up at my place."

Anne said, as she was getting up, "Could you drop Meg off. I've really got to get going. Ma's gonna' kill me."

Sean waved her off. "No problem. Go on, get goin'. I've got the bill."

CHAPTER 21

After Anne left, they chatted for a while, then Sean said, "You know, if you really would like to try the S.S. Pierce Asti Spumante, I'll pick you up a bottle on the way back to your place."

"I'd love it."

As they were walking towards his car, Sean stopped at a new blue Corvette convertible. Stopping on the passenger side, he reached down and opened the door for Meg.

With a surprised look, she said, "Whose car is this?"

"Mine."

"When did you get this? I thought you had a Buick - a blue Buick."

"I do. I just don't take this into the town."

Looking searchingly at him, she said, "Where do you keep it, if you don't take it into Charlestown?"

He pondered for a moment, then said, "Okay, I'm gonna' tell you. But, sometimes, it's better for some people not to know certain things. I do have a place out of town that nobody else knows about. Well, one other person knows."

Smiling, she said, "Tommy."

"He's the only one."

"Your mother and Anne don't know?"

"Nope, it's better for them not to know. That way, if the cops ever ask them, they don't have to lie. I don't want them to get in trouble. I can show you. They'll never have any way of tying you to the place."

"You're going to show me?"

The Real Town

"Mm hmm, we're going right by it, on the way to your place. Actually, it's not too far from your place. I'm right on Bay State Road."

"That's right up the street from me. How long have you been there?

"Couple a' months."

As they were talking, he turned into a side street, then another one and suddenly they were on the back road, appropriately named Back Street, which ran parallel with the Charles River, behind the houses on Bay State Road.

They pulled up next to a leathery looking tarp that was hanging from the overhang. Getting out, he pulled the tarp back revealing a small alcove. "This is my parking spot."

She looked flabbergasted. "You have a parking spot? Here?"

"Yup, this is mine."

"Doesn't anyone ever take it?"

"Well, when I moved in, I sort of made a deal with the guy who runs the place."

They went in the back door and up the back stairs to the third floor. The apartment consisted of three large rooms, a bedroom, a parlor and a kitchen. It also had a good-sized balcony.

He took a bottle of S.S. Pierce Asti Spumante out of the refrigerator and poured them both a glass.

"Here", he said, as he handed her the glass, "taste it."

As Meg reached for the glass, their eyes met as their fingers touched. They stood there, for a long moment, looking into each other's eyes. Not a word was said, but the chemistry was so palpable it almost caused her to squirm.

Glancing about, she waved at the rear window, "The view must be beautiful."

He opened the wide window. "Check it out."

As they walked out onto the wide terrace, Meg said, "Oh my God, it is so beautiful."

The Charles River was laid out in front of them for miles in both directions, with Cambridge as the background on the other side of the river.

After a few minutes, the November weather started to get to them. Shivering, Meg said, "I don't want to leave this view, but I'm freezing."

Pulling the cover off of a long, high sofa, Sean heartily shook it out once and it became a huge thick blanket.

"C'mon", he said, as he took her hand and walked her over to the couch. As they wriggled their way onto the couch, Sean covered them with the blanket and then swung an arm of the couch around so that they had a little table in front of them, where he placed his glass and the bottle.

"Where did you get this couch?"

"A friend of mine is into this sort of stuff and he made it for me. Do you like it?"

"I love it."

Then, almost purring, she said, "And I love this blanket. It's so soft."

They spent the rest of the bottle enjoying the view and the unavoidable sexual chemistry that, for whatever reason, caused no tension.

At one point, she asked him what he had said to Akbar.

Smiling, he said, "Akbar who?"

Smiling back at him, she said, "You know who."

He mulled it over for a moment, then said, "Ya' know, sometimes it's really better for some people not to know some things - for their own good."

Looking openly into his eyes, she nodded her head, and said, "Okay."

They were almost done with the second bottle when Sean finally kissed her. It was a sweet languorous kiss that ended with their lips still brushing as they both slowly opened their eyes. For a long moment, they stared deeply into each other's eyes. Then, unthinkingly, Sean slowly breathed in deeply, openly smelling her. The effect was instantaneous - in both directions.

The effect on Sean was obvious as his eyes glazed over with rapture. He looked hypnotized.

Staring blissfully back into his eyes, Meg was in seventh heaven as she reveled in the helpless pleasure that filled his eyes - and then she was gone too.

They just stayed there, slowly kissing, tracing their fingers over each other's faces, until, at long last, Meg charmingly tilted her head back and, with a quiver that eliminated any doubt as to where she was, she faintly nodded her head.

Effortlessly rising from the couch, with Meg in his arms, Sean slowly strolled through the parlor into the bedroom, where he gently laid her on his huge oversized bed.

For what seemed an endless time, they kissed and touched as he slowly removed their clothing. After they had both been naked, from the waist up, for a little while, Sean unhurriedly began kissing his way down her body as he gently began removing her panties. Fluidly, without even realizing that she was doing it, Meg slightly raised her hips as he slid her panties over them.

As her panties reached her knees, he rolled them over her left knee, simultaneously bending it upwards, and outwards, seemingly to facilitate the removal of her panties. At the same time, he kissed her *down there.*

Her eyes flew open, *"OH, what . . . what are you doing?"*

"Kissing you," he murmured, his fingers teasingly replacing his lips as they moved to the inner thigh of the leg that he'd just opened to remove her panties.

Slowly, he kissed his way down her inner thigh as delicately slid her panties from around her ankle, all the while, smoothly tracing her throbbing button with his thumb. As he changed his position so he could focus on lowering her panties down the other leg, he kissed her *there* again.

Again, she reacted, but to a much lesser degree. *"Oh."*

Continuing, he kissed his way down her other inner thigh as he caressed her with his other thumb.

The third time, as he kissed his way back up, after finally removing her panties, brought out only an uninhibited high-pitched moan of pure pleasure.

This time he didn't continue on so quickly.

CHAPTER 22

Meg greeted the next morning with a dreamy smile, lazily opening her eyes as she slowly stretched her neck and took a deep breath. As her beautiful blue eyes drifted up, she found herself looking into Sean's eyes which were staring amorously back at her. Her smile widened as a warm flow of pleasure engulfed her.

Then, as it all came flooding back, the vivid images of what they had actually done, she shot up into a sitting position in the bed, clutching the sheet and wrapping it around her, all the way up to her throat.

"Oh my God, what have I done?"

Sean, who'd been sitting on the edge of the bed, started to lean towards her, "You've . . ."

She pushed her hand up between them, firmly planting it on his chest.

"Stop," she said. "Don't touch me."

He leaned back, raising his hands. "Calm down, Meg. I would never touch you if you didn't want me to. And we didn't do anything wrong. Just relax."

Looking frantically about, she said, "Where are my clothes?"

"They're right here by the bed. But calm down, there's nothing wrong. And I mean exactly that, there is nothing wrong. Everything is perfect."

Still clutching the sheet up to her throat, Meg said, "I've never done anything like this in my life. I've never . . ."

Blushing vigorously, she looked away, unable to even put into words the things that so embarrassed her.

Then, looking up defiantly, she said, "I was drunk. I've never . . . I'm not saying that I was a virgin but the only one I was ever with was . . . we were engaged for years . . . I . . ."

Turning away, and looking down, she said, "The things we did, I've never done . . . anything . . ."

Again she was unable to continue. Her humiliation at what they'd done was unbearable. It was killing her.

Reaching in, he brushed her hair back from her face with the back of his hand. "Listen to me. You did nothing wrong. We . . ."

Her head shot up, eyes blazing. "I know what I did. I . . ."

Placing his finger gently against her lips, barely touching them, he said, "Shh, wait, let me say something. Please."

They sat silently for a moment. Then, barely nodding her head, she relaxed, ever so slightly.

"First", he said, "I know that you've never done the things we did."

"How do you know?" She challenged him. "How do you know you're the first . . ."

Again she faltered.

"Because I do, and, later on, when you're in a better frame of mind, I'll tell you."

Sliding back, and off of the bed, he said, as he walked into the kitchen, "First things first, though. I know you're a coffee-head in the morning."

Walking back into the bedroom, he had a large steaming cup of coffee on a tray with cream and sugar beside it.

"I've also got muffins out there if you want one."

Taking the tray with one hand as she held the sheet up around her with the other, she lowered it to the bed. "I have to use the bathroom. Would you go out into the other room while I get up?"

"Of course, c'mon out whenever you're ready."

A while later, Meg came out into the parlor. She was fully dressed and seemed more in control of her emotions. Before she could say anything, he said, "Would you care for another cup of coffee?"

"No thank you. I think I should be going."

Sean came over to her and, holding out his hand, he asked, softly, "Why?"

As he had held his hand out, Meg had instinctively touched it. But, in response to his question, she started to withdraw.

He had wrapped her fingers around his finger, now they stood there, touching, but barely touching.

Finally, she looked up with tears in her eyes. "I can't believe that I did the things that I did . . . and with *you*."

Stepping in, he gently circled her with his arms, and held her. She rested her head on his chest and they stayed that way for a while. When Meg finally leaned back, her face was wet with tears, but she was smiling.

"Were you telling me the truth when you said that you knew that I'd never done any of that before?"

"Uh huh."

"How did you know?"

"There's lots of little things, different responses. Good girls respond to things in different ways. I always knew that you were a good girl and you proved it last night."

Blushing, with a look somewhere between a smirk and a scowl, she said, "I really don't think I qualify as a '*good girl*' after last night."

Then, cocking her head to the side, she said, "Tell me."

"I will, later. We've got plenty of time. Do you have any plans for the weekend?"

"No. Well . . . I mean . . ."

He said, "Let's go away for the weekend."

That caught her off-guard. "I can't. . . . I . . ."

"Why not? We don't have to do anything if you don't want to. It's Saturday, we can go down the cape. How about Provincetown? If you want, we'll get separate rooms. Not that I'd want to, but if that's what you want to do, we can do it. C'mon, let's do it."

Looking totally flabbergasted, she floundered for something to say. Then, sticking her chin out, with a rebellious expression, she said, ""Okay, alright, I will, on one condition. You tell me one thing. One of those different responses that you say let you know that I was a good girl. And it better be the truth. I'll know."

"I can. But it will embarrass you."

Adamantly raising her head even higher, she said, "Try me."

Leaning in close, he said, softly, "Okay, but you'll have to remember clearly. Do you remember what you said, the first time I kissed you . . . down there?

And then, never closing his eyes, he faintly brushed her lips with his.

She was speechless. He was right. She was completely embarrassed, but only for a flashing second. Then, her recollection was so vibrant that it swept her off of her feet.

Still, a bit of stubbornness showed through the rapture on her face as she placed her hands flatly on his chest and, with an almost pouty look, said, "Tell me one more thing, just one more."

"Okay, but you'll have to remember. Do you remember the first thing you said after you came off . . . the first time?"

In a flash, her mind clearly recaptured the phenomenal image of herself lying naked on the bed, her legs wide open, with Sean kneeling between them on the floor beside the bed. She could literally feel the afterglow of her first orgasm and hear herself saying, "What . . . what was that? What happened?"

The memory of his response was equally vivid. She could clearly hear him answering her, in a soft whisper, "You came off, you had an orgasm." as he softly kissed her again.

The thrills of pleasure that were tingling through her brought her back to the present. Sean had slid his hands down her back and, cupping her cheeks, was gently, meaningfully, rubbing her against his hardness. Any resistance that she had left was gone as she realized that, in response, she was rubbing herself against him.

Fully knowing what was coming, she slid her arms up around his neck, rubbed her lips back against his and, never closing her eyes, said, in a tiny voice, "Could we just stay here?"

Which they did.

CHAPTER 23

On Monday morning, Sean headed into Charlestown. As he was driving up Bunker Hill Street, he saw Tommy's wife's car coming down the hill. They pulled up beside each other. The first thing she said was, "Have you seen Tommy?"

"No. I haven't seen him since last week. I've been out of touch all weekend."

That brought a look of concern to Rita's face. "I haven't seen him since he went out Saturday morning."

That was not like Tommy. Since Tommy had gotten married, the only time that he stayed out overnight was with Rita. Or, for business purposes, which would usually include Sean.

"He hasn't called?"

She shook her head. "No, nothing."

"I'll check with Artie and Gus. Maybe somethin' came up."

"I've called both of them. I can't find either of them."

"Alright, I'll find them. If you hear anything, call Kelly's and let Becky know. I'll get back to you."

He'd been heading up to his mother's house to give her an excuse for why he hadn't shown up on Saturday, but now he pulled over in front of Kelly's and went inside. Sammy was at the end of the bar.

Sean said, "You seen Tommy or Artie or Gus?"

"Nah, I ain't seen any a' your crew all weekend. I figured yez' had something' goin'."

He drove down to Medford Street to see if Barney was at Billy Driscoll's. He was, but he hadn't seen them either. He spent the rest of the morning making telephone calls and driving around to different places where they might have been. No luck.

Then, when he was starting to legitimately get concerned, he ran into Gus' brother, Frankie.

He asked him, "You got any idea where Gus is?"

"Yeah, he went to Vegas over the weekend."

'Who'd he go with."

"I don't know. There was three or four of 'em, goin'. They had a good day bettin' the college games. I know they won big time on one a' them. I think it was Boston College. Then they was partyin' Saturday night, when he called me an' asked me if I wanted to go to Vegas with them. I wanted to, but I had some stuff I had to take care of, so I couldn't go."

"You know when they're comin' back?"

"Nah, probably when their broke."

Although he felt bad for Rita, and figured that Tommy was going to have a problem when he got back, he felt better. As much as he wanted to call her and reassure her, he figured that Tommy would be home today and he'd better stay out of it.

It was now almost noon and he was pulling into a parking spot on Charles Street between the Boston Common and the Public Garden. He was meeting Meg for lunch. There was a little restaurant on Charles Street that he liked and, as it was right down the street from the hospital where she worked, they were going to meet at the Charles Street Circle.

The Real Town

Charles Street Circle is a major downtown Boston rotary. It connects two main streets, Charles and Cambridge Streets, along with Storrow Drive, the main road that runs along the Charles River and the Longfellow Bridge that comes over the Charles River from Cambridge. It's always a crowded area, especially at lunch time.

As he was standing on the Charles Street side of the Circle, a car pulled over and two good-sized chaps got out. He did not recognize either of them but, as they started to walk past him, one on each side, they both suddenly stopped. One of them, slightly opening his jacket so Sean could see his pistol, said, "Get in the car, Sean, or we'll blow ya' fuckin' brains out."

The second one, whose hand was in his jacket pocket, clearly holding a gun that was pointed at Sean, said, "Don't even think about tryna' run."

Raising his hands slightly, about waist high, Sean unhurriedly took two steps back, taking him out from in between them. Then, pointing his finger at the obviously pocketed gun that was pointing at him, he said, in a loud, clear voice, "Is that a gun? Are you pointing a gun at me? Are you trying to rob me? Are you going to shoot me . . . *in front of all these people?"*

Caught totally off-guard, the two hooligans glared around at the hordes of people surrounding them. Everyone was staring at them. Girls were standing, frozen, with their hands covering their mouths. Women were pointing. Men were staring back, some of them guiding their female companions away from the situation.

As he had been overtly making everyone aware of the situation, Sean had casually taken another step backwards, then sideways, all the time pointing and asking his questions in a loud, reproachful tone. And then he was in the crowd.

The Real Town

The two panicked. Dashing back to the car, they jumped in and it took off, wheels screeching.

Which is just what Sean wanted to do, but the people had him enclosed. Everyone was asking questions.

"What happened?"

"What was that all about?"

"Who were those guys?"

"Are you alright?"

"Did you know those guys?"

Raising his hands, Sean said, "I have no idea who they were. I think they were trying to rob me. I don't know. I just want outta here. Excuse me, excuse me, please."

In a courteous, yet firm manner, Sean slid his way through the excited herd of people, all the time saying, "Excuse me, excuse me, please."

One thing that people who knew Sean well were all aware of was that he would never let anyone take him alive. He used to joke about the old James Cagney movie where Cagney said, "You'll never take me alive, copper."

Sean would say, 'The only ones who I'd ever let take me alive are the cops."

As he reached Cambridge Street, and turned right, he saw Meg crossing the street, heading in his direction. As she reached the sidewalk, she glanced up and saw him. Her face broke into a wide beaming smile - which turned into a confused look of puzzlement as Sean's reaction was a minute shake of his head as he repeatedly darted his eyes towards the upcoming street on his right.

Reaching his hand up to ostensibly scratch his upper lip, he deftly pointed in the direction of the street that they were both approaching from opposite directions.

The Real Town

Although she had no clue what was going on, Meg was not only a very bright girl, she was also street-smart. Without any response, she turned into the side-street and kept on walking as if she wasn't even aware of him. She went up one block and, without looking back, turned left onto the next street.

The first doorway that she came to was five steps deep. She stepped up onto the second step and waited. A few moments later, Sean stopped at the doorway.

Taking her by the hand, he continued walking. "I'm sorry about this, Meg, but a coupla' guys just tried to grab me and I don't want you involved. We gotta' get outta here."

He then described what happened.

Meg's concern and worriment for him was apparent on her face. "You don't know who they were?"

"No," he responded, "but I will find out."

"How?"

"There are ways. But I don't have time right now. There are things that I'm gonna' have to take care of and, as much as I want to be with you, it's not a good time for you to be with me."

"What are you saying?"

"Don't tell anyone that you've seen me. Definitely don't tell anyone about the weekend."

Lowering her eyes, blushing, she said, softly "I told Anne."

Looking up, sharply, she said, "Not . . . no details . . . just . . ."

Gently placing his finger against her lips, he said, "Shhh, I know. You don't have to tell me. Just tell her not to mention it to anyone. We can't have anyone connecting you to me, right now."

The Real Town

As they were talking they had wandered up through the back of Beacon Hill, eventually coming out behind the State House.

He said, "We've got to split up here. I'm going to head out onto Beacon Street and I don't want you to be seen with me. Until I know what's going on, we have to stay apart."

The sorrow and disenchantment were evident on Meg's face. Still, she was a strong, sharp girl. Stepping up onto the first step of the doorway that they were standing beside, she turned towards him and raised her chin, lips protruding, not pouting, offering.

An offer he gratefully accepted, with a long, slow kiss.

Eventually, finally, they walked off in opposite directions, both continuously looking back.

CHAPTER 24

When he'd told her that he had not recognized either of the two who'd tried to take him, what he didn't mention was that, when they jumped back into the car, he'd gotten a look at the driver. Although he did not know him well, he did know who he was. He was a 'wannabe' tough guy from South Boston. While Sean did not know his real name, he knew his nickname, 'Puppet'.

One time, when they'd been in a bar over there, with Neezo, this guy had started mouthing off. Neezo was in the telephone booth when this guy had come in and stood at the bar next to Tommy and Sean. He was half-stiff and started running his mouth at them when they wouldn't tell him who they were.

"I wanna' know who the fuck you guys are. You ain't from Southie. Who the fuck are ya'? What the fuck are you doin' here?"

Sean replied, "Excuse me, officer. May I see your badge?"

Which totally befuddled the lunkhead. "Huh? What badge? What the fucka' ya' talkin' about?"

"You are a cop aren't you? Where I'm from the only ones who ask guys who they are, are cops - or stool pigeons. You ain't a stool pigeon, are you?"

That set him off. "Whadid you say? D'ju call me a rat? I'll kick your fuckin' ass."

At which point, Neezo returned to the bar. Tapping the loudmouth on the shoulder, he said, "Whattsa' problem?"

The Real Town

Spinning around, he immediately adjusted his attitude. He might not have known them, but he knew Neezo.

In a much less aggressive tone, he said, "This guy called me a rat."

Glancing at Sean, with a raised eyebrow, "He's a rat?"

Sean shrugged, ""I don't know. I just asked him if he was. He was askin' us who we were."

Which brought it home to Neezo, nodding his head with a half-smile, half-grimace, "An' you asked him for his badge."

Looking back at the now rather fainthearted hulk, Neezo said, "You want a problem with me, Puppet?"

Shaking his head, "I got no problem with you, Tommy."

Neezo repeated himself, "That ain't what I asked ya'. Do you *want* a problem with me?"

"No."

Pointing at Sean, Neezo said, "Uh huh, well, *I* wouldn't want a problem with *him*. You get it?"

That ended that. It had happened over a year ago and, while Sean had seen him a few times when he'd been in South Boston, they'd never spoken again.

Now, as he drove up Broadway, he closely watched both sides of the street. As he approached "D" Street, he saw Neezo's best friend, Matt, coming out of Sonny and Whitey's, a bar on the left side of the street. Beeping his horn, he caught Matt's attention and waved him over.

As Matt neared the car, he said, "Hey stranger, where the Hell you been? We ain't seen you in a coupla' months."

Sean said, "Yeah, we been busy. Is Neezo around?"

"Yeah, I just left him. He's right inside the door."

"Do me a favor, will ya'? Ask him to come out. I really can't hang around."

"Sure, I'll go get him."

A minute later, Neezo came out. Sean motioned him into the car and they drove off, ending up at Castle Island, the most detached area in South Boston, which is located at the far end of the beach, and projects out into Boston Harbor.

Historically, Castle Island goes back to the early sixteen hundreds when it was designated as Boston's sea defense. To this day, it still houses a two hundred year old fort, Fort Independence, which was the last place the British occupied in Boston before they were forced to evacuate in 1776.

Castle Island also has a large parking lot to house the crowds of people who come there. There is also a causeway which extends out into Boston Harbor. The causeway, which locals call 'the loop', encompasses Pleasure Bay. It runs from Castle Island to Head Island and back to Day Boulevard which runs along the beach and back to Castle Island.

As they parked, Neezo asked, "Is this car hot?"

Sean said, "Yeah, but don't worry about it. I got a Mass. Plate on it that I got out in Springfield about six months ago."

When Sean told him what happened, Neezo asked, "What did the other two look like?"

As Sean described them, Neezo was nodding his head. "Yeah, that sounds right. It sounds like the Joyce brothers. Puppet's always kissin' their ass. But what's their beef with you?"

"I don't know. Whatever it is, it ain't with them. I never saw either one of 'em before. It's something' else. You got any idea where this Puppet might be?"

"Yeah, he don't go t' too many different joints. Let's take a ride."

On the third bar that they stopped at, Neezo didn't come right back out. Sean parked up the street. A little while later, Neezo came out.

"He's in there. I can't see his car. Let's cruise around, it can't be too far."

He was right. It was parked around the corner in an alley.

It was already dark when Puppet came out the door, around suppertime. As he staggered towards the alley, where his car was, they effectively positioned themselves to intercept him. He was parked just past the first doorway in the alley.

As he reached the doorway, a voice startled him. "Hey Puppet, how ya' doin'?"

Spinning towards the door, he saw Sean standing there, pointing his pistol at him.

What he didn't see, as he froze at Sean's question "Do you want to die?" was Neezo rising up and quietly coming around from the other side of the car with a pipe in his hand.

*

When Puppet came to, he was tied up, naked, on the floor of a dark dingy room, most likely a cellar. His arms were up over his head, tied around a pipe. Sean was pouring ice water on him. Coughing, with water splattering out of his mouth, he looked up and saw Sean.

Instantaneously, a shrill whimper burst from his trembling mouth. "Aaaaah."

All he could see was Sean, smoking a cigarette and an assembly of frightening paraphernalia, including a hammer, pliers, nails, a cigarette lighter, scissors and many other things'

Sean said, "You wanna' tell me now, what today was all about, or you wanna' wait till later?"

Glancing at the paraphernalia, he said, "Either way, you're gonna' tell me."

Puppet's head was throbbing from the blow that had rendered him unconscious but his fear was so intense that he was impervious to the pain. He had been certain that Sean had not seen him at Charles Street Circle. Now he was overwhelmed with fright. "Please, I had nothing' to do with it. I just gave 'em a ride."

"Nothin' to do with what? What did they want me for?"

When Puppet hesitated, Sean simply reached in and put his cigarette out on his stomach.

His scream was muffled as someone, who was standing behind his head, covered his face with a pillow.

When the pillow was lifted off of his face, the first thing that he saw was Sean lighting another cigarette. He crumbled. "I swear to God it wasn't me . . . I wasn't the one who drove them when they got the other ones."

Almost breathlessly, Sean asked, "What other ones?"

"The other Charlestown guys who had the money."

"Tell me what happened - everything."

He did.

The Real Town

CHAPTER 25

Sean and Neezo returned to Castle Island. Sitting in the car, they went over what Puppet had told them.

On Friday night, someone from Charlestown had called Jimmy Brown and told him that Sean's crew had made a big score - over a million. Jimmy Brown was a guy from Southie who had gotten out of prison a few years earlier and had a crew pulling scores and shaking people down. He was also a known 'fence', someone who would buy stolen goods.

Jimmy had his guys looking for four of them. Whoever it was that called, called back on Saturday night and tipped them off to where Tommy and Artie were that night. Brown's crew snatched them when they were coming out of whatever joint they were in. They never had a chance. Tommy and Artie were both dead, and they had died hard. They had been tortured until they told their captors where they each had stashed their end of the score.

Puppet had no idea who it was, from Charlestown that gave them up. All he knew was that it was someone who was drinking with either Tommy's or Artie's brother on Friday night. But he did know who it was that grabbed them. There were six of them, Brown, the Joyce brothers, Brown's main shooter, 'Big Al' and two of Al's cronies, Frannie and Lee. He also didn't know where their bodies were.

The one thing that shocked Neezo was that Puppet told them that while they did get Artie to give up where his money was, they didn't get Tommy's. Tommy had given in, too, but he'd told them that Sean had his money.

Neezo said, "I can't believe that Tommy would give you up."

With a long cold look, Sean said, "He didn't. He did what I would've done if I was in his shoes. Think about it, I don't have his bread and he knew they'd be coming for me anyways to get my end."

After a few seconds, the perplexed look left Neezo's face. "Sonofabitch! He was protecting Rita."

They sat quietly for a minute and then Sean asked, "Do you think Puppet could get them to come down here? What if he told them I was down here meetin' with someone? Not you."

Neezo said, "Yeah, I think so."

Then, "Jesus, ya' know what? Ya' see those two guys that are goin' out on the loop? One a' them runs with the Mullins crew. They're beefin' with Brownie."

They just looked at each other. Then, without saying a word, they both got out of the car. They had parked at the far end of the parking lot which, in daylight, or in warmer weather, would be filled, but now was empty. They were the only ones there.

Opening the trunk they reached in and pulled Puppet out. His arms were cuffed behind his back and his mouth was covered with duct tape.

The brisk removal of the tape brought forth a gasp of pain.

As he started to say something, Sean said, "Shut up and listen."

Puppet's mouth clamped shut.

"You got two choices, live or die - and if you choose to die, you'll die a lot worse than Tommy and Artie did."

He then laid out what he wanted said and how he wanted it said.

The Real Town

As they stood by the pay phone, Puppet dialed three numbers before he found them. He caught the Joyce brothers at the Transit, a bar down at the start of Broadway. He told them that he had seen Sean driving up Broadway and that he'd followed him and that Sean had gone down to Castle Island. He told them that Paulie McGee had been waiting for him and that the two of them were walking the loop together right now. He also told them where he was parked, so they knew where to meet him.

While Sean had brought the hot car, they had placed Puppet in the trunk of his own car and Neezo had driven that down. Now they repositioned the cars. They kept Puppet's car at the deserted end of the lot. Neezo took the other car to the other side of the lot.

A few minutes later, a car came barreling along the beach down Day Boulevard and swung into the lot. It came directly towards Puppet's car. They could see Puppet sitting behind the steering wheel. What they could not see was that his hands were taped to the wheel. As they pulled up beside him, their window was rolling down. Kurt Joyce, who was in the passenger seat, started to say something, "Hey, get outta the car. Where . . ."

His question was drowned out by the cracking sound of the rifle shot that Neezo fired from across the lot, shattering the driver's head.

At the same time, Sean rose from behind the other side of Puppet's car and opened fire across the hood, with two blasts from a double-barreled sawed-off shotgun - one to the front, one to the back.

As he pulled the trigger for the second shot, he dropped the shotgun on the hood and swiftly drew two pistols from his belt, emptying both of them into the car's occupants.

As Neezo pulled up, also firing into the car, Sean was coming around the front of Puppet's car, firing from yet a third pistol.

There had been four guys in the car. The one in the back seat behind the driver tried to get out. Neezo and Sean both gunned him down.

Neezo had jumped out of his car and moved quickly towards Puppet. Then he stopped. The left side of Puppet's head was blown off. One of his own had killed him, while firing back at Sean. Sean, scooping up the shotgun and the two pistols from the hood of Puppet's car, joined Neezo who'd jumped back into the other car and they were gone.

CHAPTER 26

As Sean pulled back into Charlestown in his own car, his mind was racing. They had dumped the hot car in Southie and Neezo had given him a ride downtown, where he had stowed his car earlier. Neezo had also kept the guns, to get rid of them. They were probably already in the ocean.

As much as he knew that he had to tell Rita, he was putting it off. As much sorrow as he had buried in him, he was keeping it submerged beneath the fury which raged inside of him, totally consuming him.

He went straight to Charlie's' Bar and Grill, a bar at the far end of the town, where Artie's brother, Richie, hung out. Without going in, he peeked through the window. Richie was sitting at the end of the bar, drinking by himself. He wasn't a bad kid, but he drank too much and couldn't keep his mouth shut.

Sean went to the pay phone on the corner and called Charlie's. Clearly using a voice that was not his, he asked for Richie. When Richie got on the line, Sean said, "This is Sean. We've got to talk. Don't say anything to anyone and don't tell anyone that it was me calling. Don't rush. Finish your drink and then leave. I'm outside. I'm parked down the street past McCarthy's."

McCarthy's was the next bar going down Main Street into the town.

About ten minutes later, Richie came to the car. As he bent over to look into the car, Sean stepped out of the doorway behind him. "Get in."

Caught off guard, Richie said, "Jesus Christ, you scared the shit outta me."

Sean walked past him and got into the car. He drove them down to the other end of town and parked by 'The Oiley's', a football field across the street from the Navy Yard, at the end of the Little Mystic River, just before it flowed into the Boston Harbor.

Sean said, "Who were you drinking with on Friday night?"

"Huh? I don't know, a coupla' guys."

"Think. Who were you with?"

Furrowing his brow, he said, "What's goin' on? Whadda ya' wanna' know that for? I mean, there was guys comin' in an' out all night."

Losing his patience, Sean said, "Who did you tell that Artie made a big score?"

That made him back up, stiffly, "I didn't tell anyone. I swear it."

Giving him a greatly abbreviated account of how he knew, he said, "There are some guys that know and they got it from someone that was drinking with either Tommy's or Artie's brother on Friday night. Tommy doesn't have any brothers and you're Artie's only brother. Now tell me."

"Sean, I swear to God I didn't tell anyone . . . I . . . Artie did gimme some money, but I lost it playin' cards an' I called him an' asked for some more, but he wouldn't give me any. He told me to go home an' he'd see me in the morning. But I kept pressing him an' then I . . . I said something' stupid. I called him a cheap bastard and said 'You just made a million dollar score an' you won't give me a lousy coupla' hundred bucks."

Staring coldly, Sean said, "Who was with you when you said it?

"Nobody, I was on the pay phone by myself. But . . . someone did hear me. He made like he didn't, but I knew that he did. But I thought he was just being cool when he looked the other way."

"Who?"

"Dickie Black."

Sean took a deep breath. It fit. Dickie Black was a weasel. Sean had never trusted him.

He made Richie go back over everything that he could remember saying on the telephone.

"Alright", he said, "you keep this between me and you. Don't tell anyone anything."

Nodding his head, he said, "I won't. I give you my word, except Artie. You know I gotta' tell Artie."

Sean looked at him for a moment. "Yeah, but nobody else."

Sean spent the rest of the night looking for Dickie Black. No luck.

One of the stops that he made was at Billy Driscoll's. After checking the place out, he called Barney outside. As much as he wanted to keep everything under wraps, he knew that he had to tell Barney. He quickly told him what was going on.

Barney was stunned. "Do you think they're looking for me, too?"

"I don't know. If I had to guess, I'd say 'No'. Word is, they're looking for four of us and I don't think Dickie Black has any reason to connect you with us. I made Richie go over what he said on the phone, a coupla' times, and he never mentioned anyone's name. But, like I said, I really don't know. That's why I'm telling you. If I were you, I'd get outta town for a while. But that's your call. One thing - you don't tell anyone, and I mean anyone, anything I've told you tonight."

Barney nodded his head, almost shivering at the glacial look in Sean's eyes. "You know I won't say nothing'. And I'm not going anywhere. I know you're gonna' move alone and I'm not asking any questions, but, if you need me - if there's anything I can do - just let me know. *Please*. They were my friends, too."

The Real Town

CHAPTER 27

Early the next day, he called Rita and told her that he wanted to meet her, but not at her house. They met in the back of a restaurant parking lot in Malden, a smaller city just outside of Boston. When she got into his car, they just stared at each other.

Finally, she said, "Tell me."

He took a deep breath. "I'm sorry. I . . ."

"No . . . no, please, no."

"I don't know what to say. I . . ."

Tears running down her face, she interrupted him. "How? What happened? Please don't tell me he's dead. Please."

All he could say was, "I'm sorry."

She collapsed, burying her face against his shoulder, as they sat there, both of them drenched with tears.

In the end, she asked him again, "What happened?"

"You don't want to know. It's better for you not to know. In the end, there's probably gonna' be a lotta heat. You don't want any part of it. I'll tell you this much. It was over money. They tried to get his money."

Her eyes widening, she said, "Does it have anything to do with what happened over in Southie last night?"

It had been all over the news. "5 SOUTHIE GANGLAND SLAYINGS" "5 DEAD IN SOUTHIE GANG WAR". The media was having a blast.

He said, "Like I said, you do *not* want to know *anything*."

Then, "And I think that it might be a good time for you to go away for a while."

151

Emphatically shaking her head, she said, "No! I want him found. I'm not going anywhere until they find his body. You'll find him. I know you will."

"It's possible, but I can't promise it. You know I'll try, but, if it comes down to a choice between finding out where they left him or bringing down who did him, well, you know what he'd want me to do."

Shutting her eyes, she said, "I know."

"I really think it's best for you to get out of town for a while. Ya' never know, they might come after you for the money. And don't tell anyone where you are, just me. I give you my word, if we find him, I'll come and get you - immediately."

She finally agreed to go. Then they sat there hugging and comforting each other with tears running down both of their faces.

CHAPTER 28

His next mission was to find Gus. He had tried his number but got no answer. So, he called his brother, Frankie. Frankie told him that he had just gotten a call from Gus, wanting to know what the Hell was going on in Southie. He'd seen it on the news.

Sean asked, "What did you tell him?"

"I told him I hadn't heard nothin'. That all the paper's are sayin' it's a gang war. I did hear they picked up Paulie McGee, but they had to let him go."

"When's he comin' back from Vegas?"

"I think they're comin' back tomorrow."

"What time's his plane landing'?"

"I don't know, yet. He said he'd gimme a call an' let me know an' I can pick 'em up."

"Yeah, well, call Kelly's when ya' find out, will ya'? Let Becky know."

"Sure."

The next day, when Gus' plane landed, Frankie was waiting for him at the airport. So was Sean, although no one was aware of it. As they all came out of the terminal door, and crossed over to the parking lot where Frankie's car was parked, Sean stepped out from behind the wide pole, caught Gus' eye, nodded his head to the side and stepped back behind the pole. Gus' spontaneous smile disappeared instantly from the look in Sean's eyes.

Turning to the others, Gus said, "I'll be right back. I'll meet yez' at the car."

As soon as he joined Sean at the pole, he said, "What's goin' on? What's the problem?"

Sean said, "Go tell them you have to go with someone else. Don't tell them it's me. Tell them you saw someone you've been looking to talk to an' you'll see them later."

As soon as Gus came back, he got into Sean's car and said, "Tell me."

Sean did, in detail.

When he finished Gus sat there, unmoving, staring off, face permeated with turbulence. Finally, he said "They're both dead?"

Sean just nodded.

Then, looking up, Gus asked, "What about Barney? Does he know?"

Sean nodded, again. "Him and Rita, I didn't tell Richie that they're dead. I don't want him to go off and do something stupid that will let Dickie Black know that we know. But we're gonna' have to catch him quick. Ritchie's a fuckin' drunk. First time he runs into Dickie, he'll let him know without even knowing that he's done it."

But it was already too late. For the next couple of weeks, the hunt was on, but they couldn't find any of them. They also had people, who they knew they could trust, and who could keep their mouths shut, very stealthily keeping an eye out for Dickie Black. No one saw him.

At the same time, Neezo was keeping him up to date on the South Boston situation. There was still a lot of heat from the killings, but it was finally starting to lighten up. One thing that hadn't changed was that neither Jimmy Brown nor Big Al had been seen since the shootings.

One Sunday afternoon, after Sean had been roaming around all weekend, hunting, he was heading home to get some sleep and he decided to stop down Sullivan's Bar, for a drink.

The Real Town

Sully's, an old-time bar that went back to prohibition, had two rooms. The front room was just a bar for guys watching television. The back room had about fifteen tables and a jukebox and was more for girls, guys looking for girls, and couples.

Sean got a drink at the bar and went into the back room which, at that time of day, was empty. He was sitting in the back room, by himself, sipping a drink and listening to Irish songs on the juke box, getting ready to head home, when a guy that he knew came in, and came over and sat down at his table, a big, fat, imitation tough guy. He was nobody he'd ever hung around with, but he didn't have any problems with him, either.

He said, "Listen, Sean, I was just up Winter Hill and I got a message for ya'. They said if you don't get away from Rockball they're gonna' dump ya'."

Now, O'Rourke had made a lot of enemies over the years and since he got out, some of them had been going up to the Hill trying to instigate a problem, spreading stories that O'Rourke was recruiting Sean's crew, and that they were going to pick up his end when the trouble started.

The timing couldn't have been worse. Although Sean had never had a problem with Winter Hill, he had been awake since Friday morning and was teeming with frustration at not being able to find his enemies. He responded immediately, and, without really hurting him, got the messenger's attention. At the conclusion of his response, with a pistol in his fat face, he told him, "You go back up the Hill and tell them if they threaten me again, or move on me and miss, I'll make a parking lot outta Pal Joey's."

Pal Joey's was the nightclub on Winter Hill where they hung out.

With that, he escorted him out the door.

All thoughts of going home were forgotten. He immediately went and got two more pistols. Then he went to a friendly local druggist and got enough 'diet pills', known on the street as 'Black Beauties', to bring him back to life. He continued roaming.

On Tuesday, he came into Billy Driscoll's bar down on Medford Street. Barney Johnson and Din McCarthy, came over to him.

Barney, said, "Where the Hell have you been? Someone told Winter Hill that you were gonna' dynamite Pal Joey's."

Sean still hadn't slept and mistook his question, responding belligerently, "Where have I been? What the fuck are you talking about? I haven't left town in days. Anyone's looking for me, I'm real easy to find."

"Whoa, whoa, take it easy." Barney said. "Nobody said you were ducking. But someone told the Hill that you were gonna' blow up Pal Joey's and they're runnin' around up there like chickens with their heads cut off."

Sean said, "I never said that." Then he told him what had happened.

When he was done, Barney said, "That ain't what they heard. Listen, we'll take a ride up and tell them what happened."

Sean said, "Sure. Let's go."

He said, "Uh uh. No, no. Not you. Me and Din will go up and see them."

Sean thought about it and then said, "O.K., you go an' tell 'em. But tell 'em that I'm here and if they want to see me, c'mon down. I'll wait right here."

The Real Town

They went out and got into the car and Sean went over to the end of the bar. At the end of the right hand side of the bar, it hooked around so you could sit with your back to the corner and watch the door. He had a pistol in his waist, one on the stool between his legs and another one on the bar next to his drink, under a newspaper.

They came back about an hour later. Barney came over and said, "O.K., everything's all right. They said they got no beef with you and they're gonna' straighten out the guy that told you that shit."

Sean nodded, "Okay, thanks."

As Sean was walking out the door, Barney said, "Sean, get some sleep. You're outta control."

CHAPTER 29

Later on, that week, he got a call from Anne. She said she had to talk to him. Very discreetly, he slipped into town and went up to the house. There was a back way up, from Medford Street, that anyone hardly ever used. That was how he came in.

Much to his surprise, his pleasant surprise, Meg was there. As the kids were already in bed, the three of them and Pat, sat in the parlor.

Shaking his head, Pat said, "Nothing on Dickie Black, he ain't been around in a coupla' weeks."

Anne said, "On top of that, I haven't seen his wife lately, either. Usually, she pushes the carriage by the house on her way down to the store. You know she had a baby a couple of months ago."

"No, I didn't know that."

They talked for a while and, as it was a Friday night, they had a few drinks. At one point, when Meg had gone to the bathroom, and Pat had gone upstairs to check on the kids, Anne got up to get them all another drink. As she was handing Sean his drink, she said, "What are you doing this weekend?"

He just sort of looked off, and shrugged his shoulders.

She said, "Why don't you and Meg go away somewhere?"

"I can't. I've got things I have to do."

"I know, but why don't you give it a break. Take a couple of days off. Go away."

Then leaning in, she playfully punched him on the shoulder, "Give *Meg* a break. Take her away for a couple of days - or weeks."

Looking up from his seat, he said, "Believe me, I'd like nothing better. But, I just can't . . . I . . ."

Shaking his head, he leaned back in the chair.

Staying right in front of him, she said, "You need a break. You're so on top of everything. Maybe it would help you if you could lean back and view the situation from a different angle. Just think about it. You know there are places you could go where no one will know either of you and you can relax. Sean, you need it, you need the break . . . and so does Meg."

Later on, when they were putting on their coats, Sean asked Meg, "Do you have any plans for the weekend?"

"No."

Appearing discomfited, he said, "Look, you know I'm afraid to . . ."

Covering his lips with her fingers, she said, "Just ask me."

Smiling, he said, "Would you like to go somewhere with me for the weekend?"

Smiling back, "Yes, I would."

Not wanting to be seen together in Charlestown, they went out different ways - her through the front door, onto Bunker Hill Street, him out the back, down to Medford Street. They agreed to meet at her apartment.

When they got to her apartment, Meg wanted to go up and pack some clothes, but Sean didn't even want her to go upstairs. His plan was to just drop her car off and head right out of town.

"C'mon, we'll drive down the Cape. We can head to Provincetown right now. You don't have to pack any clothes, or anything else. There's plenty a' stores down there. It's a perfect opportunity. We both know you're a little shopaholic. So, we'll go shopping together tomorrow morning and I'll pay. That way, we both make out. You get to shop for whatever you want and I get to watch you try everything on."

Leaning in, he added, "And I get to fantasize about taking everything off of you."

Beaming, she said, "Sounds swell. But I do have to go upstairs for a minute. I have to pee."

"Okay. I guess I should pee, too. P-town's a long ride."

They went up.

A couple of minutes after entering her apartment, as Sean was coming out of the bathroom into the small narrow hallway which connected the kitchen and the parlor, he almost bumped into Meg who was coming from the kitchen with a full glass of wine in each hand.

Smiling, as she leaned back against the wall to give him room to slide by, she said, "S.S. Pierce Asti Spumante; I've still got those two bottles that you gave me. I figured we could take them with us."

The image of her, standing there, inches apart, her back to the wall, arms wide open, with a perfectly happy smile on her face melted him.

He could not stop himself. He kissed her, a long, adoring kiss, as his fingers worshipfully traced all over her - her face, her neck, her arms, her breasts, her sides, her stomach.

The Real Town

Throughout, Meg remained motionless. Finally, quivering all over, thrilled with delight and excitement and unable to take any more without reacting, she whispered, "I . . . you . . . I better put the glasses down. I'm going to drop them."

This was the first time that they had been alone since their one weekend of extraordinary pleasure, so much for Provincetown, that night.

In the morning, after very little sleep, they showered and headed out to the car. They had decided to take Meg's car, as Sean was driving his 'Charlestown car', which was rather well-known in certain circles - cops and robbers.

CHAPTER 30

They had what could only be described as a perfect weekend. On their way down they stopped for lunch in Hyannis and then wandered merrily around the town, shopping, joking and kissing. They moved on to Provincetown later in the afternoon and, after checking in to the best hotel in town, they went for dinner at Ciro's and Sal's, Sean's favorite restaurant in Provincetown.

Provincetown is an historic town - where the Mayflower landed, and stayed for over a month, before it went on to Plymouth. It became a fishing and whaling community which eventually grew into a distinguished art colony. Basically, it's pretty much a couple of miles of art galleries, cool shops that carry everything imaginable, swinging bars and night clubs, delicious food and amazing old mansions. It's also an ideal place to have a romantic getaway and, without a doubt, a haven for lesbians and gay men from around the world.

Sunday was more of the same, as they spent the morning meandering through the town, mutually enthralled, oblivious to all but each other.

After a hearty brunch, they returned to their suite and were lying on their sides, on the bed, talking and lightly kissing. As wonderful as everything was, Sean seemed to sense a feeling of uneasiness emanating from Meg. "Is something wrong? You seem, I don't know, uncomfortable."

Hesitating, she lowered her eyes. Then, looking up, she said, "There's something that I have to tell you. I've been trying not to, with all the troubles and everything that's been going on, but I think I have to."

"Please, tell me."

Taking a deep breath, she said, "I missed my period. I'm afraid I might be pregnant. I don't know. I'm seeing my doctor this week."

"What would you like to do? Do you want to get married? Do you want to get an abortion? What do you want to do?"

"Do you want me to get an abortion?"

"I want you to do whatever you want to do. If you want to have the baby, we can get married. If you're not ready to have a baby, I know a doctor who will terminate the pregnancy, and no one will ever know about it."

"You're not against abortions? I thought you would be. I mean, whatever it is you do now, you were an altar boy."

"I don't think what I think matters. I don't think what any guy thinks about abortion matters. I mean, I think we got a right to have an opinion, but I don't think we got a right to have any say in whether a girl gets one or not. That should be up to the girl, not just you, any girl. I think it's wrong that they're illegal."

"But you do have an opinion?"

"Yeah, I've got an opinion."

"What's your opinion?"

"I think if a girl finds herself pregnant, and she wants to have a baby, then she should have it. If she doesn't want to have it - for whatever reason, if she just isn't ready, that's her business - then she shouldn't have to have it. You can bet if guys got pregnant they'd be legal."

Meg was smiling now, her discomfort long gone, as she cuddled up to Sean, kissing him. "Well, I'm only two weeks late. Who knows? With everything that's been going on, it might just be stress, or something else. Maybe I'm not even pregnant. As I said, I'm seeing my doctor this week. We'll think about it then. For now, let's just enjoy the rest of the weekend."

They lay there, totally engrossed in each other, yet, each off in their own world. Although Meg was snuggled up to him with her head on his chest, Sean could actually see her joyful face, eyes closed with a dreamy, contented smile. There was a full-length mirror covering the outside of the bathroom door, and the door had been left half-open. By pure chance, if Sean turned his head to the side, he was looking at Meg's reflection.

As he lay there, pondering, he realized that he had never felt so complete, so satisfied, so fulfilled, in his entire life, as he did at that moment. Which, in light of everything that had happened in the past month, made him feel almost schizophrenic. On the one side, he and Meg had melded together so seamlessly that he could not recall ever feeling so complete, and yet, at the same time, the loss of his friends, especially Tommy, left him feeling almost empty. It was like a part of his body was missing.

He felt as if he was living in two separate worlds at the same time, or that he had gone from one world to another, or that he had become two separate people.

In essence, he was totally mesmerized by the enthralling happiness that presently enveloped him. And yet, at the same time, he was equally captivated by the overwhelming hatred that had been blazing through him, and out of him, for the past month.

The Real Town

The truth was, as much as he wanted to simply blend in with Meg and just block out the rest of the world, he couldn't. And it wasn't just the money, or self preservation. In the end, it was Tommy. They had been best friends, and partners, since they were kids. One way or the other, certain people were going to die.

As he lay there, thinking about Tommy, his mind roamed back to the day that they met and, unthinkingly, he smiled.

Sean had been fifteen years old. Tommy was fourteen, but he was already the larger of the two. They were playing penny-ante poker on the door-steps of a three-decker house at the far end of the large lot behind the Alibi, on the corner of Lawrence Street, where Tommy hung out. Sean did not really hang down there, but he used to go down there sometimes. There was a girl that he used to like to see, that hung down there and, when the opportunity arose, to make out with her. They hadn't 'gone all the way', but she did like to fool around a little bit. That was enough for Sean.

This day, when Sean showed up, the lads that hung there were playing penny-ante poker, and Sean got into the game. There were six of them playing. Sean knew most of them, but he didn't know Tommy. Three of them were standing on the sidewalk, two were sitting, on the steps, one on each side, and Sean was sitting on the floor of the hallway at the top of the steps.

One hand turned into what was a huge pot for a penny-ante game, over five dollars. Five of the six players each had a good hand and the betting, and raising, went on and on. Finally, it came down to Tommy and Sean. Tommy lost with four tens. Sean had a low straight flush, the ace to the five of diamonds.

The Real Town

Tommy was furious. His face was beet-red. He'd been so sure that he had a winner that the hand broke him. That was how the betting had stopped. Actually, he was a penny shy. He owed Sean a penny, from calling Sean's last raise. He borrowed a dollar off of one of the others and continued to play.

A while later, in the middle of a hand, Sean was calling a bet and was short on change. Although, he still had money, he needed one more penny to call the bet. Tommy had been winning since he borrowed the dollar. He'd even paid the dollar back, and had a couple of more dollars in change.

Instead of reaching in his pocket to get out a dollar to change for a penny, Sean said, 'Hey Tommy, you got that penny you owe me?"

Tommy, who was the middle one of the three standing on the sidewalk, was still pissed off at losing with four tens to someone who didn't even hang with them. He said, "Take it."

Sean said, "What?"

Belligerently, Tommy said, "You want it, come an' get it."

Without a thought crossing his mind, Sean was instantly on his feet, diving down the three steps onto Tommy. The fight was on . . . and on, and on.

The Real Town

At a minimum, they had to have gone to the ground ten times - and not alone - together. It wasn't the old-fashioned kind of fight where one would go down and the other would step back and let him get up. This was war. On their feet, they punched and grappled. On the ground they punched and kicked and bit and did everything that they could until they wound up separated and leaped back to their feet, immediately attacking each other again. Finally, at one point when they were on the ground, Sean wound up on top, and had Tommy pinned down. They both knew he had him. But Tommy would never quit. Sean got to hit him once, when Tommy's good friend, Mickey, jumped on Sean's back. Quickly, a friend of both of theirs, Edgie, jumped on Mickey and, for a few seconds, the four of them tussled. Then, it was broken up.

The fight had lasted so long, maybe a half-hour, that a huge crowd had gathered. A good number of the spectators were adults, guys in their twenties and thirties, who appreciated a good fight. At this point, though, a couple of them stepped in and grabbed Tommy and Sean and kept them apart. It took two grown men to hold each of them. They were both straining and trying to wrestle their ways back to each other. They were both so enraged that they each had tears of frustration running down their faces. But it was over. The guys would not let them go on.

One of them said, 'Enough'.

Not letting them get back near each other, they kept Tommy in front of the house while a couple of them walked Sean back across the lot towards Main Street. When they reached the front of the Alibi, they told him to keep going. He did.

The Real Town

This happened at the end of June. Sean had already signed up with the Boy's Club to go away to a camp at a golf course, down on Cape Cod, to caddie for the summer. A busload of them was leaving the next morning. When the bus took off from in front of the Girl's Club, around the corner from the Boy's Club, Sean was on it.

He spent the summer there, and returned at the start on September. On the day that he came home, he headed back down to where he had had the fight with Tommy, the day before he'd left.

As he was walking across the lot behind the Alibi, he could see the house outside of which they had the fight. There was nobody around. Half-way across the lot, he noticed someone walking down Lawrence Street.

It was Tommy.

Tommy saw him at the same time, and both of them turned, walking towards the other. As they came to their midpoint, they stopped, about five feet apart, and just stared into each other's eyes.

Tommy said, "Where ya' been?"

Sean said, "I went to caddie camp down the Cape the morning after we had the fight. I just got back about an hour ago."

Tommy nodded his head, and grinned "I knew it was somethin'. I knew you weren't hidin'. People kept askin' me how come you ain't come back. I told em', I don't know, but you wasn't duckin' me.'

Glancing over at the steps, where they had both been heading before they saw each other, they realized that a crowd had begun gathering. There were already about ten kids there - all staring at the two of them.

Exchanging looks, they both smiled.

Tommy said, "Ya know they're all talkin' about: 'Are they gonna do it again'?"

Sean said, "Over a penny?"

They both grinned.

Tommy said, "Ya want ya penny?"

Sean laughed, "Nah, I think you earned it."

They both laughed and then Sean stuck his hand out. Tommy gladly grasped it.

As they shook hands, Sean said, "That was the longest fucking fight I ever had in my life."

Tommy laughed again, "Me too."

Then they turned and walked over to the waiting crowd.

That was how their friendship began.

*

Now, as Sean lay there mulling over all that was going on in his life, on the one hand, he could truly feel himself spending the rest of his life with Meg. As much as he liked girls, he not only hadn't been with anyone else since the first time he had been with Meg, he hadn't even thought about being with anyone else. Drifting in and out, daydreaming about what could possibly lie in his immediate future, he realized that he could step out of the life. He had enough money stashed, so that he could set himself up and go straight. He could buy property and live comfortably off of the rent. If Meg were pregnant, and she wanted to have the baby, that would probably be the way that it would go.

Yet, despite the fact that he had utopia within arm's reach, he recognized that going straight was not an option at this point in time. He couldn't even if he wanted to. He knew that he had no choice. After what happened to Tommy and Artie, there was a war going on and whatever else was happening, he had to finish it. He felt bewildered and torn. Yet, he knew what he had to do.

Meg stirred from her catnap, with a slight purring sound. Looking up at him, with her entrancing bedroom eyes, she erased all thoughts of the outside world from his consciousness. They spent the rest of the day engulfed in each other, and their surroundings. Nothing else mattered.

As Meg had to be in work on Monday morning, they returned to Boston on Sunday night. On their way back, they drove out to the famous Provincetown dunes to romantically behold the ocean.

C H A P T E R 31

When they reached Beacon Street, and pulled up next to her apartment, there wasn't a parking space in sight. Meg was irked. "Parking around here is so terrible."

Sean said, "Oh, it's not that bad."

"Oh sure, you've got your sneaky little parking spot behind your building."

"Oh, I got two parkin' spots."

"Are you kidding me? You have *two* spots? Where's the other one?"

"Right there," he said, pointing at his car which he had left parked right in front of her apartment.

"Oh," she said, giggling, and punching him in the arm. "You are so evil."

"I'll pull out and you can have the spot."

After they changed spots he got out of his car and joined her on the sidewalk outside of her door.

Standing there, holding hands and looking into each other's eyes, Sean said, "It's almost midnight and I know you've got to get up early for work, so I'm gonna' let you go. But I want to tell you something first, something that I've never told anyone - although Tommy always said it.

Taking a deep breath, he said, "I love you. I'm so in love with you, I have to tell you. And it has nothing to do with what we talked about today."

Eyes glistening, her face glowing with a radiant smile, Meg answered, "And I'm in love with you."

They stood there, staring blissfully into each other's eyes, enthralled in the moment, when, out of the blue, they were blown off of their feet, as gunshots unexpectedly roared through the Sunday night serenity. The impact landed them on the steps, Meg landing on top of Sean.

Instinctively, he rolled over covering Meg and thrusting her towards the edge of the sidewalk behind the parked car. "Stay down!" he shouted

Leaping up, he dove away from her, drawing fire as he sprinted back down Beacon Street, then ducking back down behind the bumper to bumper parked cars.

The bullets were being fired from a car that had pulled up in the middle of the street. As Beacon Street is a one-way street and Sean was heading in the direction from which the traffic came, in order to chase him, the lethal car flew into reverse and started down the street after him.

Sean quickly reached the nearby street corner, and darted around the corner to his left. As the driver of the hit car was focusing on Sean while driving in reverse, he never saw the car that came around the corner from the other side of the street, smashing into the rear of the hit car.

The loud crashing noise was followed by an instant of silence, which was quickly replaced with the sounds of indignant yelling. The car that had come around the corner was filled with college students who had been out partying and were now pouring out of the car bellowing profanities.

"You fucking asshole."

"What the fuck are you doing driving backwards?"

"This is a one way street!"

"You're in trouble, asshole."

Big Al, who was in the back seat, said to the driver, "Get the fuck outta here. *Now!"*

The hit car took off and in seconds was out of sight.

The Real Town

When the cars had crashed, Sean, still fleeing in the opposite direction, threw his head back over his shoulder, to see what had happened. As the college kids came jumping out of their car, and the hit car took off, he turned and headed back at the same speed. As he reached Beacon Street and turned right, he saw the hit car, wheels screeching, taking a sharp left turn at the next corner.

Running flat out, he was at Meg's side in seconds. She was still lying where he had left her, on her back, on the edge of the sidewalk, against the parked car.

Dropping to his knees, thankful that there was no blood on her, he said, "Meg, are you hurt? Are you alright?"

When she did not respond, he repeated himself, "Meg, are you hurt. Please answer me, darling. *Please.*"

She lay motionless. He started to raise her and then he realized that she was not breathing.

"No", he screamed. *"No."*

At the sound of brakes screeching, he looked up to see a cop car coming to a stop. Rising immediately, with Meg in his arms, he ran towards them. "She's been shot. She's not breathing. You've got to get her to the hospital."

"What happened?"

"Someone shot us. We've got to get her to the hospital. She's not breathing!"

As Sean hurriedly got into the back seat, still holding her in his arms, other cop cars were pulling up. One cop, a detective, outside the car, said to him, "You'll have to stay. We have to ask you some questions."

Sean exploded, *"No! I'm going to the hospital with her. Now!"*

Spinning towards the driver he screamed, *"Go! Now! She's dying."*

Knowing that Sean was right, the driver glanced at the detective outside of the car, nodded his head, and took off.

It was too late. Shortly after arriving at the hospital they pronounced Meg dead. They said that she had died at the time of the shooting. A bullet had hit her in the back and pierced her heart, killing her instantly.

At the hospital, when the police began questioning Sean, he barely acknowledged their existence, let alone their questions.

He did give them Meg's name - and his own. That stopped everything. They knew who he was.

They bombarded him with questions.

"What happened?"

"Who did it?"

"How many were there?"

He only answered them once. "Somebody shot us from a car. I don't know who it was."

They continued to inundate him with questions. He ignored them. Finally, one of the doctors who had tried to treat Meg, came over and said to the cops, "Excuse me," she said, "I am Doctor Sim. I have to examine Mr. Brady. I believe he's been shot. Blood appears to be coming through his jacket."

As he arose, to go into the other room with the doctor, he responded one last time to their continuous pressing questions, "I told you, someone shot us from a car. I never got a look at them. Now leave me alone."

He had been hit. He'd been hit in the lower left side, just above the hip. It was merely a flesh wound - in the front, out the back, hitting nothing vital, but it gave him a respite from the questioning.

While she was cleaning out his wound, the Doctor Sim said, "You obviously cared for her a great deal."

The Real Town

With eyes still off into the distance, yet tears running down his cheeks, Sean said, "I loved her. I still love her. I'll always love her."

Looking sympathetically up at him, as he sat on the table, she said, "I know. So did I. We all did. Meg worked here. She was the sweetest girl you could ever know. How could something like this have happened?"

Sean just shook his head. He had been so engulfed he hadn't even realized that they were at Meg's hospital.

CHAPTER 32

Meg's funeral was held at Sawyer's Funeral Home at the top of Bunker Hill Street. There were so many people there, that there was a line going out the door. When Sean arrived, he was surrounded by Meg's family and friends. They shared their pain and their sympathy, but the collective message was clear; they did not blame him.

As he moved into the main room, where Meg was lying, the line of people who were waiting to kneel at her casket all stepped aside. He could not take his eyes off of her as he approached the casket. With tears flowing down his face, in agony and disbelief, he knelt beside her. She looked like she was sleeping, happily sleeping. She actually had a slight smile on her face. He could not look away. He could not get up.

At some point, he felt someone place their hand on his shoulder. Coming back from wherever he was, he looked up. It was Meg's father. Saying nothing, he simply squeezed Sean's shoulder.

They stayed like that for a long moment. Then her father said, "We have to talk."

Looking back at Meg, he was completely discombobulated. He knew that he had to get up, but he could not leave her.

Then someone else touched his shoulder, his other shoulder. It was Anne.

"You have to let go. Say goodbye, Sean."

At which point, they both removed their hands from his shoulder and stepped back.

After another long moment, he slowly stood up. Then, bending over, he touched her lips with his.

As he turned away, his body reacted on its own, with a shudder.

Anne was waiting for him and she accompanied him to Meg's family. After paying his respects, they went downstairs with Meg's father. As soon as they got there, Meg's father turned to Anne, saying, "I know that you were Meg's best friend and how much you love your brother. But it is best that you do not hear this conversation."

Looking at each of them, she nodded her head and went back upstairs.

Looking austerely at Sean, he said, "The homicide police from in-town have asked me to see if I can find out anything from you regarding my daughter's murder. They say that that will be the best way for them to solve this crime."

Returning the formal stare, Sean replied, "Tell them that you asked me and that I have no idea who did it."

Nodding his head, he replied, "I will do that."

Then, leaning in so close that their faces were almost touching, in a low voice, filled with vehemence, he said, "Kill them, Sean, kill them all."

Nodding his head, Sean mouthed the words, "I will."

*

As the wake ended, and they were all congregating outside, Sean was approached by three suits. One of them, a Charlestown detective named Mike Williams, told Sean that they would like to speak to him in private.

After they stepped off to the side, Williams introduced him to the other two, "Sean this is Detective Timothy Nolan and Detective Edward Warren. They're both members of the Boston Homicide Squad."

Detective Warren stepped forward, "We're gonna' shake ya' down, Brady. You got any problem with that?"

The heartlessness that had replaced the sorrow in Sean's eyes seemed to deepen as he stared back at Detective Warren.

Spreading his arms, he said, "Do it."

As Sean spread his arms, a flow of tension and indignation began to spread through the surrounding crowd, which quickly became apparent through the rumbling comments that could be overheard.

"What the fuck are they doin?"

"Who the fuck d' they think they are."

"What kinda disrespect is that."

"Those fuckin' assholes."

"Don't they give a fuck his girl friend's dead?"

Detective Warren, hesitating, said, almost inaudibly, to Detective Williams. "We got a problem here?"

Eyes scanning the crowd, that was starting to rustle, Williams answered, "Maybe."

Raising his hands to the agitated crowd, he said, "Take it easy, everyone. We just . . ."

At which point, Sean interrupted. Still staring at Detective Warren, he said, "Warren, Eddie Warren, you're the one from Southie."

With a belligerent look, he said, "That's right, so what?"

Eyes growing ever colder, mind obviously racing, putting things together, Sean said, "You were there the night they killed her. You're the one that wanted to question me."

The Real Town

Stepping back, Warren said, "Look, I don't know what you're implying. I . . ."

"Now I know. You're how they found out where my car was."

Completely on the defensive now, Detective Warren said, "You got it all wrong. That's not how it happened."

Stepping back towards their car, Detective Williams said, "This isn't the right time. We'll talk to you after the funeral tomorrow."

But Sean was over the edge. Death gleamed from his eyes as he started to move towards Detective Warren.

Suddenly, Anne was in between them, whispering vehemently, with her hands on his chest. "Sean, stop. They're cops. You can't do this. Not here. It's Meg's wake. *Stop*."

Then they were in their car and gone.

Looking down at Anne, he said, "He set me up. He works for Jimmy Brown. I know Brown's got cops drivin' him around looking' for some of the guys he's beefin' with in Southie. He's how they found out where my car was. How else would he have gotten there that quick after it happened - and now he's here tonight wantin' t' shake me down? I don't believe that much in coincidences. He's goin' down."

Later on, he brought it to Neezo, who'd been at the Wake, but had faded back into the crowd, when the cops had shown up.

"This Eddie Warren, is he the cop Brown's got drivin' him around looking for Paulie McGee an' that crowd?"

"No. That's another cop, Donnelly. But I know Brownie's done business with Eddie. An' you're right, he's the one Brownie would go to, to find out where your car was, if it was in town - Donnelly's stationed in Southie, Eddie Warren's in-town. Ya' know Eddie Warren's the bag-man in-town?"

Sean said, "No, I didn't know that."

Certain members of the 'law enforcement' community were known to have a tolerance for a variety of activities that, while technically illegal, were common everyday practices, e.g. bookmaking, loan-sharking, prostitution, etc. As these activities tended to result in regular profits, their practitioners felt a certain sense of duty to share these profits with those members of the law enforcement society who were kind enough to look the other way. The persons who collected this disbursement were referred to as the 'bag-men'.

Sean asked, "You know when he collects?"

"Nah, not really, but I could find out."

"Let me know."

Neezo replied, "Yeah, I will. Somethin' else, ya gotta watch ya back with him. He's a shooter. He always got a 'throwaway' pistol with him. He's whacked a coupla' guys that I know of."

A 'throwaway' pistol was a pistol that certain cops carried in case a situation arose where they had to prove that they had had to shoot someone to protect themselves. As soon as they took someone out, they would plant the 'throwaway' pistol on the body, usually in the 'suspect's' hand, ergo, justifiable homicide.

CHAPTER 33

From then on, Sean was all but invisible - except for sporadic, unexpected appearances, in bars and clubs in Charlestown and South Boston. He was always alone. Or, so everyone thought. They wouldn't see Gus who'd be parked inconspicuously, nearby. All to no avail, he could find none of them.

One night, out of the blue, Sean walked into Kelly's. Scanning the bar looking for Dickie Black, he walked to the end of the bar, and looked into the men's room. Nothing.

As he walked back towards the door, an old friend, Bug Eyes, stopped him and offered to buy him a drink. Sean declined. As he walked out the door, Bug Eyes walked out with him, telling him how bad he felt about what happened to Tommy and Artie. Bug Eyes had hung with them when they were younger.

Just as they stepped out the door, a cop car pulled up. Two uniformed cops got out of the front seats. Detective Tony Anthony got out of the back seat.

Approaching Sean, he said, "Sean, you know we've got orders to shake you down whenever we see you?"

Sean nodded his head, "Yeah, I figured."

Bug Eyes stepped forward, "Hey Tony, shake me down."

The detective just glanced at him. "Mind your business, Bug Eyes."

Looking back at Sean, he said, "You wanna' put your hands out, Sean?"

The Real Town

Sean unzipped his jacket and stretched his arms out to the side. "Go ahead."

Slowly, Detective Anthony ran his hands over Sean. Starting with one hand on Sean's shoulder and the other one under his arm, on the outside of the jacket, he manipulated his way down to the wrist. Then he did the same thing on the other arm. Spreading the jacket wide open, he slid his hands inside and meticulously ran his hands over Sean's upper body, front and back. Bending over he started patting his way down the lower body. As he touched the back pockets of Sean's dungarees, he hesitated for a second, then continued on down, thoroughly probing both legs down to his ankles.

Straightening up, Detective Anthony turned to the two uniformed officers who were standing on each side of him, with their hands on their guns, "He's clean."

Turning back to Sean, he said, "You can go, Sean."

As they drove off, Bug Eyes said, "Man, I thought you were busted."

Sean just nodded his head, and said, "I'll see ya' around."

Turning away, he walked up Concord Street. As he reached the top of the street, at the corner of Bartlett Street, Gus pulled up in the car. Sean quickly got in.

Gus said, "What the fuck happened? Howdja' get rid of it?"

Gus knew that Sean had a pistol on him.

Sean said, "I didn't. It's still in my back pocket."

Reaching into his right rear pocket, he pulled out a handkerchief and a small pistol. It was a double-barreled, over and under, .357 derringer. Whenever Sean carried it, he kept it in his back pocket, covered by a handkerchief.

Gus said, "He didn't feel it?"

Sean "I don't know."

The Real Town

They just looked at each other.

Grinning, and nodding his head, Gus said, "How much ya' figure ya' owe him?"

Sean just shrugged. "We'll see."

Gus said, "Ya' know, he mighta' just wanted to avoid a shootout."

A few days before that, they had met with Barney out of town. In the midst of their conversation, Barney told them that he had been talking to a friend, Suitcase Fidler, who had told him a story that he thought Sean should know.

Suitcase was an old-time bookie. He was one of the Alibi crowd that had survived the war.

Barney said, "Suit's tellin' me, he's down the Oiley's the other night, payin' off the two dicks, Tony Anthony and Mike Williams. They're standing by the car when, all of a sudden, it comes over the cops' car radio that you're walking up Bunker Hill Street and that someone should shake you down. They both start to get in the car and then the cop on the radio starts describin' what you're wearing, an' he says, 'And Brady is carrying a small brown paper bag.'

"That stopped them in their tracks. Suit says, 'They just looked at each other, then Tony says, 'Ya know, I don't think I counted this, did I? Let's finish what we're doin'. Someone else can shake him down.' '

"Suit said when they got back outta the car they just looked at him and grinned."

CHAPTER 34

As the Holidays approached, as much as Sean wanted to spend Christmas with his family, he didn't think that it was a good idea. At the very least, if the cops came to the Bunker Hill Street house to hassle him, it could ruin their holidays. He did not want to do that. It was common knowledge that a couple of Detectives from in-town - one of them being Detective Warren - were looking for Sean. They had gone to Grace's, and Anne's, on three separate occasions, asking if they knew where he was. The cops told them that they did not want to arrest him. They just wanted to question him.

His family told them that they had no idea where he was.

So, as Christmas was on a Monday, Sean quietly arranged to see them on the Friday before Christmas.

On Friday evening, just after it got dark, Gus dropped Sean off down on Medford Street and Sean made his way up to the back of the house on Bunker Hill Street.

He had had Gus and Sammy both drop off a number of wrapped presents, for the kids, during the week. He brought Grace's, Anne's and Pat's presents with him. He had a necklace for Grace, a bracelet for Anne - both expensive - and a pair of Red Sox season tickets for Pat. They were all quite pleased, as were Bridget and Patrick.

The Real Town

After the kids had gone to bed, Sean got ready to go. Pat had agreed to give him a ride over to Somerville, just on the other side of Sullivan Square, where he had left his car. After a heartfelt farewell to his mother and sister, Sean went out the back way, while Pat went out onto Bunker Hill Street and got into his car. Two minutes later he picked Sean up on Medford Street.

As they were heading down Medford Street, towards Main Street, where Medford Street ended and they would turn right towards Sullivan Square, Pat said, "Listen, I gotta' tell ya' somethin', but I didn't wanna' mention it in front of Anne and your mother. I ain't seen him, but a coupla' guys told me that Dickie Black's been in an' outta town, lookin' for backup - tryin' to recruit guys that you don't like, guys that'd like to see you get whacked. One guy told me he saw him down Cappy's the other night, about four o'clock in the morning, talking to . . . *Jesus Christ. Look!*"

At the same time that Pat yelled, Sean had slid down beneath the dashboard. As they were approaching Main Street, they could see Charlie's Bar and Grill on the other side of Main. Teddy Hurley was standing on the front step. Unbelievably, he was talking to Dickie Black.

Sean and Pat had both seen them at the same time. Sean had immediately ducked below the dashboard. Looking up at Pat, he said, "Don't look at them. Just take the right and keep goin'."

Pat turned right onto Main Street and continued on towards Sullivan Square. After glancing into the rear-view mirror, he said, "They never looked at us. They're still talking. Jesus, whatta' ya' want me to do?"

"Just keep going around the rotary. Go down Rutherford Ave. and drop me off at those old railroad tracks that run back by Charlie's."

Rutherford Avenue ran parallel to Main Street, in back of Charlie's. There was a set of railroad tracks, that were no longer in use, that ran alongside the building, across Main Street and then across Rutherford Avenue.

Pat said, "Okay, where do you want me to park?"

Sean said, "Go straight home. All you know is you dropped me off in Somerville, on Broadway - up by Winter Hill."

Pat said, "Sean, you're gonna need a ride. I know I ain't a wheel-man, but you have to have a ride."

"If I need a ride, I'll call ya'. Just go home, Pat. Please."

Pat pulled over, on Rutherford Avenue. "Alright, but call me if ya' need me - for anything."

Sean said, "Thanks, man, I mean it. Now get outta here. Go home."

Dashing along the abandoned railroad tracks, towards the alley that ran alongside of Charlie's, Sean pulled one of his pistols out of his belt.

As he reached Main Street, he gingerly peeked around the corner towards Charlie's, which was one building away. Dickie 'Shorty' DiVola, an ex-boxer, who'd been the New England Lightweight Champion a few years earlier, had the first building, a barber shop on the corner of the alley. At this time of night, the shop was closed. The next building, around a slight bend, was Charlie's.

Sean stepped out and moved towards Charlie's. As he reached the bend, he realized that they were gone. Edging up to Charlie's, he peeked through the barroom window.

The Real Town

There were about a dozen guys sitting there drinking. The ones in the booths were playing cards. The ones at the bar were watching television. He could not see either Teddy or Black. Although he could see the whole bar, due to the angle of the window, he was unable to see the first two booths. Going quickly past the front door, he peeked into the window on the other side, which was right behind the first two booths. They weren't there, either.

Stepping back to the door, he slid his .38 caliber snub-nosed pistol back into his waistband, opened the door, and walked in. Nodding to the bartender, Vinnie, he said, "Hey Vin, I'll have a screwdriver."

Casually, he walked to the end of the bar and went into the Men's Room. Although he gave no indication of his awareness, the tension and apprehension that flooded through the patrons of the bar was so obvious that, even if he hadn't seen Dickie Black standing outside just five minutes earlier, he would have known that someone was around or that something was going on. The fearful look on Vinnie's face when he'd ordered the drink, said it all.

He came out of the Men's Room and realized that at least three customers - guys that had been standing at the bar, and that he knew were friendly with Teddy Hurley - had already departed. Taking their place at the bar, he was, seemingly, watching the television, which was above the window.

Actually, he was watching the window. The only reason that he'd even come in, was to check the Men's Room. The drink had simply been a cover.

Knowing that he'd missed them, the frustration was boiling inside of him as he stood there sipping his drink, trying to decide what to do next. He decided to call Pat and have him pick him up where he had dropped him off, when he saw Teddy's car pulling up out front. He couldn't believe it.

Nonchalantly, he finished his drink, nodded goodbye to Vinnie, and walked out the door. He had timed it so that Teddy was just reaching the step when Sean opened the door.

Teddy's startled eyes opened wide. Before he could say anything, Sean moved in close and stuck his pistol into Teddy's stomach.

"Get back in the car."

Teddy froze; the fear was obvious in his eyes.

Cocking the hammer on his pistol, Sean said, "Last chance."

The sound of the hammer clicking sent a chill up Teddy's back. In a hoarse voice, he said, "Awright."

When they got into the car, Sean had Teddy sitting in the driver's seat, facing forward, with both hands on the steering wheel. Sean sat beside him, sideways, facing him, with a pistol in each hand.

"Where did you take him?"

"Listen, Sean, I got nothin' to do with . . ."

Sean jammed the head of the barrel of the pistol in his left hand into Teddy's cheek, as he reached across Teddy's lap and, pressed the point of the barrel of the other gun against Teddy's left knee. He cocked the hammer and said, "Where did you take him?"

Swallowing hard, he answered, "I took him to his mother's house."

The Real Town

Sean sat quietly thinking. As badly as he needed to catch up to Dickie Black, he would never invade someone's home to get him - especially his mother's home. Regardless of the public perception of Charlestown's supposed level of violence, there were certain rules and codes that were followed. That was one of them.

After a minute of contemplation, he had Teddy drive to a nearby pay phone. He said, "You're gonna call him an' tell him to meet you down on Medford Street by the 'Wiggies'."

That was what they called the Wiggins Terminal, which was on a back street that ran from Medford Street down to the longshoreman's dock on the Mystic Pier, where the Mystic River ran into Boston Harbor.

Turn his head towards Sean, he said, "Sean, I can't . . ."

Sean smashed the butt of the pistol into Teddy's mouth, splitting his lips, and shattering one of his front teeth.

"You're gonna call him or you're gonna die, your choice."

Cowering back against the door, blood pouring from his mouth, Teddy mumbled, "Awright, I'll call him."

"Tell him you were checking the trucks down 'Wiggies' and you found a trailer fulla razor blades, an' there's no one around. Then, ask him if he knows anyone who'll take 'em tonight. Or if he knows anyone who can stash 'em for yez."

One of the most important elements, of setting up a truck high-jacking, was to have someplace to store your score. Usually, you just made sure that whoever you were selling the goods to was ready to take the truck, and had a place to unload it. Where this was going to be a spur of the moment score, it became a priority.

Sean continued, "Tell him you're gonna keep an eye on it to make sure there's no one around and for him to walk down and meet ya."

Dickie Black's mother lived at the far end of the project, about a ten minute walk from where they were supposed to meet.

Teddy made the call, with Sean standing up against him, gun pressed into his ribs, as they both listened to Dickie Black on the phone receiver.

Teddy repeated what Sean had told him to say. As soon as Teddy asked him if he knew anyone who they could take the load to, that night, Black said, "Yeah, I know a guy that got a warehouse over in Southie. He uses it to stash hot shit, so I know he'll take it. That's what he does, he's a fence."

Teddy told him where he'd be parked and they hung up.

Sean had him park two blocks down the street, across the street from where he said he'd be parked, facing towards the project.

Not two minutes later, a Paddy Wagon came down Medford Street. As it was going by them, it pulled over. Two young uniformed cops got out and leisurely strolled back towards Teddy's car. It was obviously just a check-up based on their interest in two guys sitting in a car in an area that was deserted at that time of night - until they got close enough to the car to see the blood on Teddy's face. At that point, they both frantically drew their guns.

The Real Town

From the moment that they got out of the Paddy Wagon, Sean knew that he had two choices, kill them, or take the pinch. He decided to take the pinch. He smoothly slid one pistol down to the floor of the car and pushed it under the seat with his foot and slid the other gun under a magazine that was on the seat between him and Teddy, who was unaware as he was watching the policemen approach them.

The policemen arrested both of them and took them down to Station Fifteen. As there were two pistols, they charged each of them with one of the guns. They booked them and placed them in separate cells. Sean requested that he be allowed to call his attorney, Alan Jarrady.

A while later, Attorney Jarrady showed up, and bailed Sean out. After collecting his property, they went to the front door. Having grown up just a few blocks apart, they had known each other all their lives. Alan was a few years older.

As Sean started for the front door, Attorney Jarrady said, "Sean, wait."

Sean turned and looked back at him. The lawyer's discomfort was evident from his mannerisms.

"What's up, Alan?"

"Listen, Sean, I can't give you a ride - not at this hour of the night. It's almost three o'clock in the morning. I'm married with kids now, Sean. I can't be in a car with you. Not with your situation. I'm sorry."

He hesitated for a second, then said, "You know Teddy called me, too. They let him go first."

Sean nodded, "I understand, Alan. I really do."

Alan said, "Listen, let me call you a cab."

"No, that's okay. I'd rather go on foot. Let me go first."

The Real Town

Walking out the door, he turned left and walked towards Main Street. As he was going around the bend onto Main Street, he suddenly broke across the street into an old lot that ran into an alley, and suddenly he was out of sight. One of the benefits of Charlestown being only a square mile was that, having grown up there, Sean had spent a good portion of his childhood rummaging through the town, climbing fences and walls, going through people's back yards and alleys. Sean could literally go from one end of town to the other, only using the streets when he had to cross them.

CHAPTER 35

The following Tuesday, after Christmas, as Sean arrived at the Court House, to be formally charged, he was walking up the inside stairs when, as he approached the top of the stairs, he heard someone say, "Listen Teddy, we got a sample of your tooth, your lip and your blood from one of the pistols. *You* know he was gonna kill you and *we* know he was gonna kill you."

As they came into sight, Sean saw two detectives leaning over talking to Teddy, who was sitting on a bench.

Teddy responded, "Nobody was killin' anybody. I got nothin' to say."

Attorney Jarrady was already in the Court Room, waiting for them. The hearing went quickly and they were both released on bail.

Two days later, another local lawyer, Ben O'Donnell, got in touch with Sean, through Gus. They had done business together in the past, so Sean went to his office to see him.

After their initial greetings, Ben said, "Looks like they got you on this one, Lad."

Sean nodded his head, waiting. He knew that Ben would not have contacted him if there wasn't something in the wind.

Smiling, Ben said, "Listen, I'm not getting involved in the case, but if you come up with twenty-five hundred, the prosecutor will let you off with a year. Maybe less, if he can. But the most you'll get is a year. You interested?"

Sean said, "Tell him I'll take it. But I'll need a little time to come up with the money."

"No problem. Your next hearing's scheduled in two weeks. If you don't have it by then, he'll go with a continuance. One thing, don't tell your lawyer. Keep it between us."

Sean said, "No problem."

Three days later, a local hustler, named Jackie Cain, approached him, with a different deal.

He said, "Judge Gilman got a deal for ya. He says if you come up with five grand, he'll keep you on the street."

Sean said, "Tell him I'll take it. But I'll need some time to get the money."

"No problem. He'll give you all the continuances you need."

A week later, Jackie Cain reached out for Sean. They met at the North Station, outside of the Boston Garden.

Jackie said, "Listen, Judge Gilman's been looking at your record. He was gonna give you probation, but he can't, you already got two pistol convictions. That's a mandatory five to seven."

Sean said, "Well, I don't have to pay for that."

"Yeah, well he's got an idea. He says if Teddy Hurley will plead in to both guns, he can let him off with a fine. He's got no guns on his record."

Sean said, "Okay, but he's duckin' me. I won't be able to get in touch with him till the next hearing. That's tomorrow. Tell Gilman I'll need a continuance."

Jackie said, "No problem."

The next morning, when Sean appeared at the Court House, he came a little early. He met his lawyer upstairs in the lobby where everyone waited outside of the court room. Teddy wasn't there yet, so he took Attorney Jarrady off to the side so they could speak privately.

The Real Town

"Listen, Alan, I've been, shall we say, plea-bargaining. I don't want to go into too many details - sometimes it's better not to know things - but the offer was, if I pled in, I could get off with probation. Unfortunately, because of my past record, they can't give me probation. I'd have to get a mandatory five to seven. But, if Teddy pleads in to both guns, they'll let him off with a fine, and we'll both walk away."

As they were talking, Teddy had come up the stairs into the lobby. He didn't come over to them, staying on the other side of the lobby.

Alan said, "Alright, I'll go tell him and see what he wants to do."

Alan walked over to where Teddy was standing, and they talked for a few minutes. Now, Teddy came over to Sean.

"Lemme get this straight. You want me to plead in to the guns you were gonna whack me with?"

Sean said, "It's either that, or we're both gonna be found guilty. When that happens, we'll appeal it in town. I'll get the cases severed and buy my way out and you'll wind up in Walpole. It's your choice."

Teddy stared silently at Sean. They had been in other situations together and he knew what Sean was saying was possible. Turning away, he walked back to their lawyer.

A few minutes later, Alan came back to Sean. He said, "Alright, he says he'll go for it, but you have to give him your word that you won't kill him."

Sean said, "Okay, I'll give him a pass till the case is over."

A look of incredulity crossed Alan's face. "So you want me to tell him you won't kill him for two weeks?"

Sean shrugged, "What? He can shoot at me but I can't shoot at him? I don't think so."

Alan went back over to Teddy and spoke to him for a minute, then returned to Sean.

"He says he gives you his word that he's out of it. He says he'll leave town."

Sean thought for a moment then said, "Okay, I'll take his word. You tell him he gives me his word he's out of it, he don't have to leave town."

Alan went back over to Teddy. After a minute, Teddy looked over at Sean and nodded his head.

When they appeared in front of the judge, the case was continued for two weeks.

CHAPTER 36

Two weeks later, on the morning of the scheduled trial, Sean had Gus drive him down to City Square. They parked on Chelsea Street. As Sean got out of the car, Jackie Cain got out of a Cadillac that was parked on the other side of the street, outside of Dot's Diner. Dot's was the heart of City Square, a restaurant that was opened twenty-four hours a day, seven days a week. Sean recognized the car. It belonged to a local politician.

When Jackie came up to him, Sean handed him a brown paper bag that contained five thousand dollars in cash. "It's all there."

Jackie smiled. "Okay, we're on."

Sean walked up Chelsea Street and crossed over the Square to the Court House. Teddy was waiting for him on the steps, and they went upstairs together.

In a muffled voice, Teddy asked, "Is it all set?"

Sean nodded, "Yep."

As they entered the lobby, a court officer who was staring at Sean raised one eyebrow. Sean covertly nodded his head. The court officer walked across the lobby and went down the steps.

Sean watched him from a window that looked out onto the square. The court officer crossed the square and got into the politicians car. A few minutes later, he got out of the car and headed back towards the court house.

Suddenly, Sean heard Teddy mutter, "Oh, fuck."

Glancing in the direction where Teddy was staring, Sean saw four plain clothes cops; an F.B.I. agent, a State Police detective, Eddie Warren, and a local Charlestown detective, Bill Doyle. They were all staring at Sean.

Teddy said, "They're here for you. That fucking Doyle hates your guts."

"Yeah, I know."

Just then the court officer came back up the stairs, and went into the judge's chambers. Five minutes later, he came back out into the lobby and announced that the day's sessions were about to begin. Everyone filed into the court room.

After the court room had filled, and everyone was seated, the judge entered the room from his chambers, behind his desk.

The court officer stated, "All rise."

Everyone in the room stood up until the judge was settled into his chair. Then as everyone was in the process of sitting back down, the judge said, "First case, Sean Brady and Theodore Hurley. Brady, 'Not Guilty', Hurley, 'Guilty', fifty dollar fine, ten dollar fine, motor vehicle violation, next case."

As soon as he said, "Brady, 'Not Guilty'", Sean turned and discreetly drifted towards the door. Just before he reached the door, the judge finished his finding and slammed his gavel on the desk.

There was a moment of dead quiet, broken by an incredulous voice.

"What the fuck did he say?"

It was one of the four plain clothes cops.

The Real Town

As it was said, without breaking stride, Sean stepped through the door, walked about a half a dozen steps, took a left around a corner, and sat down in the lobby pay phone booth. He dialed Anne's number. As the phone was ringing, he was watching the lobby. From his angle, he could not see the court room door, but he could see the steps that went down to the street. As Anne's phone rang, the four plain clothes detectives came running across the lobby from the direction of the court room door, and darted down the stairs.

Anne answered her telephone. "Hello."

Sean said, "Hi. I just wanted you to know that everything went okay. I was found Not Guilty."

Relief flooding her voice, she responded, "Oh my God. How did . . . never mind. We'll talk later. Are you coming up the house?"

"I don't think so. I think it might be better for all concerned if I go away for a while. But don't worry, and tell Ma I'll keep in touch"

CHAPTER 37

About a week later, Sean got a message from Neezo. Neezo was one of a select few who knew how to get in touch with him. You had to go through Becky, or Gus. Whether you did it down Kelly's, or somewhere else, it had to be in person. Becky would get word to Gus. Gus would talk to Anne.

They met in a restaurant named Barney's, another of Sean's choice eating places, at Harvard Square, in Cambridge. Harvard Square had always been one of Sean's favorite meeting places. Everything was cool, anyone could blend in and nobody would expect to find him there.

As soon as they sat down and ordered their drinks, Neezo said, "I know who was in the car the night they killed Meg."

Sean sat, staring.

"It was Big Al, Davey Elliot and Walter Glennon. Davey was drivin' and Al and Wally did the shootin'."

Sean sat pondering, "You getting' any heat?"

"Nah, we did at first, guys were kinda' stayin' away. Then, I did what you said. Whenever your name comes up I just tell 'em I ain't seen hide nor hair of ya'. Then, when I ain't around - you know people know we're friends - an' someone brings your name up, Matt tells 'em you ain't havin' nothing to do with anyone from Southie anymore, so we ain't havin' nothin' to do with you."

Sean said, "Good. Keep it up. You don't need the heat."

Then, "Have any of them been around?"

The Real Town

Neezo said, "No. They're all still hidin'. But that's the other thing I gotta' tell ya'. There's a story goin' around that they're comin' back soon because the cops are gonna' bust you, and as soon as they do, Brown and his crew will be back. There's another story, that Eddie Warren's gonna whack ya.

"Y' know, maybe you oughtta think about getting' outta town for a while."

Sean said, "I've been thinking' about it. Maybe if I'm gone, they'll come back. If they do, get word to me, right away. Something else you can do, the next time someone mentions my name, tell 'em the word in C-town is that I'm on the lam in California, that I know the cops are looking' for me. People know I got friends out there."

As they were leaving, Neezo said, "Jesus, I'm stuffed. That shrimp was delicious, but I think I'm gonna' smell like garlic for the next three days."

Smiling, Sean said, "You will, but I bet you'll be back here before I see you again."

CHAPTER 38

In February, Sean got a message that Jack Laby wanted to see him.

He set up a meet with him at The 108, a watering hole in Everett, just across the city line outside of Charlestown. Sean was sitting in the last booth at the back of the pub. Jack stopped at the bar for a moment, said something to the bartender and then came over to the booth.

As he sat down opposite Sean, he said, "I heard about Tommy and Artie. What the fuck happened?"

Sean said, quietly, "They got set up - for money. We made a good score and someone found out about it."

Jack asked, "D'ya' know who did it?"

Steering clear of the question, Sean said, "I'll take care of it. What's up?"

Jack stared at him for a moment then, slightly nodding his head, said, "The reason I called, I got a score - a two man score. It's a drop, one guard, two bags, and he don't even carry his gun. I figure about two hundred grand, maybe more. You interested?"

After a long moment, he replied, "Yeah, I am."

The truth was, Sean wasn't just frustrated and angry, he was also bored. He'd been staying alone at a cottage that he'd rented in Northern New Hampshire. He'd done nothing since he'd gone undercover except read books, watch television and ruminate on everything that had happened and everything that he intended on doing. He was at his wits' end. He needed to do something and if he couldn't do what he wanted to do, he could do a score.

The Real Town

"Look, Sean, I know you're in the middle of a thing. If you need a hand . . ."

Sean held up his hand, "Thanks, Jack, but there's nothing that can be done right now. When there is, I'll take care of it. If I do need you, I'll get in touch."

*

Sean and Jack pulled into the parking lot of a huge shopping mall, outside of Boston, and parked at the far end with a clear view of the bank, which was at the front of the lot, set off from the rest of the mall. They were separated from the main shopping area by hundreds and hundreds of parked cars.

They were sitting in the car watching the bank, waiting for the armored truck, when Sean suddenly sat up straight. He'd been looking back into the enormous parking lot when suddenly he saw someone. It was Dickie Black.

With a voice hoarse with stunned fervor, he said, "Score's off, Jack."

The intensity of his voice caused Jack to snap his head around. "What?"

Pointing past him, Sean said, "That's the guy that set up Tommy and Artie."

Then, without removing his glaring eyes from his target, he said, "I'm not tryna' get you involved, Jack, but I need the car. There's a bus stop right on the other side of the mall. It'll take you right back to Boston."

Quietly, Jack said, "Go do what you gotta' do. I'll be right here, unless you want me to move to another position."

Sean started to protest when Jack cut him off. "Listen, you know as well as I do, it don't matter if it's a hit or a score, ya' get ready for both of them the same way. You're covered well enough and this is the car to do it in. Go on, I'll be here."

Sean had no more time to argue. Dickie Black was walking through the parked cars and if Sean let it go any longer, he might reach his car and be gone. Getting out of the car he walked at a parallel angle in the same direction as Dickie, who was coming from the shopping area and cutting through the cars. There were about twenty cars in each of the many rows separating them. As Jack had said, Sean was disguised well enough so that, even if Dickie should notice him, he wouldn't recognize him. They reached the point where there were only about a half-dozen cars between them when Dickie turned left and was walking towards him. Sean kept going straight, but kept him in his peripheral vision. Dickie stopped at a car and, turning his back to Sean, took his keys out and started to unlock the car. Sean immediately turned right and headed back towards him. There were now only two cars between them. Sean was timing it so that he would reach the car just as Dickie got in and shut the door. With one car left he slid his gun out and took one last quick glance around. As the door slammed shut, Sean's eyes were skimming over the top of his car.

He stopped, in shock, then instinctively turned the other way, and kept on walking. Coming from the same direction that Dickie had just come from was Dickie's wife. Even worse, she was carrying a little baby in her arms.

The Real Town

Jamming the gun back into his pocket, fury radiating from him, he kept walking in the other direction, glancing back as Dickie's car pulled out, going in the other direction. He never had a clue how close he had just come to dying.

As he got back into the car, Jack said, intensely, "Did you get him? You were so far away I couldn't see yez' in the cars. I didn't hear anything'."

Pounding the dashboard, Sean said, "His fucking wife was there - with a fucking baby!'

Glaring up through the windshield, he said, "Where's that fucking truck!"

Jack said, quietly, "It came. It's gone."

CHAPTER 39

In March, he finally got the message for which he'd been waiting. By that time, it was common knowledge that Sean was in California. It was so widely known that the FBI actually raided the house of a friend of his who lived in San Francisco, around the start of March, looking for Sean.

Anne was the only one who could contact Sean. Far from California, Sean was still lying low in New Hampshire, under an alias. Anne knew his telephone number. She would only call from a pay phone, and not in Charlestown.

The day after she got the call from California, Gus stopped her at the supermarket. In a casual conversation, he told her that he had a message for Sean.

That day she had Grace mind the kids. She told her that she had to go in town to do some shopping. After taking the train in town, she browsed around Filene's Basement for a while. Then, as you could actually walk directly from Filene's Basement into the underground subway, she went back from the Basement into the subway and was on the train in less than a minute. She went two stops, got off at Haymarket Square, went upstairs and back out onto the street, picked up one of the pay phones and made her call.

When Sean answered, she kept it brief, "Gus says he has to see you. He says it's important and for you to get back to him right away."

Sean said, "Tell him I'll meet him tonight. He'll know where. I'll be there at twelve."

Then, "How are you? How's Ma? How're Pat an' the kids?"

She said, "Everyone's fine. We all miss you. How are you?"

He said, "I'm fine. I'm bored."

"By the way," she said, "Your pal, Al, called from 'Frisco. The FBI raided his house looking for you."

"You're kidding. Did they give him a problem?"

"No. He just told them that he hasn't seen you in ages. He said the best thing was, he didn't have any grass in the house. He said he knew that they were watching him for about a week before they hit him. That's why he didn't have any grass. But he had no clue why they were watching him until they asked for you. He asked me if you were really out there."

"What d'ya' tell him?"

"I told him that that was what the word was, but that I hadn't heard from you since Christmas."

"Good girl. You know they're listening to your house phone."

CHAPTER 40

That night, he met Gus in Harvard Square, at Barney's. He said, "Neezo wants you to know that they're comin' back. He heard that they're gonna' be here by St Paddy's Day. Some guy that's been collecting money for them, from the bookies, was half-stiff the other night, an' he was leanin' on some guy that's been bookin' an' not payin' anyone off, an' he told him that if he didn't come up with the bread he was gonna' be in deep shit because the boys are gonna' be here on St. Paddy's Day."

The look that came into Sean's eyes was scary. "So won't we."

They had two weeks to get ready. Sean had Jack Laby rent an apartment for him in South Boston. Jack was from out of state and thereby unknown to any of the locals. Naturally, he rented it under an alias.

By St. Patrick's Day, the apartment was filled with all of the required apparatus, guns, gloves, disguises, etc. That morning, they placed the necessary escape vehicles in three separate locations, each strategically positioned. One would take them south or west, depending on which highway they chose to take, the second would take them north, or into Charlestown, the third would take them straight into downtown Boston.

The plan was to make their move after the parade was over, when it got dark. It was just going to be Sean and Gus. Sean had sent Jack out of town. Even though there was no intention of anything happening at the apartment, where Jack had rented the apartment, Sean wanted him to have an alibi.

The Real Town

Brown and his crew were holding shop at the Transit, down on Broadway, at the back of the bar. Sean's plan was to go in through the back door and open up on them. Gus would stay in the car. Not that he was afraid to go in, he wanted to go in, it just wasn't his job. He was the wheelman - the best wheelman. They had been in situations where there had been no way out. They were done. Then, after a few sharp lefts, a few sharp rights, a couple of blurry spins, and, on more than one occasion, a few missing doors and front fenders, they were away.

As they were going over things, one last time, the telephone rang. It was Neezo. Part of their plan was to keep Neezo out of it. So, he was spending the day at The Celtic, a bar where Brown rarely, if ever, went.

"Sean, you know where I am. You're not gonna' believe this. Dickie Black just come in. He's with a kid from Southie that I know. The kid just asked me if Brownie's in town an' if I know where he is. He told me Dickie's lookin' for him. He says Dickie's got some money comin'."

Sean's mind was flying. He had different thoughts. As much as he liked the set-up at the Transit, if he had his choice, he'd rather have things go down at the Celtic. There was an alley on one side and an empty lot on the other. Moreover, it wasn't on Broadway, it was on a side street, out of the main stream.

He told Neezo what he thought. Neezo liked the idea. Then he said, "What about the rain?"

It had started raining during the Parade, and now it was pouring. "I like it. There'll be less people around. According to the papers, today's supposed to be the biggest St Paddy's Parade in history."

The Real Town

Up at the Celtic, Neezo hung up the phone and went back to the spot at the bar where he and his pal, Matt, had been standing. They talked quietly for a few minutes and then they slowly blended into the crowd, ending up at a different spot at the bar. They were standing next to a guy that they had never had anything to do with. But they knew who, and what, he was - another 'wannabe'.

Standing next to the 'wannabe' who was facing in the other direction, Matt ordered them a drink and then turned back and said to Neezo, "I tell ya', man, someone oughtta' give Jimmy Brown a call an' tell him that guy Dickie Black, from Charlestown, is here lookin' for him."

Neezo said, "I know, but I ain't gettin' involved. Someone else'll call him. Enough people know Brownie's down the Transit today."

They had both spoken in ostensibly low tones, but still voluble and comprehensible enough for their neighbor to hear and understand what they were saying - known in some circles as an Irish whisper. Picking up their fresh drinks, they meandered back into the crowd. After about four steps, Matt glanced peripherally into the mirror. The 'wannabe' was already moving towards the pay phone.

CHAPTER 41

After talking to Neezo, Sean and Gus headed out. The car was already equipped with what they needed. Five minutes later, they were at The Celtic. Gus parked across the street and Sean got out of the car and scampered over to the bar. As he reached the sidewalk he veered slightly to the left and ducked into the alley. He positioned himself behind a pole on the side of the building next-door, from where he could see Gus who was still sitting behind the steering wheel watching the lot on the other side of the bar. The rain was coming down so hard he could barely see Gus. Something that Gus obviously realized, because, a few minutes later, without taking his eyes off of the lot, the driver's window suddenly went down half-way and Gus raised his hand and held up three fingers.

Sean immediately stepped out from behind the pole, walked out of the alley and turned left, going straight past the front door of The Celtic. He was wearing a ski hat, pulled down to his eye-brows, and a long coat, over a hooded sweatshirt, with the hood up covering the sides of his face, which was all quite in keeping with the miserable cold wet weather. The coat also had a tailoring alteration. Although it was unnoticeable to the general public, the inside of the right-hand pocket had been removed, thereby allowing him full access to the double-barreled sawed-off shotgun that he was carrying.

Just as he passed the front door, Big Al, Wally Glennon and Davey Elliot came around the corner from the lot. With no hesitation, Sean whipped the sawed-off shotgun up from under his coat and fired both barrels. The first shot hit Big Al, who was on Sean's right hand side and Wally who was in the middle. The second shot hit Wally and Davey.

The three of them were blown back into the lot. Davey and Wally landed on their backs and Al was slammed against a pole. With the sound of the shotgun blast still reverberating through the night, Sean swiftly drew two pistols from his belt and started firing.

He wasn't the only one shooting. Big Al wasn't just big. He was also tough and fast. As soon as he had smashed into the pole he pulled his pistols and returned Sean's salvo, matching him shot for shot.

For a stretch of time that seemed to be unending, but was actually no more than a few seconds, Sean and Al stood there, in the torrential rain, firing bullets into each other. Then one hit Al in the face, dead in the eye, shattering his head and dropping him on his back. Sean automatically turned and fired his pistols into the other two who had killed Meg.

The Real Town

Simultaneously, out of the blue, as he shot the other two, a car coming out of the lot slammed on its brakes, coming to a screeching halt just inches from Big Al's body. Spinning in the direction of the car, both pistols pointed at the driver, Sean saw someone he knew, not well, but he knew him. His name was Jimmy Kearns. He came from Revere and he was into the life. He was known to be a stand-up guy and a sharp guy. Things had happened so quickly that he had had no chance to turn around or shield himself. So, when Sean glanced at him, he already had one hand held out, about chest high, clearly empty. The front passenger window was already coming down.

Leaning across the passenger seat, with both hands plainly in sight, he said, "I'm not with them. I got nothin' to do with this. I didn't see anything"

Their eye contact, though fleeting, said many things. Turning away, Sean quickly slid into the back seat of their car, which Gus had just pulled up behind him. In less than five minutes they were changing cars in the parking lot of Anthony's Pier 4, ironically, one of Sean's favorite restaurants. Gus had decided to take Northern Avenue - what many people considered the back way - out of South Boston. This way gave him the options of going north on route 93, or to go into downtown Boston or Charlestown.

As they got into the second car, Gus saw Sean stagger. He said, "I knew you was hit. How bad is it?"

"I'm okay. Just get us outta here."

"Listen man, you're bleedin' bad. You gotta' go to a doctor."

Looking down, he spread his coat wide open. His shirt was covered with blood.

"Alright, head back to the 'Town. We'll see if Jim Ryan's in."

The Real Town

*

Jim Ryan was a doctor who practiced in Charlestown. He was not your regular doctor. Under certain circumstances, he would perform procedures that most doctors would not. If a girl found herself in the position of carrying an unwanted fetus, Dr. Jim would remove it. If a guy found himself in the position of carrying an unwanted bullet, Dr. Jim would remove that. There were requirements. He had to know you, or whoever vouched for you, well enough to know that you would never tell on him.

It had all started years earlier. Dr. Jim was rather a ladies' man. One night, an irate boy-friend of one of his acquaintances showed up outside of his office, just as he was leaving. The conversation quickly degenerated to the point where the boy-friend pulled a weapon from his pocket and told Dr. Jim what he was about to do to him.

Unfortunately for him, his threat, and the pointing of the pistol, coincided with a third party coming around the corner in their direction.

The boy-friend's instinctive first move was to turn and point his gun at the stranger. He yelled, "Don't move."

He picked the wrong person. As the words were coming out of his mouth, his target was already whipping out his own pistol. With no hesitation, he fired and the boy-friend was down. Charlestown wasn't the best place to pull a gun on someone that didn't know who you were.

They quickly carried him into Dr. Jim's office. He was dead. They worked out their stories so that they were both covered. However, after a while when the cops didn't show up, they agreed that it would be better for all concerned if the boy-friend simply went away.

A quick telephone call had a car there within five minutes, and the boy-friend was gone.

The Real Town

After that, Dr. Jim's relationship with the 'Town became more personal.

CHAPTER 42

As Gus pulled up in front of Dr. Jim's office, he said, "Shit. I don't think he's here. His car's not here and the office is dark. Sean, you gotta' get to the hospital. You're hit bad, you're pouring blood."

Shaking his head, Sean said, "No way. I'll wait till tomorrow. I ain't turnin' myself in. Take me up the monument."

When they got to the apartment that Sean kept across from the Bunker Hill Monument, Sean was too weak to get out of the car. Gus had to help him. As they entered the apartment, Sean said, "Put me in the tub."

Then he passed out.

When he came to, Gus said, "You're goin' to the hospital, man."

Sean lay silently, trying to think clearly. After a few moments, he said, hoarsely, "Alright, but first check me. If the bullets went through, I'll do it. If there's any bullets left in me, I ain't goin' in. And call Sammy, he'll be down the Mirror."

A quick, but thorough check-over revealed three entry wounds, all between the waist and the neck. There were only two exit wounds in his back. As Gus was frantically trying to find a third exit wound, Sean reached his right hand up to his left shoulder, and squeezed, causing a low, involuntary gasp of pain.

"Shit", he said, removing his hand, and pointing at his shoulder, "what's this?"

Gus, hovering, prodded the area where the flesh was protruding. "Oh fuck. I think it's the third bullet."

"Is it showing? Can you see the bullet?"

"No, but there's a lump there, I know it's the bullet."

The Real Town

After a moment of silence, Sean said, "Take it out."

"Huh? What? Take it out? Are you nuts? I ain't Dr. Jim."

"Get a razor, split the skin and take the fucking thing out now."

Gus turned around, opened the bathroom cabinet and came out unwrapping a razor blade. "What am I gonna' use to pull it out with? I won't be able to get a grip on it with my fingers. Whatta ya' got I can use? Ya' got pliers"

"Yeah, under the sink, and there's tweezers in the cabinet."

As Gus rummaged under the sink, Sean said, "And gimme me a wet towel."

Just before he placed the wet towel in his mouth, Sean said, "Do it and do it quick."

Then, pushing the dripping towel into his mouth and firmly sinking his teeth into it, he nodded his head.

Following the instructions that Sean had given him, Gus placed his left hand around the bulge and pressed down, causing it to protrude even more. Then he ran the razor blade firmly across it. As blood spurted up, the head of the bullet popped out.

Gus quickly dropped the blade and picked up the tweezers. Still pressing down with his left hand, he tried to get a grip on the bullet. The tweezers kept slipping off.

After the third try, each of which provoked an involuntary flinch from Sean, Gus' anxiety and frustration exploded. He barked, "I can't get a grip on it. There's not enough of it sticking out."

Removing the towel from between his teeth, Sean said, "Then dig the fucking things in deeper. Go in as far as you have to, but do it. *Now!*"

Taking a deep breath, Gus leaned over and, pressing around the bullet as hard as he could, both down, and out, in an attempt to spread the skin even more, he pushed the tips of the tweezers into the wound along the sides of the bullet.

An involuntary muffled growl of pain came through the towel jammed between Sean's firmly clenched teeth. But he never pulled away.

After a long moment of Gus wrestling with the bullet, the tweezers slid off of the bullet once again. He said, "Fuck!"

Then, excitedly, he said, "I almost got it Sean. It's almost out."

Looking down, he picked up the long narrow pliers. Slowly he got a good grip on the bullet. Then, suddenly, he yanked. Blood gushed out, but the bullet was gone.

The relief on Sean's face was obvious.

The bell rang. It was Sammy.

They quickly filled him in on what was happening. Then, Sean told them that he wasn't going straight to the hospital. That he wanted to do it slightly differently - and how. As he talked, they re-dressed him in the same clothes. Then they got him back down the stairs and into the car.

Sammy got into Sean's car and took off first.

A few minutes later they pulled up in front of Sullivan's Bar. Sully's was on the corner of two narrow, dark, back streets that had houses on one side and a wire fence on the other. The fence separated the street from warehouses and train-yards that ran along the railroad tracks. At night, except for Sully's customers, the street was usually deserted - as it was now.

Sammy parked Sean's car in the closest parking spot and hustled back to where Gus had pulled up outside of Sully's.

The Real Town

He helped Sean out of the car into the downpour, and staggered over to the stairs with him, laying him on his back. As Sammy jumped back into the car, Gus stuck his gun out the window, and fired three shots into the wooden stairs, then emptied it into the air, out over the railroad tracks, as, wheels screeching piercingly, he took off.

Pandemonium broke out inside of Sully's. About ten seconds went by before someone carefully opened the door. Sean was lying on the steps, barely conscious. One of the guys who stepped out slowly looked down and said, "Jesus Christ, it's Sean Brady."

That caused an uproar, not only was Sean well known, he was well liked.

"Call an ambulance!"

"Someone shot Sean Brady!"

"Someone call the cops."

One man pushed his way through the crowd and dropped to his knees next to Sean. "Sean, it's Jeff, can you hear me? Sean."

Slowly, Sean opened his eyes and tried to speak. He was past that point. He could barely mouth the word. "Hospital."

That was enough for Jeff. He and Sean had grown up together. They were good friends. Pushing his way through the crowd, he ran up the street, jumped into his station wagon, and pulled it up next to Sean. Very carefully, four of them lifted Sean up and laid him down in the back of Jeff's wagon.

As they were pulling onto the Prison Point Bridge, heading for the hospital, they heard the sound of a police car siren in the distance. There were three others in the wagon with Jeff, two of them were in the back with Sean.

One of them said, "You wanna' wait for them?"

Jeff said, "Fuck them. They'd stop for a drink an' let him die."

"Well, not all of them. But you're right. Some of them would."

CHAPTER 43

When Sean opened his eyes, he was lying in a hospital bed.

Anne, who was sitting on the right side of the bed, jumped up, crying out "Ma, he's awake. He's gonna' live. Oh Sean, how do you feel?"

Looking to his left he saw his mother sitting next to him, tears running down her face as she bit her lip, trying not to cry.

Sitting in a chair in the far corner, behind the door, was a uniformed police officer. At that point, Sean realized that his left wrist was attached to the side of the bed by a handcuff and his right ankle was attached to the other side of the bed by a handcuff.

The police officer rose from the chair and stepped out of the room. A minute later, he returned. He was accompanied by two plain-clothes detectives, Detectives Nolan and Warren. They approached the bed, one on each side.

Detective Warren said to Anne and Grace, "We'll have to ask you two ladies to step outside."

Anne said, "Why?"

"This is police business, now step out."

Anne and Grace exchanged looks, then Grace said, "Do not hurt my son."

Warren responded, "Nobody's getting hurt. We've got our job to do."

As they walked out the door, they both stared at the detectives, then at Sean.

When the door closed, Warren turned back to Sean, "Well, now we got ya'. Ya' wanna' tell us what happened?"

Sean laid motionless, silently staring back at Warren.

"Who shot you?"

Sean remained silent.

Reaching back towards the bottom of the bed, Detective Warren grasped the handcuff that was binding Sean's ankle to the bed.

"This feels kinda' loose," he said, suddenly squeezing it tight. "Where were you before you got shot?"

Sean's leg tightened, as it jerked in reaction, but he never made a sound.

Detective Nolan interjected, "Didja like the parade, yesterday?"

Sean remained still, never responding, never removing his eyes from Detective Warren's.

Warren moved in closer to the bed. "We got ya'. We know you were in Southie. We know you killed Big Al an' Wally an' Davey. You're goin' down. We're gonna' put you in the chair."

Still no reaction from Sean.

Bending over the bed, his voice filled with anger, pointing his finger belligerently in Sean's face, Warren said, "Ya' shoulda' whacked the other one, asshole. He gave you up. We're gonna' fry your ass. You got it?"

Putting emphasis on his remarks, he jabbed his finger into Sean's chest. That caused a reaction as Sean's body instinctively flinched from the pain.

It also brought out a reaction from the doctor who came through the door just as Detective Warren poked Sean with his finger. It was the same doctor who had treated him the night that Meg had been killed.

"What do you think you are doing?" She demanded in an outraged tone.

Warren spun around, angrily. "We're questioning a murder suspect. Now step back out that door, before I place you under arrest."

The uniformed officer said, "Detective, this is . . ."

The doctor interrupted him, walking straight towards Detective Warren. "Will you? Then maybe I will have you arrested. My name is Doctor Sim. I am Mr. Brady's doctor and I just watched you assault my patient. Who told you that you could abuse a gravely wounded victim of gunshot wounds? Let me see your badge. Now! I am going to report you."

The detective was taken aback.

Detective Nolan attempted to intervene. "Please, let's all just take it easy for a minute. I think if we . . ."

Which was as far as he got; spinning towards him, Doctor Sim, said, "I didn't hear you saying that to your colleague when he was mistreating my patient. I wish to see your badge also."

Turning back to Detective Warren, she said, "Are you going to show me your badge, or not? How do I know that you are a police officer?"

At which point, Detective Warren took his badge out and flashed it at her. As he started to put it away, she said, "Not so fast."

For a long moment, they stood there, glaring at each other, him with his badge almost back in his pocket, her with a pen and a pad of paper in her hand. He slowly brought it back out and held it up while she copied down the information.

After repeating the procedure with Detective Nolan, she said, "You will both leave this room, now. I will inform the officer when Mr. Brady is well enough to be questioned.

As the door closed behind them, Doctor Sim approached Sean, and said, "How are you feeling?"

Barely whispering, he replied, "I'm fine. Thank you, Doctor, for everything. There is one thing. Can you have them loosen up that cuff on my leg? It's killing me."

As she looked down at his ankle, her eyes widened, "Oh my God! Officer, please loosen this up right now. It's so tight it's broken his skin."

The uniformed officer got up from his seat and came over to the bed. Without saying a word, he removed the cuff from Sean's ankle, leaving the other end of the bracelet hanging from the bed.

The door flew open as Anne and Grace came hurrying in. "What happened? What did they do to him? Is he alright?"

Doctor Sim responded, "He's fine. I just could not abide with the manner in which they were questioning him. But he's fine."

Anne said, "We heard them talking when they came out. One of them was saying to the other one that he shouldn't have put his hands on Sean. What did they do to him?"

When Doctor Sim explained, Anne glared at the uniformed officer. "I'm not going to leave Sean alone with these people. I'm staying."

The uniformed officer said, "I have no problem with your staying here, ma'am. But it's not up to me. It's up to the hospital. They set the visiting hours."

Doctor Sim said, "Officer, I am instructing you that no one is allowed to question Mr. Brady without my permission. Is that understood?"

He said, "Yes, Ma'am."

"If those two officers return, will you prevent them from entering the room?"

Now he looked uncomfortable, lowering his eyes, then looking up at Sean, who was returning his look.

Doctor Sim said, "Officer . . ."

They all turned in Sean's direction as he said, in a raspy voice, "There ain't nothing' he can do. They're dicks. They got the weight."

Tilting her head, Doctor Sim said, "Dicks?"

Half-grinning, as she rolled her eyes at Sean, Anne said, "He means Detectives. They outrank the officer."

Just then, the door opened and Jeff and the other three who helped him bring Sean to the hospital came into the room. "Hey Sean, how ya' feelin'?"

Sean smiled as Anne went over and hugged Jeff. "Thank you so much for what you did." She whispered in his ear. "You saved his life."

Grinning, he responded, "Yeah, well, you don't have to whisper. They know it was us that brought him here. A coupla' dicks just stopped us outside an' wanted to question us. We told 'em everything that happened. We heard shots an' a car pulling away. We looked out an' Sean was layin' on the steps."

Turning to Sean, he said, "Man, those cops don't like you. What a dirty look one of them gave Jackie when he said he'd do it again."

Waving the other three over to the bed, he said, "Sean, you know Jackie and Freddie, but you don't know Cass. He's from outta town. They helped me bring ya' here."

Sean nodded to them, "Thanks guys, we'll get together for a coupla' drinks when I get outta' here."

After Doctor Sim left they all stayed and chatted for a while. As they were getting ready to go, Anne said, "Jeff, can you give my Mom a ride home. I'm going to hang out here."

He said, "Sure, but I thought visiting hours were over?"

"They are, but Doctor Sim said that I could stay."

Sean said, "Listen, I really don't want you to stay. Go on home. The kids are gonna' need you. I'm okay."

Sensing that there was a problem, Jeff said, "What's up?"

Anne told him what had happened.

"Really?" he said. "Ya' know, I'm off work for the next two days an' I really ain't got nothing' to do tonight. Hey Sean, you up for some chess?"

When Sean smiled, Jeff said to Anne, "You take your Mom home. I'll stick around."

When she started to protest, he said, "Listen, I been waitin' for this shot. He's the only one who ever beats me in chess, now's my turn. Go on, get outta here."

Turning to Jackie, he handed him his car keys and said, "Do me a favor, will ya', Jack? Bring me up my chess set. It's in the back. Thanks."

After they were gone, he said to the cop, "You ain't got no problem with me being here, do you?"

The cop shook his head. "Uh uh, not me. But I'll tell ya', if you got any heat on ya' . . ." He just shrugged his shoulders.

Jeff grinned, "I got no heat. I'm a fireman. Me and Sean grew up together."

CHAPTER 44

The next day, Detectives Warren and Nolan returned early. When they asked Dr. Sim if they could speak to Sean, she told them that they could.

"However", she added, looking directly at Detective Warren, "there will have to be somebody else present."

Detective Nolan said, "I'm sorry, Doctor, but we can't allow that. We have an investigation to conduct. He's not the only one who got shot, Sunday. There were at least three others, and they're all dead."

"I know. I saw it in the newspapers, and it's been all over the television. That still doesn't mean that I am going to allow my patient to be physically abused."

Placatingly, Detective Nolan said, "I promise you, nobody's going to be abused, Doctor. We merely want to conduct our investigation."

Before she could respond, a tall, young gentleman, in a light blue suit approached them. "Excuse me, are you Dr. Sim?"

Turning, she said, "Yes, what may I do to assist you?"

Reaching out, smiling, he shook her hand and said, "Hi, I'm Alan Jarrady. I'm Sean's Attorney. Before we go anywhere else, I'd like to thank you for taking such good care of my client. I hear he was in pretty rough shape when he got here."

Immediately brightening up, Dr Sim said, "Yes, he was, but he's much better now. I must tell you though; one of the police was very abusive to him."

"Yes", he answered, "so I've heard. Well, that won't happen again. My client will no longer be questioned without my being present."

Then, for the first time acknowledging their existence, he turned to the detectives and said, directly to Warren, "Do you understand that Officer? My client is not to be questioned or spoken to by the police, unless I am present."

Obviously infuriated, Detective Warren said, "Then let's go in and question him now, while you're here."

"Certainly, that's why I'm here."

As they walked into the room, Sean looked up and smiled at Dr. Sim and Alan. Then, as Detectives Nolan and Warren came in behind them, he said, "Oh yeah, good thing you guys are here."

Detective Warren stared at Jeff, who was sitting in the chair next to Sean's bed. "What are you doing here?"

"Visiting a friend."

"Well, you're gonna' have to leave. Now."

Jeff said, "Sure."

As he rose from the chair he turned to the lawyer. "Hey Alan, good to see you here."

Alan replied, "Hi Jeff, good to see you here."

Jeff turned back to Sean and said, "Take care, Lad. I'll be back to see you. We'll finish our chess game. I gotcha."

Alan walked over to the bed, touching Sean's right calf as he looked at the cuff around his ankle. "How are you feeling, Sean? I hear you had a rough night."

"Yeah, kinda', I'm alright now, though."

The Real Town

"These detectives would like to question you. I want you to know, for future reference, that I have told them that they are not to question you without my being present. If they should attempt to question you, you will refuse to answer. You will then contact me as soon as possible. Understood?"

"Uh huh."

Then, nodding towards Detective Warren, he said, "But I'll tell ya' what, I got nothin' to say to them. I ain't puttin' up with their shit, not after last night."

At which point, Detective Nolan stepped forward, "Mr. Brady, we're just trying to find out what happened. Do you know who shot you?"

Sean said, "No."

"Tell us what happened."

"I was going into Sully's for a drink and someone called my name. I turned around and they shot me from a car."

"How many of them were there?"

"I don't know."

"You couldn't see them?"

"Not really, they shot me as soon as I turned around."

"What time were you in South Boston that day?"

"I wasn't."

"Mr. Brady, we have witnesses placing you in South Boston on St. Patrick's Day."

"Then they're mistaken. I didn't go to the Parade this year."

"Do you know 'Big Al' Grundy?"

"No. I know there's a guy from Southie they call 'Big Al', but I don't know his last name."

"Do you know him?"

"No. I've just heard the name."

"Word is, you haven't been around much lately. Tell us where you've been."

"No. I'm not getting into my whole life because someone shot me."

"Alright, if you weren't in South Boston on Sunday, where were you?"

Looking up at his lawyer, he said, "Alan, I'm done."

Turning back to Detective Nolan, he said, "I have nothing more to say. If you have any more questions, ask my attorney."

Then he closed his eyes.

Detective Nolan tried again. "Mr. Brady, I would suggest that you be more cooperative."

At which point, Alan stepped in. "That's all, gentlemen. My client has nothing more to say. I think that he has been quite cooperative. He told you what happened. I think he needs to rest now.

"There is one other thing. I notice that you have both his arm and his leg cuffed to the bed. Why is that? Why both?"

Detective Warren said, "Security, we consider him to be an escape risk."

"Really? I've had other clients in the same situation and only one of their legs was cuffed to the bed. You have a man lying here that's been shot three times, you have a police officer sitting right here watching him and you don't think that it's enough to just cuff his leg to the bed? I think that this might constitute harassment - especially where there is an obvious bruise on his ankle from the cuff."

Detective Nolan said, "It is not harassment."

As they were walking out the door, Detective Nolan said to the uniformed officer, "I'd like to speak to you outside."

The new officer, who had replaced the one who was there the night before, got up and went out with them.

After they went out, Alan said to Dr. Sim, "I don't mean to be rude Doctor, but could I speak to my client in private for a few minutes."

"Of course", she said, and left.

As soon as the door closed, Sean said, "Have they charged me with anything?"

"Technically, not yet, but they say they're charging you with three murders in South Boston, they say that they've got a witness placing you at the shooting in Southie."

"Yeah, well, if it comes to it, I've got witnesses that will place me somewhere else."

The door opened and the uniformed officer re-entered. He came directly to the bed and uncuffed Sean's wrist from the bed.

He said, "They don't want you to feel that you're being harassed."

The door opened again. Anne peeked into the room and said to Alan,. "Is it okay to come in?"

"Sure, come on in."

Anne and Pat came in, smiling.

Pat went over to Alan and said, "Thanks for coming in, Al."

"Thank you for calling me, Pat. Sean's not only my client, he's my friend."

Anne said, "We met Jeff as he was leaving. He's such a good guy. He said if you hadn't fallen asleep on him, he would've won the chess game."

Sean just smiled, "We'll see. He'll be back, if for nothing else, to win the game."

Glancing down at the chess board that was set up on a small table next to the bed, he said, "And he is winning."

CHAPTER 45

For the next couple of days, Sean's room was filled with a constant stream of visitors. The Detectives never came back. Then, late on Friday night, after the visits had all left, a nurse came into the room and told the officer that he had a telephone call. It was the original officer, back on shift.

He returned a few minutes later. He came over to the bed and uncuffed Sean's leg from the bed.

He said, "I'm outta here. They dropped all the charges."

Sean, who had been dozing, off and on, said, "What time is it?"

"A little after midnight."

"They dropped the charges at midnight? Who called?"

"It was Warren."

They stared at each other, then, eyes widening, the cop realized where Sean was going. He said, "No way. He wouldn't . . ."

But his uncertainty was obvious. After a long pause, with a grim scowl settling on his face, he said, "Can you walk?"

Sean said, "Yeah, I just gotta' get up."

Even though they played on opposite sides of the fence, there was no animosity between them. They actually got along pretty well, and were on a first name basis. His name was Bill.

The Real Town

Strenuously, Sean rolled over and tried to sit up. Gently, Bill helped him, with one hand around his waist while Sean clutched his other hand. As he got to his feet, the door opened.

Bill froze, a man wearing a stocking cap and a long dark coat stepped in, staring at him, intense loathing flowing from his eyes. His hands were in his coat pockets. Bill said, "Who are you?"

Before he could respond, Sean said, "It's all right, Bill. He's with us."

Then, to the man at the door, he said, "This is Bill. He's a good cop. He's not with them. He's trying to help me."

The stranger nodded as the ice disappeared from his eyes. Without wasting a second, he said, "You know they dropped the charges?"

Sean said, "Yeah, Bill told me. He just got a call."

Looking at Bill, the stranger said, "They tell you to get outta here?"

"Yeah, they said I'm off duty, to go home."

All three of them exchanged glances.

The stranger said, "I got a call, too. We've gotta' get you outta here. Can you walk?"

"Yeah, not good, but I can do it."

Bill said, "Where are you parked?"

"Out back."

Thinking for a minute, Bill said, "Hang on."

Passing Sean to the stranger, he opened the door and peeked up and down the corridor, then stepped out. He was back before the door even closed - with a wheelchair and a long towel.

Sitting Sean in the chair, he wrapped the towel around his head and shoulders. "C'mon", he said, "there's a freight elevator around the corner at the end of the corridor that comes out by the back."

As the elevator reached the bottom floor and the door opened, Bill said, "You see that door there? It goes out to the back of the building, by the high-rise apartments. Is that where you're parked?"

"Yeah, that's right where I'm parked."

Bill said, "I'm going back up. I'll take the other elevator down and go out the regular way. Good luck."

Sean said, "We won't forget this Bill. But, of course, it never happened."

As the elevator closed, they exchanged smiles, and nods.

Less than a minute later, they were on the sidewalk, outside the back door, as a car pulled up beside them. Barney Johnson was driving. "Need a lift?"

As they pulled out, Sean was sitting behind Barney, with his feet up on the seat. He said, "Thanks, Uncle Kevin."

Kevin turned around, and said, "Don't thank me, thank Barney. He's the one who called me."

Barney and Sean exchanged smiles in the rear view mirror. They each knew what the other was thinking. A few days after Harry Gannon was found, Barney had approached Sean, alone. He said, "Listen, I ain't askin' nothin, I don't wanna' know nothin', okay? I just want you to know, if there's ever anything I can do for you, you let me know."

Winking at Barney in the mirror, Sean said, "I know. Thanks, Barn."

CHAPTER 46

Uncle Kevin was Grace's brother. Although they were all very close, they really didn't see him that often, anymore. For the most part, they only saw him on the holidays. He'd moved out of town about five or six years earlier, shortly after the Irish gang war had broken out.

Kevin, like so many others, had had friends on both sides. He was highly respected and friends on both sides had tried to persuade him to join them. He refused. Kevin had made it clear from the very start that he was not going to pick sides. He was far from the only one. There were so many guys that had friends on both sides that, to some, it was almost like a family feud.

One day, shortly after the troubles began, Kevin and two of his friends, Nick and Sam, were pulling up outside of Kelly's at the same time as four other local guys were getting out of their car. They all knew each other, all rogues, no enemies, and some of them were friends that had pulled off a few scores together - and they had all hung in the Alibi.

They exchanged greetings and one of them said, "I hear Johnny O'Malley got whacked last night."

Kevin said, "Shit, I hadn't heard that."

Nick said, "That sucks. He was a good bum. What happened?"

"I don't know. We just heard they found him on Medford Street, down by Billy Driscoll's joint."

As they started to walk inside, Kevin said, "I'm goin' in Guy's an' get a sub. I'll be in, in a bit".

The Real Town

While the other six went into Kelly's, he went next door to O'Guy's, a submarine sandwich shop.

A couple of years earlier, 'for the good of the city', Boston's politicians had torn down an entire neighborhood, known as the West End. It was probably just a coincidence that their political cronies made all of the money rebuilding the neighborhood into high-rise apartments. The only thing that they left standing was the Massachusetts General Hospital.

The West End was a diverse neighborhood which, while it housed people of all ethnic backgrounds, was, at the time of its demolition, largely Italian. The unfortunate dispossessed were scattered about the city. A number of them moved to Charlestown, which was nearby.

Gaetano Maegna, a.k.a. "Guy", was one of those who chose to come to Charlestown. Guy was an old-school Italian, who made great Italian sandwiches, a.k.a. 'subs' and the best slush you could find. When he moved into Charlestown and opened up his sub shop, he named it "O'Guy's". The town adopted him. Not only did they love his subs and his slush, they loved him.

Kevin stayed in O'Guy's for about fifteen minutes, eating his sub, and chatting with Guy. When he came into Kelly's, the six were down at the far end of the bar. They were deep into conversation and it was obvious, from the collective body language, that the conversation was intense. That, and the fact that there was a noticeably large empty space at the bar between them and the next patron, emphasized the intensity of the conversation - everyone else was staying clear.

Kevin ordered a drink, sent a round down to the others, and then went over to the table where the card game was being played.

The Real Town

There was usually a game of poker going on in Kelly's. There was always one on the weekend. Every Friday afternoon, a small game would start, gradually growing, which would run right through the weekend. In the summer, when the bar closed at midnight, guys would take the game across the street into the housing project. There was a wall about three feet high, in the courtyard, behind the buildings, where they would continue the game. They would bring their beers with them and, even though the bar was 'closed', they still had access and would take turns, during the night, going back over to replenish their supply. When the bar reopened at eight o'clock in the morning, the game would move back inside - same thing on Saturday night. In the winter, they would just lock the doors at closing time and let the game go on all night. More often than not, the cops would stop by, have a couple of drinks and watch the game.

After watching the game for a while, and talking to the players, Kevin finished his drink and walked to the end of the bar. Stepping around the others, he went behind the bar, which placed him next to Nick and Sam. They were standing at the end of the bar, while the others were standing in front of it, directly across from Kevin.

Turning towards the bartender, he said, "Give us another round here, will ya', Charlie?"

The conversation, as he'd assumed, was about the troubles. The fellow directly across the bar from Kevin, said, "What about you, Kev, which way you goin'?

Kevin replied, "I'm not."

One of the others said, "C'mon, man, you're too close to too many of those guys. I mean, Stevie Hughes and Tommy Ballou are both good friends of yours. No way you can stay out of it."

Kevin said, "Yeah, I can. It's not my beef. And Stevie and Tommy are on opposite sides. When friends of mine beef, if I can do somethin' to square it, I will. If I can't, I don't get involved. There's no way I can square this, there's no way anyone can square this, it's gone too far."

Trying another tack, the guy said, "Yeah, well, even if ya' stay out of it, who d'ya' think is right? I mean, look, we all know . . ."

Kevin held up his hand. "I don't wanna' hear it. I don't know nothin'. I wasn't there. All I know is what I've heard, and I've heard both sides. Ya' gotta' remember, there's three sides to every story, yours, mine, and what really happened. And just because the stories are different, don't mean anyone's lying. Sometimes, people just see things from a different direction. Either way, there's good guys on both sides an' I'm stayin' out of it."

Just then, the bartender brought down the round of drinks that Kevin had ordered, and placed them on the bar, in front of them.

As Kevin reached into his pants pocket to get the money to pay for the round, his jacket opened slightly, revealing the revolver that was stuck in his waistband.

One of the four, who was sitting on the stool across the bar, said, "Hey, you still got your pistol on ya'."

Looking at him questioningly, Kevin responded, "Yeah?"

"We got a deal. Everyone puts their gun behind the bar."

"Why? What's the problem?"

The Real Town

Nick said, "We was talkin' about Johnny O'Malley gettin' whacked, an' then we got talkin' about the troubles, and who's gonna' be with who, and who's right and who's wrong, an', you know, it started gettin' a little hot, and nobody here's lookin' for a beef, so we all agreed to put our shit behind the bar."

Kevin, glancing down at about ten pistols that were on the shelf right in front of him, under the bar, nodded, "Okay, I get it."

The guy across the bar said, "So you wanna' put yours down, too?"

Kevin said, "Uh uh, not my beef, not my conversation. I'll go watch the card game"

As he started to pick up the drink that the bartender had put down next to him, one of the four, a younger one, in his twenties, said, "So, what, you're gonna' be standin' over there, ten feet away, with a gun on ya', while we're standin' here with nothin' on us? I don't think so."

Taking a sip of his drink, Kevin said, softly, "If you want to put your gun behind the bar, that's your business, not mine. If I want to keep mine on me, that's my business, not yours. Like I said, it's not my beef and it's not my conversation."

Angrily, the young guy responded, "So whatta ya' figure, you got a gun on ya' an' we ain't, so you can do any fuckin' thing ya' want? *Fuck you. I'm tellin' ya. Put your piece down with ours.*"

The youngster's voice had risen aggressively. Instantaneously, the bar went silent. The only sound that could be heard was coming from the television down at the front of the bar.

The Real Town

Kevin guardedly extended his left hand out to the side, placing his drink back on the bar, all the while maintaining direct eye contact. Then, with the same hand, he reached down, picked up one of the pistols, and placed it on top of the bar directly between him and the confrontational young man. At the same time, as he leaned back from the bar, he pushed his coat back, displaying his pistol.

Softly, he said, "You want your gun? There it is. Go for it."

As Kevin was not touching his pistol, it was now a dead even challenge. It was anyone's ball game. It was quick-draw time. Anything could happen. Nick, Sam and the other three, all stepped tactfully away from the two of them.

After a moment's hesitation, all animosity gone, the young fellow stepped back from the bar, saying, "Listen, man, I ain't lookin' for a beef. I just . . . I . . . I didn't mean . . . I was . . ."

One of his three compatriots interrupted, "Kevin, please, let it go. Dougie's just a kid. But he's a good kid."

Never removing his eyes from his adversary, Kevin responded, "Then someone better teach Dougie to keep his mouth shut or he ain't gonna' grow up."

That ended the incident. Nick and Sam retrieved their pistols. Then, the others did the same and quickly left.

The Real Town

At that point, Kevin began to develop a little paranoia about what was going on around town. It wasn't fear. He had no problem dealing with a situation regardless of how much violence was necessary. He just didn't like violence, if it wasn't necessary. The bottom line was, friends were beefing with friends, so who could you trust? He was aware that he was being paranoid. But, he was also a believer in the old philosophy that, 'Just because you were a paranoid, didn't mean that someone wasn't trying to kill you'.

Then it all came into fruition.

One night he was leaving The Stork Club about four o'clock in the morning. When he got outside, he was approached by two rogues that he'd seen, but hadn't spoken to, upstairs in the Club about an hour earlier. He'd known one of them, Jerry, since they were kids. They had gone to school together, and they were friends. The other one, Albie, was about ten years older. Although he and Kevin knew each other from a distance, they had never associated. Albie was looked up to, and considered to be a dangerous player. He was a known shooter.

Jerry said, "Listen, Kev, we know you don't wanna' get involved in the beef, but people are sayin' you been hangin' around with some of the other guys."

"I hang with who I want to, Jerry, but when friends beef, I don't get in the middle. I stay out."

Albie cut in, in an accusing tone. "You were in-town drinkin' with Ronnie Murphy the other night. He's with them."

Shrugging, Kevin said, "Who I drink with's, my business. It ain't got nothing' to do with the beef."

Raising his hands, waist high, Albie slowly pushed back both sides of his unbuttoned jacket with his thumbs, revealing two large pistols stuck in his belt. "Yeah? Well now it does."

Kevin said, "You gonna' use 'em?"

Albie answered "You gonna' pick a side?"

Pushing back the right side of his jacket, revealing a pistol, Kevin responded, "I just did. Touch 'em an' you're gone."

Albie instantly drew both guns. They were all the way out of his belt when Kevin blew him away with three quick, deadly shots.

Jerry was standing there, hands held clearly away from his body. Eyes wide with fear, he said, "I told him not to, Kevin. He's been wantin' to talk to you, and when he heard you was with Ronnie, he said he was gonna'. I tried to talk him out of it, but when we saw you tonight, I couldn't stop him. An' nobody sent him. I swear to God, he did it on his own. Please don't."

Kevin lowered his pistol, which had been pointed directly at Jerry since the third shot.

"Nobody sent him?"

"I swear to God. He's been wantin' to talk to you since that shit happened down Kelly's with that kid, Dougie, an' when we saw ya' tonight it was a spur a' the moment thing."

"Alright, you tell them I said if they got no problem with me, I'll still stay out of it. It's their call."

The next day, Kevin got a message from Jerry. Nobody had a problem with him.

The Real Town

Still, it brought it home to him. It was time to step back. He'd been having a good run and had made some money. So, unbeknownst to all but his family, Kevin circumspectly purchased a farmhouse in New Hampshire, and simply disappeared. By the time that the troubles ended, he had gotten settled in, and decided to stay. He liked it in New Hampshire.

Now he was back.

CHAPTER 47

A while after they left the hospital, they pulled into the parking lot of a motel up on Route One, on the north side of Boston. The trip took a little longer than usual, as they had to stop on the way in order to exchange cars.

Instead of the usual building with a number of rooms, this motel was a series of separate small cottages. As they pulled up in front of one of the cottages at the rear of the property, Sean said, "Are we going in this one?"

Kevin said, "Uh huh, we rented it this afternoon."

Sean said, "This is weird. I was only up this place once before. I was with a cutie I met over in Harvard Square. But, what's weird is, this is the same room we got. Two times an' I get the same room both times."

Grinning, he said, "I don't think tonight's gonna' be as good as that night was."

As he was helping him out of the car, Kevin said, "Ya' never know. We'll see."

Barney had gone straight to the door, so when Kevin and Sean got there, the door was open. The first thing Sean saw when he walked in was Jimmy Kearns sitting on the chair.

He said, "How ya' feelin?"

As he lowered himself onto the bed, Sean said, "A lot better than I did a while ago."

Jimmy said, "I'll bet. The first thing I wanna' tell ya' is, 'Thanks'. A lotta guys woulda' whacked me too."

The Real Town

Sean nodded, "Yeah, I know, and if I thought you were a rat, I woulda'. Ya' know the cops been tellin' me that you gave me up. How'd they find out you were there? I figured you woulda' got the fuck outta there as quick as I did."

"I did. But they tracked me down. The thing is, I drove those guys up there."

That caught Sean off-guard. "*You* drove them up there? You were *with* them?"

"Uh uh, not *with* them, just giving them a ride. For whatever reason, none of them had their cars down at the Transit. Either that, or they didn't wanna' give up their parking spots. You know what parking's like on St. Paddy's Day, in Southie. Whatever it was, I was on my way out the door - I wasn't there for the Parade, I was there to see Brownie on business - and, 'cause I was leaving, he asked me if I'd give them a ride up The Celtic to pick some guy up.

"But here's the thing, you asked me how they tracked me down. I don't know. Maybe someone got my plate, or maybe someone who knows me, saw me. I don't know. I really can't tell ya'. But I don't think so, especially with all that rain. I don't go over there that much, so there ain't that many guys around there that know me, and as far as the plate goes, the car I was drivin' ain't registered in my name. The car's legal, but it ain't in my name, an' the cops ain't been to the person whose name it is in. What I *can* tell ya', is this; The only one who knew that I was there, was Jimmy Brown."

Sean said, "You think he ratted you out?"

The Real Town

Jimmy took his time before he answered. Glancing up at Kevin, then looking back at Sean, he said, "Kevin taught me something years ago. Never call someone a rat unless you can prove it. So, no, I'm not gonna' say he gave me up. On the other hand, that ain't what you asked me, is it? You want to know if I *think* he gave me up. Lemme put it this way. I been doin' business with him for about six months, so, he does have some shit on me. He's got a warehouse down on "A" Street and it's a convenient place to dump stuff. He could get me for a coupla' truck-loads; cigarettes, razor blades, you know. The thing is, the stuff's all gone so the only way he could get me is if he comes outta the closet and testifies. I don't see him doin' that. What I am gonna' do is back up. I'm not gonna' *tell* him that I'm not doin' no more business with him, but I ain't. I just can't let him know."

Sean said, "I get it. Don't give him any reason to think you know. Lemme ask you something else. What cops tracked you down."

Looking up at Kevin, again, he said, "Did you tell him what happened?"

"No. I figure it's better if he hears it from you."

Looking back at Sean, Jimmy said, "Warren and Nolan, the two dicks from down-town. I was having a drink at the Intermission, down the combat zone, when they come in and picked me up and took me over to headquarters, up on Berkeley Street. They hassled me for about four hours. They're tellin' me that they know I was there, that they know I was with the guys that got whacked, that I saw the whole thing. I keep tellin' them they got the wrong guy, I don't know nothin', and I got nothing else to say. Finally, they kick me out, tellin' me I'll be back.

The Real Town

"This was Monday, by the way, the day after it happened. That night, the feds came to my house. They tell me the same thing, that they know I saw everything. But that wasn't why they were there. They said they had to tell *me* something but that it had to be off the record, because it ain't a federal beef so they weren't supposed to be involved. They said they've been following your crew and they picked up some information from a phone tap. They said the reason they know I was there was because they heard your guys talkin' about it and that your crew was gonna' whack me because I'm a witness - because I saw you "*execute*" the three guys in Southie on St. Paddy's Day. That's how they put it, "*execute*"."

"I tell them that, if your guys are saying that shit, then they got it wrong, that I wasn't there, that they must have me mixed-up with someone else.

"So they say 'Okay, we just figured we had to tell you that your life may be in jeopardy. Just don't mention it to anyone'. I tell them I won't.

"That night, about three in the morning, someone machine-gunned my house. They blew out all the windows on the second floor."

Sean instantly said, "Was anyone hit?"

"No."

"You know it wasn't my guys. Even if we wanted to whack you, we'd never go to your house."

"I know. But I had to tell you. That's why I asked Barney to reach out for Kevin. I knew he was your uncle. Kevin and I go way back. The first thing he said when we talked was, 'Sean would never do that and neither would his friends'.

Sean asked, "Do you think it was the cops, or Brown?"

Jimmy answered, "I don't know. But the feds came back the next day. They said your guys did it. They said they heard them talking about it on the phone, but they can't use it against them. The tap's not legal. They just wanted me to know. After they were gone, Warren and Nolan showed up. They tell me the same thing. They tell me they can't tell me the source but they know someone shot at my house and they know who did it. Same story, your crew, 'those bastards from Charlestown', is how Warren put it.

*

Kevin said, "Alright, I'm going to tell you all something that I just found out today. When Anne told me on Tuesday, what happened with the Boston cops at the hospital on Monday night, I made a phone call. I'm not getting into any names, but you'll know who I'm talking about. He's a guy I grew up with. Now he's a fed. Anyways, he got back to me right away, he called me at Ma's - we got a history - and I told him what was going on. He already knew and he told me he'd get back to me, again. He did, today. That's when I found out that they were dropping the charges tonight."

Sean said, "A fed knew?"

"Uh huh, and lots more."

Looking over at Jimmy, Kevin said, "He's one of the ones who came to your house, not the one who was doing the talking, the other one, his partner."

Jimmy was stunned. "What did he tell you?"

The Real Town

"About you, nothing. Actually, when I brought up your name, it caught him off-guard and he let it slip that he was at your house on Monday. After that, he pretty much said he didn't wanna' go there, or he couldn't go there, that all he was calling me about was Sean. What he said was, they were going to drop the charges on Sean and that I had to get him out of the hospital as soon as I could.

"When I asked him about the cop Warren, he told me not to trust him. When I asked him about Jimmy Brown, he said the same thing. He kinda hemmed and hawed at first, but when I pressed him, he told me - in a roundabout way - that Brown has a rather close relationship with his partner. He didn't actually say Brown's a rat. What he did say was that, while Brown and his partner's relationship is close, their relationship is not the same kind of relationship that him and I have."

Sean cut in, "You figure what he's sayin' is, the difference is, you don't tell him nothin'?"

Kevin nodded, "That's what it sounded like to me. Ya' gotta' understand, this guy and I do have a close relationship."

Taking a discrete look at each of them, he said, "What I am going to tell you, not only stays here, it dies here. After we leave this room, I do not want you to ever even discuss it amongst yourselves."

Silently, all three nodded. They were mesmerized. All three of them had the same mentality as Kevin. He knew that, and they knew that he knew that. What he had just said was unnecessary, and they all knew that - including Kevin. So, for him to say it, had them totally captivated.

"My relationship with this guy goes back to when we were kids. We used to play sports together. We always played hockey together down the Oiley's."

Jimmy Kearns interrupted, "Down the Oiley's? Where the fuck d'ya play hockey down the Oiley's?"

Although Jimmy wasn't from Charlestown, he had friends there and he knew that the Oiley's was a football field.

Kevin said, "They flood it after football season. That's where we skate."

Continuing, he went on, "Anyways, me and this guy were close. Then, when we were sixteen, his sister got raped. It was kept real quiet. You know how things were back then. No one could know about it. The girl's reputation would be ruined. But he knew about it. He heard her crying to their mother one night and eavesdropped on the conversation. The guy that did it lived down on the Somerville line, up the street from the Royal Cafe. The guy was in his twenties and he had a rep' for bein' wild, and he was supposed to be a tough guy. The next weekend, someone beat him to death. No one was ever caught, but there were witnesses that said that they saw two teenagers beating him, one with a baseball bat, the other one with a bar or a pipe.

"Anyways, a couple of years later, I got busted for something stupid, but I got a deal and they let me off in exchange for joining the Marines. While I was in, the war started and by the time I got out, he had moved on. But we're still friends. We both always recognized that we're on opposite sides of the fence. But, he never asked me to tell him anything, 'cause he knew I never would, and I never asked him for a favor - till now. And I'll tell you what, he is uncomfortable with what he told me, but he knows it's family.

The Real Town

"Anyways, the reason that I told you that was so that none of you would have any doubts as to what's going on. The bottom line is this: It don't matter if it was the cops, or Brown, who shot up your house, Jimmy. For all intents and purposes, they're the same. It was all a set-up. Whoever did it, did it to convince you that Sean and his guys are gonna' whack you and your family. That way, they figure they got a shot to get you to roll over."

Sean said, "Ya' know, Jimmy, I've been thinking about what ya' said earlier. I think you could use this shooting to your advantage. You can tell Brown, or even just get word to him, that you're gettin' outta town for a while because someone shot up your house. You could even tell him that someone told you that it was a Charlestown crew - ya' just can't tell him who told you - but you don't want any problems with those guys. Ya' hear they're nuts. Better yet, do it over the phone. If his 'friend' happens to have his phone tapped, it gets the message across to them that you bought their message but you ain't giving them up."

Jimmy said, "I like that. I think that's just what I'm gonna' do. Me and Kevin already talked about me getting outta town for a while. I'm takin' off right after I leave here. I already got my stuff in the car."

Sean said, "Ya' know what I'd do, if I was you? I wouldn't make the call till I was on the road. Like, if I was headin', say, for the West Coast, I'd head south first, an' maybe make the call from someplace like Maryland or Delaware or Virginia or someplace in the opposite direction from where I was really gonna' be. I mean, it ain't like you got a schedule."

Jimmy said, "I hear ya'. Having the feds looking for me down south, while I'm sittin' on the West Coast ain't a bad idea."

Jimmy got up and they all shook hands. As Barney was the only one staying in town, they made arrangements to make contact through him, if it became necessary.

They all left together.

After Sean was in the car, he looked back at the cottage. "Ya' know, this really is my lucky room. I'll have to remember it. The next time I bet a football game I'm gonna' come here to watch it. Hell, I may even come here and call the bet in."

CHAPTER 48

Kevin brought Sean to his farm, where he spent the next couple of weeks recuperating. Even though he'd been out of Boston for years, Kevin still read the Boston newspapers every day. One morning, after he had gone into town to pick them up, they were each sitting in the parlor reading separate papers.

Suddenly, Kevin said, "Oh, Jesus."

Sean looked up, "What's wrong?"

"Do you know a guy named Bobby Stewart?"

"Yeah, he's a diddler. He gets high on speed and goes out picking up kids hitchhiking an' takes them back to his place and gets them high and takes them to bed - boys or girls, it don't matter."

"Did you ever do anything with him?"

"No. Well, yeah, I slapped him in the face one night."

"Yeah? Well, he ain't just a diddler, he's a rat, too. He says you did a bank with him."

Handing him the paper, he said, "Here."

Sean quickly took the newspaper and stared at the blazing headline:

"MILLION DOLLAR BANK ROBBERY RING BROKEN"

"The FBI announced today that they have cracked an organization of bank robbers. A long-time bank robber, Robert Stewart, has come forward and given up the robbers of at least seven banks. The amount of money taken in these robberies is estimated at well over a million dollars.

"Informant Stewart has identified at least seven of his partners in crime. Amongst those charged were, Lawrence (Larry) Hapley, 4 banks, John (Jack) Laby, 3 banks, Paul Dudley, 3 banks: Thomas King, 2 banks, Edward Foley, 1 bank, James (Barney) Johnson, 1 bank and Sean Brady, 1 bank."

The article went on to say that the FBI had already arrested all of the suspects except for Sean and Jack Laby.

Looking up at Kevin, who was waiting for him to finish reading, he said, "I never did nothin' with that piece o' shit. I'd heard of him, and I met him once, with Jack Laby and Barney, over at Larry Hapley's bar. Stewart and Larry worked together and I guess Jack did a coupla' scores with them.

"Anyways, we stopped there one night - Jack had to see Larry about somethin'. So we're standing at the bar in the corner havin' a drink when Stewart comes in with this guy that I know is a skinner. I don't know the guy. I couldn't even tell you his name. But one night me and Rockball were in-town having a drink when this guy comes in the door. He spots Rockball and says, 'Hey, Joe, I heard you got out. How's it goin'?'

"Rockball says, 'Did I ever talk to you inside, you fuckin' skinner? Keep steppin'.

"Of course, the guy took off. Now here comes Stewart an' he's got this skinner with him. They come over to where we're standin' and Stewart says, 'Hi" to the other guys.

"Then he says to me, 'You're Sean Brady, right?'

"I say, 'Do you know this guy ya' got with ya's a skinner?'

"As soon as I said it, I knew he knew. It was all over his face. But he tried to duck it and play the tough guy. He gets loud and starts pointin' his finger in my face, "Hey listen, man, I don't know who the fuck you think you are . . .'

"I slapped him across the face. That ended that. He shit the bed and started yellin' for Larry. We just walked out."

Kevin nodded, "I'm sure."

The fact that Sean had slapped Stewart, and not punched him, told Kevin all he needed to know. Where they were from, a punch was a fight, a slap was contempt.

Sean said, "That's the only time I ever had anything to do with him. I did hear he got busted a while ago, but I don't think I even heard what he got busted for."

Kevin said, "I'm gonna' go make a phone call."

Sean said, "Yeah. Listen, see if you can find out anything about Barney, if ya' can, will ya'?"

Although Kevin had a telephone in the house, he only used it to make local calls. As to incoming calls, Grace, Anne and Sean were the only ones who had the number. Whenever he had to make a call that he did not want to chance being traced, he drove into Massachusetts to make it. It was three hours before he returned.

The first thing that he said was, "They're all on 'no bail'. But, they are having a bail hearing this week. My friend says that they'll probably give 'em bail, but it's gonna' be high. He says if they get you, there won't be no bail. They figure you've gone off the deep end and that you're comin' after Brown. His partner's got Brown stashed somewhere, so that answers any questions about that.

"He also said that my name has come into it. He says it's just a matter of time before they track me down and come here lookin' for you - and it could be soon.

Sean was already getting up off of the couch. "I hear ya', time to move on. They got anything on you?"

"No. They just want you off the street. The cop at the hospital never told 'em a thing. He said you were by yourself, sleeping, when he left."

Exchanging smiles, Sean said, "Good guy."

It was now three weeks since Sean had been shot. He had recuperated remarkably and was already into walking a good distance through the woods every day. They had recently been discussing what they thought would be the best avenue for him to resume his agenda. Up till now, they had generally agreed that he should lay low for a while and continue to recover, and let the heat from St. Patrick's Day continue to dissipate. This changed things dramatically.

"It's time for you to see the country, Sean, maybe the world."

"Yeah, I know. There's just a coupla' things I gotta' do, first."

"Look Sean, I know what you want to do. And we will, just not now. The feds got Brown stashed. Ya' gotta' understand somethin', even the Boston cops don't know he's tied up with the feds. From what I gather from my friend, not many feds know either, just him, his partner and a coupla' big shots, upstairs. Bottom line, you gotta' get outta' Dodge for a while.

"I'll tell ya' somethin' else. He didn't exactly say this but he made sort of an off the wall remark about his partner and Brown's relationship. How it *really* ain't like ours, but in a coupla' different ways. I think he was lettin' me know, in a roundabout way, that they're fags."

"You gotta' be shittin' me. I never had much use for Brownie, but I never heard anything like that."

"There was story about him, years ago, when he first got out. I don't really remember what it was. Something happened upstairs over Blinstrub's one night, somebody walked in on somethin'. I don't know. But what makes it weird is, Stevie Hughes and 'Punchy' McLaughlin used to joke about this fed being a fag and how he used to dance with J. Edgar Hoover."

"That is weird. And now your guy's sayin' it's true?"

Shrugging, Kevin said, "Maybe. But like I said, he never really said it, so don't repeat it."

While they had been talking, Sean had been getting dressed. Now, as he put on his jacket, he said, "The first thing I have to do is contact a friend of mine, to get some ID's."

"Who, Mickey Morrissey?"

"Nope."

Looking slightly taken aback, Kevin said, "You know someone better than him?"

Sean was grinning, "Nah, I'm just playin' with ya'. Any time I wanna' see Mickey I either go over The Stone Lounge or I call Pixie."

"Pixie, who the Hell is that?"

"His partner, Chester Poliskey."

"Oh, Chester, I never heard anyone call him Pixie."

"That's what we all called him when we were Jokers. I think his mother used to call him that when he was a kid, and it stuck, with us."

"Yeah, that's a good move. Mickey always had the best I D's around."

"They're even better now. Someone broke into the Registry and stole one of their cameras and a bunch of blank driver's licenses. Mickey and Pixie got them."

"You should get a *couple* of I D's."

"I am."

CHAPTER 49

As they drove back into Massachusetts, Sean and Kevin put together a series of stratagems. They started with calling Pixie and arranged to meet with him and Mickey.

They met at a Chinese Restaurant, The Kowloon, up on Route One, in Saugus. Ironically, The Kowloon was just up the road from the motel where they had met with Jimmy Kearns two weeks earlier. They had agreed to meet at a table in the far corner of the back room. They got there early. Pixie and Mickey were already there, waiting at the table.

As they approached the table, Pixie got up and grabbed Sean by the shoulders, "Man, you look great. I heard what happened the day after St. Paddy's Day. I was gonna' come over the hospital, but, I figured, with all the heat . . . you know. So, I went and found Jeff. I heard he brought you to the hospital. He said you were out of it, when he left ya', but you were still alive. He said they were goin' over to see you. I told him to tell you I was askin' for ya'. Did he tell ya'?"

"He might've. I was so in and out for the first coupla' days, I couldn't tell ya'."

"We saw that piece in the paper. Who's this fuckin' Stewart? We never even heard of him."

"Piece a' shit. And, no, I never did any scores with him. The only time I ever met him was over Larry Hapley's joint one night. I slapped him in the mouth. He's a fuckin' diddler."

The Real Town

They all sat down and ordered a huge meal. After the waiter brought them their drinks, Mickey said, "Okay, what can we do for you?"

"I'm gonna' need some I D's. I wanna' buy a couple of 'em, maybe three or four."

"First of all, we don't sell I D's, we use 'em. Second, we ain't sellin' *you* nothin', we're giving them to you."

Sean started to say something, but Mickey just held up his hand and kept talking.

"Third, we figured that's what you needed, so we brought them with us. We got the camera in the car. After we're done eatin', we'll go to a motel and take your picture. You'll be on the road before the night's over. Now let's eat."

CHAPTER 50

Sean spent the next few days surreptitiously drifting around, collecting money that he had salted away. In the meantime, Kevin went to see an old friend that they both knew. Joey DeValli was an old-time rogue who had gotten out of the life years earlier and opened up a car dealership. Although Sean and Joey had never worked together, they knew each other well through Kevin. Kevin and Joey had been cohorts back in the day. Kevin, like many of Joey's former colleagues, always recommended him to people that he knew who were looking to buy a car - as did Sean, who always bought his own cars there. Joey's business spiraled.

That night, after the business was closed and all of his employees were gone, Kevin and Sean showed up. They parked in the back and went up the rear stairs to Joey's office. As soon as they walked into the office, Joey got up and came over and gave Sean a hug.

"Jesus, when I first heard you got shot, the word was, you weren't gonna' make it. You look great. C'mon, I got the paperwork all ready. It's all filled out except for the name. I didn't know what name you wanted to put it in."

With a rather facetious grin, he said, "I'm sure it ain't gonna' be Sean Brady."

Sean reached into his pocket and took out one of his new driver's licenses, and handed it to Joey.

Joey looked at it. "Raymond Johnson, I like that. You wanted a new blue Buick, right?"

"Yeah."

"It's parked out back."

The Real Town

Picking up a pen, Joey filled in the spaces where the new owner's name was required. One of Joey's many talents, years ago, had been forgery. He was very good at duplicating someone's signature. When he reached the lines where the purchaser's signature was called for, he stopped for a moment. Then, grinning, he signed the paper.

"I know it says, 'Raymond Johnson', but do you know who just signed that?"

"Who?"

"J. Edgar Hoover."

Sean said, "Great, now I'm a fag."

The three of them laughed.

As Sean and Kevin were leaving, Joey said, "Listen, I don't imagine I'll be seeing you any time in the near future, but if anything comes up and you need me, for anything, not just a car, anything, you call me at this number."

He handed Sean a card with a number hand-written on it.

Sean looked at it and then said, "Thanks, Joey. Does Kevin have this number?"

"No, I haven't seen him since I had it put in. I'm gonna' give it to him now."

Handing Kevin the card, Sean said, "Let him take this. You don't need me to have your number on me. I got his number in my head. If I need you, I'll just call him and get it."

They all agreed.

CHAPTER 51

The next day, Kevin went to see Alan Jarrady. After he explained the situation, Alan thought for a bit. Then he said, "Yeah, we can do it. Can he give me a day to get the paperwork together?"

"Yeah, *he'll* give you as long as you need. But *I'd* appreciate it if you can get it done as soon as possible."

"I will. Tell him I'll see him tomorrow. He knows where I'll meet him."

There were times when Sean and Alan would have to meet, but the meetings had to be circumspect. They would usually meet at an Italian restaurant in a suburb north of Boston.

Kevin said, "No, not this time. He says that he doesn't think it's safe to meet in your usual spot. He wants you to do something different."

He then laid out the upcoming scenario.

The following day, Alan took the subway train into downtown Boston. After he got off of the train, he went upstairs and out onto the street, where he picked up a pay phone, and called the telephone number that Kevin had given him.

Kevin answered, "Hello?"

"I'm at point "A"."

"I'll see you in a few minutes."

The Real Town

Alan went back down the stairs into the subway and got on the train going back to Charlestown. But he didn't get off in Charlestown, he went right on through. There were three train stops in Charlestown; City Square, as you entered the 'Town, Thompson Square, in the middle of the 'Town, and Sullivan Square, as you left the 'Town. After that there was only one more stop, Everett Station, the last stop on the MTA's Orange Line that had come all the way from the other side of Boston.

As Alan walked out of Everett Station, he saw Kevin standing across the street, on the corner of a side street. As soon as they made eye contact, Kevin turned and walked down the side street. Alan followed him. When Alan came to the first corner he turned left, as Kevin had done. Kevin was already in the car, with the motor running. Alan quickly hopped into the back seat.

"There's a guy behind me that was on the train with me. He's about halfway down the block."

The car rolled out and, in a matter of seconds, was around the bend and out of sight of the corner that they had come around.

They met Sean in a bar in Lynn. The place was empty. The barmaid, who was a very cute girl in her young twenties, brought them their drinks with a very flirty smile.

Alan said, "Wow, she's a sexy little thing."

Sean said, "You probably don't wanna' mention that. The last guy that did that here, got his head split open."

"What? She got a jealous boy-friend?"

"Something like that. It's a lesbian joint."

'What?"

Sean and Kevin were both grinning. Sean said, "We don't figure we'll run into too many people we know down here."

Alan opened his briefcase and took out some papers. Within a minute Sean had signed them.

"There is one thing," he said. "As you can see, I dated my signatures a little early, April first."

Alan thought for as second and then nodded, "Uh huh, I get it."

When they were finished, Sean handed Alan some money. "Here, this is your fee."

"Not this time, Sean. This is just between friends."

"Yeah, I know. But I want you to take it and declare it on your income tax. I want it on the record that you were paid for this transaction. Besides, if things go bad and I need some money, I'll come an' borrow it from ya'."

Alan just snickered, "Yeah, sure you will."

The Real Town

CHAPTER 52

The next step was Anne. Kevin went into Charlestown the next day, ostensibly to see his sister. He spent the day with Grace, Anne, and the kids.

At one point, Kevin said, "Ya know, it's really nice out today. Why don't we take a ride down the beach. I bet the kids would love to see the beach and all the rides, even if they ain't open yet."

They all piled into his van and chitchatted lightly as they drove to Revere Beach. Once they got there, Bridget and Patrick couldn't wait to get on the beach. They all walked along the sand with the kids scampering in front of them, picking up sea shells and throwing little rocks into the water.

Anne said, "Okay, what's up?"

"Sean wants you two to have the houses. It's up to you guys how you want to do it - one in each name, both in one name, however you want to do it."

Grace asked, "What's he going to do?"

"He's gonna' take off for a while. It's what he's gotta' do. But he wants to take care of some business before he goes - stuff like this."

Anne said, "Are we going to get to see him before he goes?"

"I don't know. To be honest, I wouldn't recommend it. He's just got too much heat on him."

Grace said, "I understand. We all do. Well, the kids don't. They want to know why he hasn't been coming around. But, how do we go about transferring the property, without meeting with him?"

The Real Town

"We've already taken care of it. You just have to go see Alan Jarrady. It'll all be perfectly legal. One thing, when you sign the papers, date them April first."

"Why April first?"

"Two reasons; First, it means it was a done deal before that indictment came down the other day for the bank. This way they can't pull one of their stunts and try an' seize the property. By the way, it's not a gift. You gave him four grand for both of the houses."

"*Really*, we certainly got a good deal."

"Uh huh, which brings us to the second reason. If it ever comes up, if anyone ever asks, that's why he sold the houses. After he got shot on St. Paddy's Day, his life was obviously in jeopardy, and he needed the money so he could go away."

Nodding her head as she got the picture, Anne slowly began to smile.

"Oh, this is so Sean. You realize we're signing it on April Fool's Day."

All three of them stood there, smiling, as the kids came running up to them, "Mommy, look, there's the pizza place Uncle Sean took us to! Can we have some pizza?"

They were across the street from the famous rollercoaster, The Cyclone, underneath the Cyclone was a restaurant/bar called The Dixie.

As they walked into The Dixie, the bartender, who also owned the place, said, "Hey Kev, long time no see."

"Hey Christy, how ya' been?"

"Great. Hey, how's Sean. I saw that piece in the paper."

"He's fine."

As soon as Kevin introduced the others, Christy came out from behind the bar. He went straight to Grace.

The Real Town

Taking her hands, he said, "Mrs. Brady, I must tell you, there is no one that I respect more than I respect your son, even though he is nuts."

Smiling, and rolling her eyes, she asked, "Oh God, what did he do here?"

Grinning, and shaking his head, he said, "C'mon, I'll show ya'."

First, they put Bridget and Patrick in a corner booth with a waitress sitting with them, playing games. Then, he took them out through the back door, onto a broad back deck. Looking up, they were completely covered by the tracks going back and forth on which The Cyclone soared. At one point, the tracks came down low and actually ran right alongside the edge of the deck on which they were standing.

"We're sittin' inside havin' a coupla' beers one day - me, Sean, Tommy and Rita. We wind up comin' out here. We're watchin' the Cyclone fly all around over our heads, and I'm showin' them the way the it shoots right by my back deck an' Sean says it's so close he could take a bottle a' beer outta my hand from the Cyclone. I tell him he's nuts. So we're goin' back and forth and we bet a round on it. So, him and Rita go out front and get on The Cyclone. Next thing ya' know, here they come, on the Cyclone. He's hangin' over the side and Rita's holdin' onto the back of his shirt and me and Tommy are standin' here with a bottle a' beer. Tommy's holdin it."

When Christy paused, Anne said, giggling, "What happened?"

"He grabs for the bottle, but he loses his grip and the bottle bounces on the deck. So me and Tommy go back inside and a coupla' minutes later here he comes. The first thing he says - pointin' to Tommy - he says, 'You almost pulled me outta the goddamn seat. Ya' didn't wanna let go of the bottle'.

"So he buys the round and we have another drink. Then we're back out on the deck. He's gonna do it again. This time he tells Tommy not to hold it with his hand wrapped around it. He shows him. He's gotta just let it stand straight up on his palm. It had to be a full bottle, not opened, and it had to be wiped dry.

"He heads out the front and Rita goes with him. About five minutes later, here they come on the Cyclone. Just like the first time, he's hangin' over the side and Rita's holdin' onto the back of his shirt, but this time she's pullin' on it and yellin' at him to get back."

When Christy paused, Anne said, giggling, "What happened?"

Christy just shook his head, with a half-grimace, half-grin. "Let's just say I bought the next round. He really is nuts!"

The kids loved the pizza.

CHAPTER 53

The following day, Sean and Kevin parted company in Harvard Square. Kevin was heading back to New Hampshire, Sean was heading west. Before leaving, he stopped at Bailey's, a sandwich and ice cream store, in Harvard Square. He loved their Sundae's and figured he'd have one more before he hit the road.

While he was eating his Sundae, he noticed something that he'd never seen before, a huge chocolate bunny. When he was finished, he asked the waitress how much the bunny would cost. She told him that it wasn't for sale. As he was playfully nagging her, the manager happened to come out of the back room. She went over and spoke to him.

When he came over to Sean, he said, "Excuse me, Sir, the young lady tells me that you are interested in purchasing the Easter Bunny?"

"Yeah, I was wondering what it would cost."

"Sir, the Easter Bunny is not for sale. It is strictly for advertising purposes."

"Yeah, I get that, but it's what, four o'clock in the afternoon? It's over, tomorrow's Easter. I mean, there's nothing more to advertise for."

The manager looked truly perplexed, but Sean could see that he was also thinking. He said, "You know, you're right. But I've never thought of it before. I wouldn't even know how much to charge."

"How much does chocolate cost a pound?"

Smiling, the manager said, "A dollar and twenty-two cents a pound. Are you aware that the Bunny weighs seventy-five pounds?"

Laughing softly, Sean said, "No, I wasn't. But what the Hell, let's do it."

After the manager and his staff packed the Easter Bunny into a cardboard box, and helped Sean load it into his car, he called Gus on the phone. No answer. Then he called Kelly's Bar. He got Becky.

Sean and Becky had a system worked out where they could communicate without even hinting that it was Sean. By the time that they hung up, Sean knew that Sammy was there when he called and that he had already left to go to a different phone where Sean could reach him, without being concerned that the phone was being tapped.

Five minutes later, he was talking to Sammy on a pay phone in Sullivan Square. When he told him what he'd like him to do, they quickly arranged a get-together.

They were meeting in Union Square, in Somerville, which was about halfway between Harvard Square and Charlestown. The first thing Sean noticed as Sammy was pulling up was that he had someone in the car with him. When they came over, it turned out that it was an old friend, Billy Coyman.

Sammy said, "Listen, I was tellin' B.C. that you got a seventy-five pound Easter Bunny for Anne's kids, and he just had to see it. He's gonna' bring it over to them."

Sean immediately realized that something was going on. Why else would Sammy stay with him, without a ride?

After talking for a few minutes, they loaded the Easter Bunny into B.C.'s car, and he took off. Sean said, "Okay, what's up?"

"You ain't gonna' believe this. I been tryna' find you since last night. I called Anne. She said you were gone."

"Yeah, she thought I was. I was leaving, when I stopped for a Sundae and saw the big Easter Bunny. I had to get it."

"Yeah, well it's a good thing ya' did. Dickie Black got busted last night."

"What! Where? Where is he?"

"He's out. He got busted for beatin' his wife up. He was drunk an' they got into an argument and he punched her in the face."

"He *punched* her?"

"Yeah, an' the cops were ridin' by and saw him do it. They pinched him right there."

"Where did he get busted? When did he get out?"

"He got busted right here in Somerville. He's livin' here!"

"You got his address?"

Smiling, Sammy said, "Uh huh, he's got a place right up on Pearl Street. Petey Murray called his brother Cubey last night and told him. Cubey came and told me."

Peter Murray was a Somerville Police Officer who grew up in Charlestown. Petey was a one hundred percent straight shooter - but he was also a Townie.

"Where is it? Where's he livin'?"

"C'mon, let's take a ride."

It wasn't that long of a ride - about five minutes. It was also about a five minute ride from Charlestown.

From a distance, Sammy pointed out which house Dickie was staying at. He said, "Is this car hot?"

"No. It's clean as a whistle."

"Okay, that's what I figured. Let's go put it someplace else. I already got cars in position. C'mon, I got one right up the street."

The Real Town

Sammy changed cars, and followed Sean as he drove back to Cambridge, where he got a room at a hotel. After Sean stashed his car in the hotel parking area, they returned to Pearl Street, and parked three houses up the street from Black's house, on the other side of the street. It was already dark, and had been for a while. As they sat there, with Sammy in the front and Sean in the back, Sammy explained where he had parked the other two cars.

He said, "Ya' know, Gus is gonna' be bullshit if we catch this weasel without him. He got the cars for me and helped me put them in place. As soon as I talked to you, on the phone, I called him to tell him to meet me, but I got no answer."

"Well, if that's the way it goes, that's the way it goes. What is, is - just gettin' the cars, and putting them in place, he did his end."

"Ya' know, I been thinkin', I know you won't go in anyone's house for a hit, but this time it might be different. There ain't gonna' be no one else there. His wife left him after he beat her up. She took the kid and she's back in Charlestown at her mother's house."

"You're probably right. The problem is, ya' never know with broads. For all we know, he could have already talked her inta' goin' back with him. Wouldn't that be swell? Go in to whack him and find her sittin' there with a baby in her arms. No thanks. I'd rather wait."

They sat there as the night dragged on, into the wee hours of the morning.

Sammy said, "Well, it's after one, so the bars are closed. If he don't show up soon, I'd guess he's hidin' in the house."

"Maybe, but ya' know, he might not even be comin' back here. He might be scared his wife's gonna' give him up, not to the cops, they know where he's at, to us, let people know where he's livin'."

"Fuck! I hadn't thought . . . Jesus Christ! Look, here he comes!"

Coming in their direction, but on the other side of the street, was Dickie Black.

Without a second's hesitation, Sean slid silently out of the car, on the driver's side, and stealthily crept around the back of the car and crossed the street. While Black was clearly visible passing under a street light, the area where they had parked was in-between the street lights and totally without light. Moreover, Sean was wearing a black hooded sweatshirt, with both of his hands buried in the pouch. For all intents and purposes, he was barely visible, until you were almost on top of him.

As they walked towards each other, Black glanced up once, looked back down, and then quickly looked up again. They reached Black's house at the same time - one on each side. Black stopped, staring with ferocious intensity, unable to make out Sean's face, as he had his hood pulled forward over his head. They were twenty to thirty feet apart.

Sean kept walking.

Suddenly, Dickie Black realized who it was. His horror was unmistakable, not only from the look on his face but from the frantic manner in which he clawed at his pocket, obviously trying to get his gun out.

Sliding his pistol out of his pouch, as he closed the distance between them, Sean shot him in the lower part of his body, in the pelvic area. As Black fell backwards, to the ground, with his gun partially out of his pocket, Sean shot him again - in the hand that was clutching the gun.

The Real Town

Leaning over him, Sean said softly, "My only regret is that I can only kill you once. But Tommy and Artie will be waiting to talk to you."

With Black's eyes widening even more, in horror, Sean emptied his pistol into his chest as he watched the life disappear from his eyes.

Turning away, Sean stepped off of the sidewalk and got into the car which Sammy had pulled up beside him. A few minutes later, they swapped cars, and headed to the hotel.

They both spent the night at the hotel. Neither of them considered it a good idea to be driving around in the middle of the night, so soon after a hit, with the cops out looking for the shooter.

They sat up talking for a while, before they went to bed.

At one point, Sean said, "I know I gotta go, but it's killing me to leave with that fucking weasel, Jimmy Brown, still alive."

"Yeah, I know, but ya' gotta' go, Sean. You know the feds are looking for you. Trust me, they're all over the town. They been pullin' all kinds of guys in, tryin' to get them to give you up. They even hassled Jeff and those guys, just because they took you to the hospital, and they know they're citizens. And I've seen that dick, Warren, drivin' around town a lot, lately. He's never in Charlestown, but he's around all the time since that rat Stewart gave you up for the bank."

"Yeah, I know."

The next morning, before they left the hotel, Sammy said, "I guess I won't be seein' ya' for a while. We just want you to know, don't worry about Anne and the kids, we'll keep an eye on them. I already told her to call me if anyone ever bothers her."

The Real Town

Sean said, "Thanks, Pal. I won't forget it. When the time comes, I'll be in touch."

CHAPTER 54

Sean pulled out of the hotel and drove through Harvard Square one last time. It was a warm, sunny day and he hated leaving. He headed for Memorial Drive, which ran along the Charles River. He was about to turn right and head west when, unthinkingly, he turned left, then right, onto the bridge and then he was across the Charles River and into downtown Boston.

He parked the car at a public parking garage downtown. He went into the MTA, took a train three stops and got off and called Gus from a pay phone.

"Hello."

"Meet me outside the World Series bar. Go now."

He hung up the phone and got back on a train.

About an hour later, Gus slowly cruised by the bar where they had spent the day of the World Series, The Rathskellar. Sean was across the street, in a doorway, carefully watching any cars that might be following Gus.

Gus kept on going. A few minutes later he was back. Sean quickly slid into the car.

Gus said, "I thought you were gone."

"I was on my way, when Sammy told me about Dickie Black gettin' busted. Thanks for the cars."

"Yeah, I saw it on the news this morning. Why didn't ya' call me?"

"I did. I got no answer, so I called Kelly's. That's how I got Sammy. After that, we were pretty much in place all night, waitin' for him to show up. Listen, I gotta take one more shot at findin' Jimmy Brown. I wanna' head over to Southie an' talk to Neezo."

The Real Town

"Sean, ain't nobody seen him since St. Paddy's Day. He ain't around. But the cops are. They been followin' me. Ya' see I ain't drivin' my car. That's what took me so long to get here. I ain't goin' nowhere near you in *my* car."

"Yeah, I know. I knew it as soon as I saw ya' drive by, the first time. Look, Gus, I understand how much heat there is, and you don't have to come. But I need the car. I just can't leave town without taking one more look for that bastard. I'll drop you off at the MTA, before I head over to Southie. You can just grab the train back to 'Town."

"I don't think so. If we're gonna do this, we might as well do it right. Let's go get some equipment. Besides, Neezo ain't gonna be around this early."

It was late afternoon by the time that they got to South Boston. They each had a sawed-off shotgun and extra pistols and they had put another car in place, in the event that they had to swap cars. Also, they were both wearing disguises. They were ready.

They found Neezo at The Celtic, where he'd been hanging out since St. Patrick's Day. When Gus walked in, Neezo glanced up at him with no sign of recognition, and looked past him. Then he looked back and his face showed that it had come to him.

They took Neezo's car, and went to where Sean was waiting. Neezo looked at him and said, "Jeez, I never saw you with blonde hair before. You look cute. But I bet Dickie Black didn't think so."

"No, he didn't. But he didn't see the blonde hair. I saved that for Brownie."

Neezo shook his head. "Sorry, man, he ain't been in town since St. Paddy's Day. Ya' know I been watchin' out for him."

The Real Town

"Yeah, I know. And I know I gotta get outta town. But I couldn't leave without comin' by one more time. I probably wouldn't even have thought of it, if it wasn't for the Dickie Black thing - the way I found out about him bein' back in town. It was pure luck. I was on my way outta town, and I stopped to have a Sundae."

He then told him about the chocolate Easter Bunny. When he finished, Neezo was laughing and shaking his head. "You found a seventy-five pound chocolate bunny? Only you. But I get it. After that, you had to take one more shot to see if Brownie was around, too. Sorry, Sean, he ain't. But I'll tell you what - if you want, we can take a ride around town an' I'll drop into the different joints that I think he'd be in, if he was in town. I'll tell ya' in front, he ain't gonna be, an' I think yer takin' a big chance with all the cops lookin' for ya', but if that's what it's gonna' take to get you the Hell outta town, then let's go."

Which they did, they spent the rest of the night cruising around South Boston, in different cars, looking for Jimmy Brown. Nothing, Neezo and Gus had been right. Deep inside, Sean had known that they were going to be right. But he had to try.

In the wee hours of the morning, after checking the after-hours clubs, he bid farewell to Neezo, and had Gus drop him off at a downtown hotel, just a few blocks from the garage where he had left his car.

As he was getting out of the car, Gus said, "Good luck, Sean."

Sean nodded. "I'll be back."

The Real Town

CHAPTER 55

He slept late the next day and finally, after lunch, he reluctantly left town. He was on the Mass. Pike, heading west. As he cruised along, well within the speed limit, he saw someone up ahead, thumbing a ride. Unlike the warm day before, today was a wet and chilly day. The hitchhiker was wearing gloves and had their hood up.

Sean pressed the button, lowering the window on the passenger side, as he pulled over. The hitchhiker scampered up to the door and pushed her hood back as she bent down to look into the window. They both just stared at each other. Then, as if they were harmonizing, at the same time, they both said, "Oh my God."

It was Jenny, the same girl that they had picked up hitchhiking in the other direction after the score last year and dropped off in Harvard Square.

After a long moment of equal astonishment, Jenny's face took on a look of mixed reactions, curiosity tinged with a slight indignance. "You never came to my play."

"I know. I'm sorry. You have no idea how sorry I was. But I couldn't help it. Some personal problems came up. They just came out of nowhere. But hop in, you gotta' be freezing out there."

Opening the back door, she placed her backpack on the floor. She started to close the door, then she said, "You know what, I'm going to jump in the back seat for a minute. I'm dripping wet."

Which she did.

As she removed her soaking wet jacket, she said, "Oh, it's so nice and warm in here. You were right, I am freezing. I didn't dress for the rain. I never watched the weather report this morning and it was so nice yesterday, I never thought about rain.

"So, what happened that you couldn't come to my play?"

"I'll tell you what, Jen, I'd really rather not talk about it. It's a personal thing and it's been going on for some time now. Actually, that's the reason I'm on the road today. I'm taking a little trip to get away from everything. But I'll tell you what I will do, to make up for my not showing up that night - which, believe me, killed me - I'll take you wherever you want to go. Where are you heading, back to Sturbridge?"

"Well, yeah, maybe, but first, can I do something back here? Can I change my clothes? My slacks are soaking wet."

"Sure, go ahead."

With a teasing smile, she said, "But you can't look."

Sean said, "Well, that'll be kinda' hard, but I'll try to be good."

After rummaging through her backpack, she said, "You're not going to believe this. I don't have any other slacks. The only thing I've got is a pair of pajama bottoms."

Wrinkling her nose, with a slightly embarrassed look, she said, "Is it okay if I put them on?"

"Of course it is."

Then, with a slight smile, he said, "What guy wouldn't want to see you in pajamas? I can look once you've got them on, can't I?"

Giggling, she said, "Yeah, but not yet, not till I get them on."

The Real Town

After a minute or two of squirming around, Jenny said, "Okay, you can look now. Can I climb in the front seat?"

"Sure, just try not to kick me in the head on your way."

After she was settled in the front, she said, "Okay, now, you said that you'll take me wherever I want to go, right?"

"Yup, where d' you wanna go, Sturbridge?"

"Well, yeah, we can pass through there while I pick up my stuff, but I really wanna go to Colorado. You gonna take me there?"

Sean glanced at her. She was smiling coyly, with a teasing look on her face.

Sean said, "Okay."

Her voice was flooded with disbelief. "Get outta here! I was only kidding. I . . ."

Sean said, "Oh, okay, if you don't want to go to Colorado, you don't have to."

Hurriedly, she said, "Oh I do. I really do. But I was just teasing you 'cause you said you'd take me wherever I wanted to go. I thought you meant around here."

"Nope, anywhere you want to go, anywhere."

After a moment of silence, she said, "I have to pick up my stuff. I've got a couple of suitcases in Sturbridge. That's why I don't have any slacks or anything in my backpack. I went back to Cambridge yesterday to say goodbye to my friends. I was going to take the bus back to Colorado. Where are *you* going?"

"Anywhere I want. Like I said, it's time for me to get away for a while. I hadn't really decided where I was going, but the West Coast was one of my considerations. I guess it's just moved up to the top of the list."

The Real Town

She said, "I can't believe this. I can give you the money I was going to spend on bus fare for gasoline."

"Why? I'd be buying gas anyways, whether you were in the car or not. Don't worry about it. Besides, I don't need it."

When they pulled into Sturbridge, Jenny had him pull over to the side of the road. She said, "I'm going to get back into the back and put my jeans back on. I can't have my friends knowing that I drove all the way out here with you, just wearing pajamas. They're so gossipy and nitpicky and, like, 'You can't do this', or 'You have to do that.' I mean, don't get me wrong, I love them, but sometimes it's like they think they're babysitting me. I'm not a kid anymore, ya' know, I'll be twenty-one in September."

After she changed her clothes, she said, "You know what? I don't think I'm even gonna tell them about you. If I show you where the bus stop is, can you pick me up there? Will you?"

"Sure will."

Later on, when they met at a restaurant near the bus stop, she said, with a pixie-like grin, "I had them drop me off two hours before the bus is scheduled to leave. I knew they wouldn't want to wait that long. I told them that I had to read a script, anyways."

Sean said, "You hungry? I think we should have something to eat before we take off."

She said, "Yeah, I'd love something to eat - and the food here is swell."

The Real Town

After a long leisurely meal, they went out and settled into the car. As they drove off into the twilight, with her shoes off and her pretty little feet up on the dashboard, wiggling her toes, she said, "I love that sunset and I love this car. It's so big and so comfortable. Boy, we're gonna have a great trip."

T H E   E N D
(for now)

CPSIA information can be obtained at www.ICGtesting.com
Printed in the USA
LVOW080737041112

305741LV00006B/95/P